The Willful Slaughter of Hope

Based on True Events

David Lee Corley

DEDICATION

To the men and women that fought and died for their countries, your sacrifice will not be forgotten.

"The more you try to control something, the more it controls you."

- Unknown

MURPHY'S LAW

November 24, 1955 – Laos and South Vietnam
Border

A sea of green swept below the wings of the Douglas C-47 Skytrain as it flew over the Annamite mountains toward the border between Laos and the newly formed nation of The Republic of Vietnam, aka South Vietnam. The Dakota, as the C-47 was nicknamed, was a loud beast. The drone of the twin engines could be heard from miles away and made talking within the aircraft a challenge. The CAT logo was prominently displayed on both sides of the aircraft's fuselage, giving onlookers the impression that it was a civilian aircraft. It wasn't. While CAT – Civil Aviation Transport - headquartered in Taipei, Taiwan, did fly civilian air transport throughout Southeast Asia, those flights were a cover for their real purpose – an undercover CIA aviation company.

CAT had flown covert operatives and their cargo to wherever they needed to go for the last ten years. The aircrews were mostly American veterans that had served in World War II or Korea. Many had served under the command of Brigadier General Claire Lee Chennault, the Flying Tigers and CAT founder. In 1950, the CIA bought CAT from Chennault and his partner.

Tom Coyle sat in the pilot's seat. Coyle first started flying for CAT near the end of the Indochina War. He and thirty-six other Americans flew cargo and reinforcements into the French garrison at Dien Bien Phu. It was supposed to be a cakewalk. It wasn't. When the Viet Minh overran the airstrip, the French replacement troops and supplies were dropped by parachute, often under massive enemy anti-aircraft fire. Coyle's best friend James "McGoon" McGovern and his co-pilot, Wallace Bufford, were killed in a crash shortly before the fortress fell. Like many survivors, Coyle blamed himself for McGoon's death. It haunted him.

CIA officer Rene Granier, dressed in combat fatigues with no insignia, poked his head through the cockpit doorway and said, "How're we doing?"

"Ten minutes out from the Laotian border. Might wanna wake your guys up," said Coyle.

"They're awake and ready."

"That's some mean terrain down there. Helluva way to spend Thanksgiving."

"All my guys are 5th Bureau. They don't even know what Thanksgiving is."

"I was talking about you."

"Mess sergeant made me a turkey sandwich before we left," said Granier tapping his shirt pocket holding the sandwich.

"Ain't it gonna get squashed by your parachute straps?"

"I don't care how it looks. I care how it tastes."

"Jarhead," said Coyle under his breath.

"What's that?" said Granier.

"I said 'Bon Appetit'."

"Yeah. Right. So, are we clear on the pickup point?"

"We'll be there but don't dilly-dally. The longer we're on the ground, the higher the risk."

"My team doesn't dilly-dally. If we ain't there on time, it's cuz we're dead. You and your flyboys can head back to your clean sheets and cocktails."

"Good to know. I like clean sheets and cocktails."

Granier grunted as he exited the cockpit, closing the door behind him. Coyle didn't like Granier, but he tolerated him. Having flown several covert missions with the CIA officer, Coyle recognized that Granier knew his business, and that was something Coyle respected. He could have lived without Granier's abrasive attitude.

As the aircraft crossed into Laos, the vegetation on the mountain slopes below darkened, and the forest grew denser. Not a place for man.

Staring out the open door in the back of the cargo hold, Granier knew what to expect. He knew the jungle. The intense heat and humidity trapped below the canopy. The thin shafts of sunlight that made a man's irises spring open and close as he searched for the enemy, who could be hidden in foliage a few feet away and he wouldn't even notice. Ankle-twisting tree roots tangled across the forest floor. Quarter-inch long ants with a bite that seared like a red-hot iron. And snakes. Those damned snakes. Some beautiful. Some deadly. There would be water. Cloud bursts or a steady downpour depending on the mountain's mood. The rain wouldn't drop directly on him and his men. The droplets would hit the canopy above then trickle down one leaf after another. They would collect it with their helmets, pouring into their canteens or over their heads and necks to cool down—anything to cool down. Rain would be welcome whenever it came. It would keep them alive.

The drop light changed to green. Granier kicked his leg bag out the door and jumped, followed by ten Vietnamese soldiers.

The leg bag holding his sniper rifle gave a hard tug as it reached the end of its strap. His parachute snapped open. Just as Coyle had predicted, Granier's chest straps tightened, squashing the sandwich in his pocket. It was a low-level jump—no time to pick your spot. Fate would decide where and how he landed. He was not a big fan of fate. He looked down at the mountain ridge. Coyle had been right about that too – it was mean terrain. Primordial. A dense layer of fog filled the valleys. *Good cover if it doesn't burn off*, he thought.

As he descended, he did a quick count of his men to make sure all their chutes had opened and they were heading in the same general direction. They were good to go. He searched the surrounding area for the radio tower he and his team had been sent to destroy. He saw nothing but trees and fog as he fell. He wondered if his commander, Colonel Edward Lansdale, had made a mistake. He didn't have more than a few seconds to ponder Lansdale's judgment before his boots crashed through the forest canopy.

The sky changed from blue to black as he moved through the dense canopy. Branches snapped with a loud crack and leaves poured down like a green typhoon. Expecting to get hung up in the trees, he was surprised when he heard the thud from his leg bag landing. A moment later, the forest floor slapped the soles of his feet. Relaxing his legs, he tumbled. Only idiots tried to remain standing when they landed. He was no idiot. He rolled down a steep slope and became tangled in his straps. When he finally stopped, he felt something cutting into his throat. He tried to take a breath. No go. As far as he could tell, one of the parachute straps had wrapped around his throat and was choking him. He would blackout and choke to death if he didn't free himself quickly. He felt lightheaded and his mind began to cloud. There wasn't much time. He pulled out his Ka-Bar from its sheath on the utility belt around his waist and sliced the strap, nicking his jaw and freeing himself. He gasped for air. It came. He would live.

He scrambled to his feet and glanced around to see several of his men land on the ground while others hung up in the trees. They knew what to do. He had trained them well. He removed his parachute harness and his leg bag strap. He followed the strap and grabbed his leg bag. He pulled out his sniper rifle case with a blanket wrapped around it for extra protection. He unwrapped it and checked for damage to the rifle. He could see nothing wrong, but he would disassemble it, clean it, and reassemble it first chance he had to make sure it was functioning correctly. He was a marine-trained sniper, and his rifle was an extension of himself. He pulled out a second blanket-wrapped package and opened it. It was his telescopic sight. Also, undamaged. He removed a small screwdriver from a pouch on his backpack and screwed the sight onto his weapon. He pulled a magazine from his belt pouch, pushed it into the bottom of the rifle, and chambered the first round. The bolt snapped shut. He was ready to fight.

Granier was a trained killer through and through. He showed no mercy to his target. Head or heart, that's where he aimed. There were no second chances. If he pulled the trigger, someone was dead. That's just the way it was. He didn't question it.

Blood trickled down the side of his throat from where he had nicked himself with his knife. He would tend to it once he knew his men were okay and had formed a defensive perimeter. Cuts were serious business in the jungle. If not tended to, they could quickly turn gangrenous, followed by blood poisoning that could kill a man in a couple of days. It was hard to accomplish your mission if you were dead.

With security established, the team's gear checked for damage, and injuries from the jump treated, Granier turned to the mission, and more importantly, figuring out where the hell they were. It wasn't easy.

The forest was thick. He could barely see the location of the sun through the canopy. He was doubtful he could find a clearing to survey the surrounding area and identify landmarks. Instead, he sent his scout up a tall pine tree to have a look around. In the Pacific War and Indochina War, it was Granier that had shimmied up the tree. But Lansdale had made it clear that as the commander of the team, Granier had no business taking risks when younger men were available for the task. The sun would set within the next thirty minutes, so if he was going to locate their position, he had to do it quickly.

When the scout shimmied back down, he informed Granier of a long valley positioned northeast to southwest with what looked like a sheer rock cliff on the northeast end. He also identified a mountain peak to the west that was slightly taller than their current position. Granier and his second in command, Sergeant Dung, pored over the map until they found what they both agreed was their position.

Dung was a good soldier and a veteran of the Indochina War fighting on the French side. Originally from a small village near Haiphong, he had traveled south during the transition period. He had no desire to see how the communists would treat him once they discovered he had fought for the French. That was the kind of secret you just couldn't keep to yourself. There was always someone who held a grudge and would rat you out. It was safer to move even though he missed his aging parents that had stayed behind.

The team would travel through the night under the cover of darkness. It was a risky proposition considering the Viet Minh's habit of placing booby traps around their camps and nearby trails. If they stumbled on a booby trap, there was a good chance a firefight would follow it. Granier and his team were too far for any artillery or air support and would probably be overrun. Besides, they were in Laos, where they weren't supposed to be according to the Geneva Agreement. Nobody would be too anxious to help them if they got into trouble.

The best Dung and he could figure, they were about four kilometers from their target—an easy stroll on flat ground but a hard night's march through the steep terrain. The forest floor was covered with pine needles and tiny cones, which proved to be incredibly slippery on the downslope. His men frequently fell backward on their asses while a few fell forward and tumbled down the slope until a tree or boulder stopped them. It wasn't a stealth trek by any stretch of the imagination. Shafts of moonlight were the only illumination. The gentle mountain breeze was enough to make the shadows of tree branches seem like an enemy reaching out. The sounds of nocturnal animals didn't make things easier either. There was a lot of stopping, watching, and starting again. The soldiers, some on their first mission, saw danger everywhere they looked and in everything they heard.

Moving up and across the ridgelines was hard work, even for soldiers in great shape. The heavy foliage made the trek even more challenging, often requiring the use of machetes to hack their way through the undergrowth. Rain turned the slopes to mud and slowed the men as the soles of their boots filled with brown sludge, and they lost traction, some slipping back down steep slopes. Trivial streams and waterfalls turned to cascading torrents, impassable, forcing a detour. Mountains, jungle, and rain were a bad combination for anyone on foot. Fortunately, the soldiers were not carrying heavy packs.

It wasn't a particularly difficult or complicated mission. Their target was a wooden radio tower built on the tallest peak in the area. The axes they carried would make short order of the pine logs used for the tower's four legs. Gravity would do the rest. Once the tower was downed, their work would be done, and they could head for the rendezvous point where Coyle and the C-47 would be waiting – an abandoned French airfield two valleys over. With luck, the mission would be over in twenty-four hours, and his men could take a nap on their way back to the airbase in Hue. Granier hated the idea of luck. It was a variable he couldn't define and therefore couldn't plan for. It just happened, one way or another, and he had to deal with the consequences. Luck sucked.

The next morning, his team crested the ridge and spotted the radio tower. Granier looked through the scope on his rifle. No enemy in sight. Easy-breezy.

"Hey, Boss…" said Dung.

"Yeah?" said Granier.

"Intelligence report said that the tower was made of wood, right?"

Granier didn't need any further information. He swung his scope over and examined the tower more closely. Its legs were made of steel, not wood. "Oh, for shit's sake," said Granier. "Tell me you brought some explosives."

"Just grenades."

"Grenades ain't gonna do jack shit if that's steel, and I'm pretty sure it is."

"What do you want to do?"

"I don't know. Let's get over there and have a closer look."

Lansdale had warned Granier to plan his missions to the utmost detail. But Granier didn't like to be too rigid when it came to operations. He planned in broad strokes then relied on his instincts and experience to ensure the mission's success. Now he was wondering if Lansdale had been right all along. They should have brought explosives… just in case. He had made a mistake, but he was determined to make it right.

The team maneuvered their way over to the tower and a small shack holding the transmitter. Dung had his men set up a defensive perimeter while Granier kicked in the shack's door and went inside. It was vacant. A tape recorder was attached to a transmitter that broadcast a prerecorded message from the communist leaders in Hanoi. The system ran on batteries that were brought in freshly charged with each new recording tape. The messages were instructions for the Viet Minh units in Laos and South Vietnam. A simple but efficient system. Granier bashed the tape recorder and transmitter with the butt of his rifle. They were useless but easily replaced. The tower was the key to stopping the messages for an extended time. He left the shack.

He walked over to Dung, already examining the tower's leg. "Yep. Steel. Just like you thought," said Dung tapping one of the supports with the head of an axe as if to make a point. "What are your orders, Boss?"

Granier took a moment to think through the problem and then said "We pull it down."

"How are we supposed to do that?"

"We rig ropes to the tops of those trees over there and attach them to the top of the tower. We build a fire underneath the legs and heat them until they're red-hot, then the men pull the tower over."

"That gonna have to be one big fire."

"Four fires, actually. One for each leg."

"It's gonna create a lot of smoke that will be seen from far away."

"Real far away."

"Viet Minh are gonna come for us."

"I would imagine. But look at the bright side."

"What's that?"

"At least we've got a lot of wood."

"That's the bright side?"

"Sorry. Best I could do."

"I'll tell the men," said the sergeant moving off.

Granier knew it was a lousy plan for a lousy situation. He considered abandoning the mission, but he knew that Lansdale would just order them to return with the proper equipment, the only difference being that the Viet Minh would be expecting them. *Better to get it done the first time,* thought Granier.

The team shimmed up the pine trees and tower to rig the ropes as Granier had instructed. They gathered dried wood and aged pinecones from the surrounding forest. The pitch in the pinecones would act as a catalyst to start the fire quickly. He examined the stacks of wood beneath each leg to ensure there were no wet pieces that would create more smoke.

Once they were ready, the team took up firing positions and checked their weapons while Granier started the fires and Dung kept the ropes away from the flames. Granier used a box of waterproof matches that he always carried in his backpack. The pinecones caught fire quickly with mini-explosions like popcorn. The rest of the wood fire caught after a minute. All four fires were burning bright and hot. He guessed thirty minutes to heat the legs to the point they could be pulled over.

Dung looked up at the morning sky filled with smoke. "No way they're gonna miss that," said Dung. "How long do you think before they arrive?"

"No idea," said Granier throwing more logs on the fires. "But you can bet they're gonna be pissed. Somebody had to haul all that steel up here. Now they're gonna have to do it again."

"It's not smart to poke a tiger."

"Yeah, but it sure is fun."

It took longer than Granier expected to heat the steel red-hot. He had to send some of the men out to collect more wood. Aggravated that it was taking too long, he reverted to throwing handfuls of pinecones on each fire. The pinecones kicked the flames into high gear, and the steel legs turned cherry red, then orange, and finally yellow. It was time to pull. He ordered half the team to man the ropes while the other half kept guard at the perimeter. They pulled on the ropes, and nothing happened. The tower didn't budge. Granier was irritated. Then things turned from bad to worse. He heard several rifle shots, and Dung yelled, "They're coming up the hill. Looks like a full company."

Ten to one with no artillery or air support. Not good, thought Granier.

In less than a minute, the gunfire turned from sporadic rifle shots to a cacophony of machine-gun fire and grenade explosions as more Viet Minh came within range and joined the attack. Even though they held the high ground, Granier knew his men defending the perimeter would not last long. He grabbed an axe and pounded on one of the legs with the flat end of the axe head. Still nothing. He whipped the axe head around and hit the support with the blade. To his surprise, his blow created an indentation in the steel. He hit it again harder. The indent grew deeper. He whaled on the steel leg with everything he had. The nearby fire burned his hands and arms, but he didn't let up. After twelve hard hits, the support began to buckle. "Pull, you bastards. Pull!" he yelled at his men.

They pulled as hard as they could, wrapping the ropes around their chests and putting all their weight into it. Granier moved to a second support leg and hammered it with the axe blade again and again. The tower groaned and tilted to one side as the second support buckled. "Out of the way!" he shouted.

The men released their ropes and ran away from the falling tower. As the tower tipped, the legs snapped, sending sparks and pieces of red-hot metal flying. The tower crashed down the side of the hill and slid thirty feet until it stopped.

The men grabbed their rifles as they rushed to help their comrades fighting off the approaching Viet Minh. Granier grabbed his map and looked for a new way out. He decided to move along the ridge so his men could retain the high ground. There was a brief but furious flurry of gunfire before Granier ordered his men to pull back. They leapfrogged backward, several men firing at the enemy as it advanced, others moving backward to take up new firing positions farther up the ridge.

Granier kept ahead of the group, scouting the ridge for a way down into the next valley. When he found it, he ordered his men to abandon their fighting retreat and run down the mountain into the valley. Granier stayed behind. He slipped on his eyeglasses hidden within a hard case in his pocket and unslung his sniper rifle. He knew he couldn't stop the Viet Minh. There were too many for just one sniper. But he could give them pause and slow their advance. Watching their comrades die from a sniper's bullets would be demoralizing. He could also decapitate their command structure and create confusion. He picked off the Viet Minh squad commanders first. He dropped two, then adjusted his targets to the closest soldiers coming up the ridgeline. He killed another three soldiers. As he suspected, the Viet Minh soldiers recoiled and took cover. He kept firing in different directions, pinning them down.

When he saw the last of his men run over the side of the ridge, he took two grenades, pulled their pins, and hurled them toward the Viet Minh. The explosions kicked up enough dirt and dust to hide his escape.

He pulled off his glasses, slipped them into the case, then his pocket, and galloped down the ridge as fast as he could without losing his footing. He carried his rifle in his right hand, knowing that if he fell, it might survive better than slung across his back.

A few moments later, the Viet Minh reached the top of the ridge and opened fire at the fleeing sniper that had killed their commanders and comrades.

With bullets whizzing past him, Granier abandoned all caution and broke into a full run down the mountainside. The problem was not running fast but stopping when he reached the bottom. The mountain slope was steep and covered with foliage that prevented him from seeing where he was stepping. His leg muscles were sore from hiking all night and burned like hellfire when he tried to slow his descent. He decided to keep running, hoping to reach the mountain base where the terrain would level out before trying to stop again. He could see his men running in front of him. It occurred to him that he never told them to stop at the bottom to provide him with covering fire. *Dung will be there*, he thought. He was right. Dung and several of his men took up firing positions at the foot of the mountain while the others continued to escape across the valley floor. "Here," said Granier as he tossed his sniper rifle to Dung as he passed.

His hands now free and the terrain leveling out quickly, he hit the brakes. Bad move. His legs gave out. He stumbled, tumbling to the ground, out of control, using his hands to protect his head. After a dozen yards, he came to a stop when his body slammed against a tree. The wind was knocked out of him. He tried to catch his breath. Dung ran over, "You okay, Boss?"

Unable to respond, Granier gave him a thumbs up. Dung set Granier's sniper rifle beside him. Several bullets whizzed over their heads. Dung yelled to his men to pull back. He fired at the enemy on the mountainside covering his team's retreat. As the last team member ran past him, Dung bent down and helped Granier get to his feet. Granier grabbed his rifle. They ran together, alternating every ten yards with firing a volley at the enemy. The foliage on the valley floor was mostly brushwood mixed with broadleaf evergreens and meadows covered with cogon grass. Mangrove trees grew in the swampy soil near a stream that ran through the middle of the valley. There was little cover to stop a bullet, but the shroud of broadleaf plants did cover their escape.

When the Viet Minh lost sight of the covert team, their scouts were forced to look for footprints and broken leaves that revealed their enemy's path. It slowed them down, putting distance between the two groups of combatants. They wouldn't give up, but neither would Granier and his men.

Granier's team scout was careful not to lead them into an area too dense to pass through. If they got stuck in vines or dense undergrowth, the Viet Minh would catch up quickly. Still vastly outgunned, the team would be finished in short order. The pursuit continued all day with no time to rest or refill their canteens in the stream. Both sides were exhausted and dangerously dehydrated.

Sitting at one end of an abandoned French airfield, Coyle and his flight crew formed a defensive perimeter around their aircraft. Each was armed with a Thompson machine-gun and a bandolier of extra magazines. Coyle knew it was overkill for a guard detail, but he figured it was better to be safe than sorry. The vegetation around the runway was overgrown and seemed impenetrable. "Where the hell are they?" said Coyle glancing at his wristwatch.

"The entire Viet Minh army could be hiding in that forest, and we'd never know it," said his crew chief.

"How long we gonna wait?" said his co-pilot.

"Until they get here," said Coyle.

"Yeah, but… what if they were captured or already dead?"

Coyle didn't answer. He knew it was a possibility but didn't want to give credence to the idea. "I don't suppose any of you want to volunteer to go search for them?" said Coyle.

Nobody volunteered. "I didn't think so," said Coyle grabbing a canteen from the aircraft. "You guys, stay here. If I'm not back in an hour, you can take off and head for home."

Coyle walked toward the edge of the runway and heard distant gunshots. He froze and waited. The gunshots drew closer. He saw movement in the distance. He tried to focus on the wall of green in front of him. The sun was in his eyes, and the forest was dark, but he was sure he saw leaves moving. He pulled back the bolt and chambered a round in his machine-gun. He leveled the barrel at the forest in front of him and flipped the safety lever from "Safe" to "Fire." More leaves moved. Whatever it was, moved closer. "Granier, is that you?" said Coyle.

A dark face appeared. Coyle slipped his finger around the trigger. Two more faces appeared, one in anguish. A wounded soldier helped by his comrade. It was Granier's team. Several men were wounded. They walked quickly across the runway toward the plane without invitation. Dung appeared limping. He had been shot in the leg, and his pants were covered in blood. "Where's Granier?" said Coyle.

Dung, out of breath and in pain, motioned toward the jungle. More men appeared and trotted toward the plane. Finally, Granier ran out like something was chasing him. He saw Coyle with his Tommy gun and said, "Mind if I borrow that?"

"Sure," said Coyle as he switched his gun for Granier's sniper rifle. Granier whipped around, leveled the barrel, and fired the entire 30-round magazine, strafing the jungle back and forth. He wasn't expecting to hit anyone. He just wanted to make some noise. "Got any more magazines?" said Granier removing the empty magazine.

Coyle pulled off his ammunition pouch and handed it to Granier. Granier pulled out another magazine and reloaded. "I suggest you get that thing cranked up," said Granier motioning toward the plane.

Coyle looked toward the jungle, half expecting Viet Minh to appear. He wasn't far from wrong. "Yeah. Good idea," said Coyle as he ran back toward the plane, signaling his co-pilot to start the engines.

Granier knelt at the edge of the forest, waiting, watching. For the moment, it was quiet and still. He heard the plane's engines cranking to life, never taking his eyes off the forest. Then movement in the distance. Granier didn't wait to see who it might be. He sprayed the woods with another magazine until the bolt locked back, indicating it was empty. He rose and marched toward the plane while reloading. He was measured and in control. He knew the Viet Minh would hesitate to encroach onto the runway after hearing a machine gun rattling away in front of them. But they wouldn't hesitate long. Courage would grow as the numbers of Viet Minh at the edge of the forest increased.

Coyle appeared in the cockpit and yelled out the side window, "Move your ass, Granier!"

Rifle fire erupted from the forest. Granier aimed at the muzzle flashes and opened fire, emptying his last magazine. He sprinted toward the plane's back door where Dung stood with his rifle firing into the forest, covering him. The aircraft started to roll forward. Granier ran, leapt into the open doorway, and pulled himself inside the plane. Dung finished his magazine and closed the door. "Go!" yelled Granier toward the cockpit.

Coyle gunned the engines, and the aircraft picked up speed. A bullet shattered the side window and plowed into the control panel above Coyle's head. More bullets punctured the cockpit's skin. One caught the navigator in the upper leg. Another hit the co-pilot in his headset, smashing one of the earpieces and knocking him cold but not penetrating his head. Minutes later, he would wake up with a bad headache but unharmed.

The Viet Minh commander watched from the forest as the plane lifted off the runway and banked over the forest. He studied the plane's flight path and surmised where they were going – a pass heading east between two mountain peaks. It made sense; the pilot would want to exit the valley at the lowest elevation possible. Fortune had smiled on the commander who had lost the radio tower. Another company of Viet Minh was using the same pass to enter South Vietnam from Laos. He could redeem himself in the eyes of his leaders if he could capture the saboteurs. He motioned for his radioman to come over. He removed the handset, twisted the dial to a new channel, and radioed the company commander.

Coyle was feeling lucky. His flight crew and the covert team had survived what could have been a nasty situation. The flight crew and paramilitary team were tending to their wounds. In another five minutes, they would be back in South Vietnamese airspace. As the Viet Minh commander had guessed, Coyle flew through the pass between the two peaks in Laos. The sun was setting behind him. The sky was picturesque as the last beams of the sun reflected off the cloud layer. The green forest covering the mountains changed to a black silhouette. It was at that moment that he noticed the tracer bullets rising from the forest canopy. There was no room to maneuver without crashing into the mountain peaks. He was flying over an entire company of Viet Minh, firing their weapons into the air.

Several Viet Minh light machine gun crews fired skyward. The loaders held their machine guns' bipod legs over their heads, giving the gunner a stable platform to fire upward.

The aircraft flew into a wall of bullets. Inside the cargo hold, dozens of bullets pierced the fuselage's bottom, killing one of the team members and cutting the control lines for the rudder and elevators. Granier ran forward into the cockpit and said, "We're getting shot to pieces. What the hell's going on?"

"Little busy. Can't chat now," said Coyle struggling with the flight controls.

Several bullets entered the cockpit, smashing the instruments, sending sparks through the cabin. The plane shuttered. Coyle looked out the side window and saw the left engine pour out black smoke. "Well, hell. That ain't good," said Coyle. "Starboard engine's been hit."

"Can this thing fly on one engine?" said Granier.

"On flat terrain, sure. But in the mountains… not so much."

Another shutter and Coyle again looked out the window to see the engine on fire. He decreased the power to the engine, hoping the wind would blow out the flames. The plane dropped to just above the treetops and headed straight into the mountain pass.

The flames decreased, but the engine kept burning. As the plane descended, Coyle was running out of options. He increased the engine's power, hoping to make it over the pass. The flames increased again as the plane increased altitude. The engine exploded, blowing off the surrounding sheet metal. The propellor ground to a halt. "Shit. We almost made it," said Coyle.

"What do you mean 'almost?'" said Granier, alarmed.

With only a few seconds of flying remaining, Coyle searched for a place to crash. It was all bad. Trees everywhere. "Hang on," he said.

Granier watched wide-eyed as the sky disappeared and the windshield filled with dark green. He looked around for something to grab. There was nothing that would hold his weight. He crouched down and covered his head with his hands and arms forming a ball.

At the moment before impact, Coyle pulled the nose up as much as possible, so the plane's tail hit first. There was no good way to crash, but he figured the more of the fuselage that hit the trees, the less chance of the plane flipping over. Even at stall speed, the aircraft was moving at sixty-seven mph when it hit the forest canopy. The plane's momentum was massive. As the fuselage and wings slapped down on the treetops, the right engine's propellor clipped leaves and branches, kicking them into the air. The plane descended into the forest. The left engine made the first contact with a tree large enough to affect the aircraft's path. The tree's trunk hit the propellor and spun the plane counterclockwise. The tree slammed into the fuselage just behind the cockpit, tearing the aircraft in two. The torn cockpit kept tumbling forward while the wings and cargo section spun wildly around the tree trunk and plunged to the forest floor. The cockpit did not come to a stop for another two hundred feet when it finally crashed into another tree trunk.

Twenty minutes later, Granier woke up. When the Dakota had hit the tree, he had been thrown forward. His head had plowed into the cockpit's center control console. He had been rendered unconscious; his helmet saved his life. The other members of the flight crew were strapped into their seats and fared better. They all had the wind knocked out of them, along with cuts and bruises. The radio operator had broken his wrist when his flailing arm smacked into the side of his seat.

At first, Granier had no idea where he was. The pain from his concussion was all he could think about. He was lying on the ceiling of the cockpit. It had landed upside down. His eyes focused, and he saw Coyle kneeling next to him, speaking, "Granier, are you okay?"

"Been better," said Granier, groggy.

"Yeah. You smacked your head pretty hard when the cockpit broke off from the fuselage."

"My team?"

"They're dead. The wing tanks ruptured. There was a fire."

"All of them?"

"As far as we could tell, yeah. I'm sorry."

"Jesus."

"Listen, we have to go. The Viet Minh are coming. Can you walk?"

"I don't know. I think so."

Coyle helped him to his feet. He was dizzy and was about to topple over when Coyle caught him. "We gotta move now," said Coyle moving toward the cockpit doorway. "Lean on me."

"My rifle?"

"It was in the rear. It's gone."

"Do we have any weapons?"

"Just our crew pistols. Everything else was in the back."

They climbed out of the cockpit onto the forest floor. Granier looked at what remained of the rear of the plane, crushed, engulfed in flames. Black smoke rose through the forest canopy. He felt sick to his stomach. He had trained those men. Now, they were all dead. "We need to get as far away from the wreckage as possible before the Viet Minh arrive," said Coyle. "I took a look at the map. There's another pass to the North. We can get out of these mountains and across the border.

"We need to head west," said Granier groggy.

"Why west? The Viet Minh are west."

"You can bet the Viet Minh know about the pass to the North. They will assume that is where we will head. We can't do what they expect."

"My navigator has a bad gunshot wound in his leg. He needs a doctor. We don't have time for a game of cat and mouse."

"If we go north, they'll catch us. You need to trust me. I'm heading west."

Coyle considered for a moment. He knew Granier was their best chance at survival. "Alright. We go west," said Coyle.

The banged-up flight crew led the way. Coyle followed, supporting Granier. They disappeared into the undergrowth.

Fifteen minutes later, the Viet Minh company arrived at the crash site and searched the wreckage and the surrounding area. Coyle had been wrong when he said everyone was dead. Dung and two other team members had been thrown clear of the plane when it was torn apart. They had landed in the forest, unconscious and covered by the heavy vegetation. They were all injured but alive. The Viet Minh found them and took them prisoner. The company commander inspected the wreckage and several pieces of equipment his men had found. The equipment was U.S. issued.

The commander examined the cockpit and found more evidence that the crew was not Vietnamese or Laotian – American candy bar wrappers and a well-worn 1953 Playboy magazine with a naked Marilyn Monroe on the centerfold. He had his men gather evidence, including Granier's broken and charred sniper rifle, which would accompany the prisoners on their long trek to Hanoi. It was the first evidence that the Americans were operating beyond South Vietnam's borders, a clear violation of the Geneva Agreement. Evidence was important, but the commander wanted to capture the flight crew. The foreigners were the prize that would guarantee him a promotion. He ordered his men to spread out and find the Americans.

It didn't take long before they found footprints in the soft forest soil and drops of blood from their wounds that identified the path they had taken. The Viet Minh company formed a staggered line and moved through the forest, searching for the Americans.

THE DRAGON LADY

Saigon, South Vietnam

Dressed in his white suit with black tie, Ngo Dinh Diem, President of the Republic of Vietnam, entered a reception held in his honor with Madame Nhu, his stylish sister-in-law, on his arm. It was an odd pairing with Diem looking like a grumpy Pillsbury Dough Boy and Madame Nhu, beautiful, dressed in the latest creation from Paris, her hair up like the Europeans, and a smile that would light up any room.

Diem's brother and Madame Nhu's husband, Ngo Dinh Nhu, followed a few steps behind. It was a convenient arrangement. Unmarried, Diem enjoyed the company of his beautiful sister-in-law. Madame Nhu and her husband saw her position as Diem's official escort as a way to maintain control over Diem. She was not Diem's mistress as many had secretly suspected. A profoundly religious man, Diem was celibate and had once considered becoming a Catholic priest like his brother, Noh Dinh Thuc, the Bishop of Hue. Brother Nhu was Diem's head of security and his closest advisor. Nhu was happy to lend his wife to his brother. Another woman might become an inconvenience and undermine Nhu's plans.

While Diem seemed cordial and shook the hands of his guests, he did not enjoy it. Since becoming president, he had become more and more reclusive. Many, including the American Ambassador Frederick Reinhardt and the head of the Saigon Military Mission, Colonel Edward Lansdale, believed this was the doing of Brother Nhu and his wife. By sowing doubt about others' motives and intentions, Diem's family became the only people he believed completely loyal. The longer he was in power, the more autocratic he became, keeping all significant decisions for himself and his family. It was a good way to run a fiefdom but a lousy way to run a government the size of South Vietnam.

Surprisingly, the one-man outside his family that Diem trusted was Lansdale. Early on, Lansdale had suggested several strategies to help Diem gain control of the country. The strategies had worked, and Diem never forgot Lansdale had been instrumental in helping him. Diem also saw Lansdale as a direct conduit to American President Eisenhower. Although Lansdale had to go through CIA director Allen Dulles to communicate with the president, he never bothered revealing that fact to Diem. It was a sin of omission, something Lansdale had mastered.

Madame Nhu saw that the receptions and parties thrown in Diem's honor were always lavish events. She didn't care what they cost. She knew Diem would not refuse her. After all, she had his best interests at heart... or so she let him believe. The cheese and champagne always came from Paris, a place she enjoyed visiting often. The chefs were French-trained from the finest restaurants. The band was the best in Saigon and always played the latest tunes. Coming from a wealthy family, she had no sense of money except that more was better, and it was meant to be enjoyed. Her husband's brother, Diem, had no sense of style and wouldn't know fun if it slapped him in the face. And that was okay with her. As president, Diem had other things on his mind. Important things. Things she cared little about. Her job was to entertain and protect Diem so she could continue to spend the American's money as aid poured into South Vietnam.

Madame Nhu stood beside Diem, surrounded by South Vietnam's elite and diplomats from around the world. As persona non grata, few French attended the gathering, yet many of those in the room spoke French to impress others with their education. Madame Nhu was only too happy to converse in French with a flawless accent. "Do the uprisings in the countryside concern you, Mr. President?" said a Spanish diplomat.

"Far too much attention is being paid to the peasant farmers. They sway back and forth in the political winds like the reeds in the delta. Honestly, the country would be better off if they all defected to North Vietnam and left us that believe in the Christ to rule as we see fit," said Madame Nhu cutting Diem off before he could respond. "Don't you think that's true, Mr. President?"

"Well, it would certainly make things easier. But we need their labor to plant and harvest the rice," said Diem. "However, I would prefer it without their criticisms and complaints. It seems impossible to keep them happy no matter what I do. I give them tools to farm, and they complain they are not sharp. I send them doctors, and they refuse their help. I send them food like mana from the sky, and they say it is sour and will not eat it. We in government must reconcile the fact that we cannot win their loyalty no matter the cost."

"So, what do you intend to do?" said another diplomat.

"What else can we do?" said Madame Nhu with a smile and shrug. "Let them eat cake."

Everyone laughed. Madame Nhu has once again charmed the audience, protecting Diem from a difficult conversation. She could sense that he was grateful.

After the reception was over and Diem was carefully tucked into bed, Madame Nhu and her husband went to their private quarters within the palace. She slipped off his jacket, untied his bow tie, pulled off his dress shoes, and laid him down on their bed. It was during this time of relaxing, they often devised schemes to skim away more American aid and where they could hide it from Diem and the American pencil-pushers. The opportunities seemed endless. She treasured those moments with her husband more than anything except shoe shopping.

Untrusting of her servants, especially the younger women, she personally prepared her husband's opium pipe, rolling the dark brown gum into a ball and placing it over the intake on the pipe. Before offering the pipe to her husband, she would slip on her latest French lingerie, remove his pants, and straddle him for five to ten minutes, depending on how much he had to drink. When finished, she would gently place the pipe's mouthpiece between his lips and light the opium using a long match. He would inhale the brown smoke, and within a few seconds, his eyes would roll back, and his penis would become flaccid. She knew what he wanted and made sure he needn't look elsewhere to find it.

The following day after a light breakfast with his wife, Nhu headed into his office inside the palace. His office looked more like a trophy room than a place of business. Mounted animal heads from his numerous hunting trips covered the walls, and tiger skins were spread across the marble floor—the musty smell of the dusty trophies mixed with the odor of cigarettes from his chain-smoking.

Nhu looked through his mail and opened a letter from his brother Ngo Dinh Can. Can was a warlord with his own private army of well-traded mercenaries, which he used ruthlessly to control the opium trade and the other businesses in which he had his fingers. He was a very wealthy man. Can and Nhu had a falling out several years earlier after a dispute over the rice trade in the Central Highlands, which Can controlled. When Can refused to share in the profits with his brother, Nhu had hired an assassin to secretly place a poisonous snake in Can's bed chambers. The uncooperative serpent had struck too soon and killed the assassin. When Can's bodyguards discovered the assassin's body, Can knew immediately who had been the man's employer. Can had the assassin's head stuffed and mounted, then sent it to Nhu for his office walls. After that, things were tense between the two brothers.

Nhu did not dare travel to Hue, Can's headquarters, unless he was accompanied by one of the well-armed special force units he commanded. In turn, it had been years since Can had visited Saigon, where Nhu was headquartered.

Strangely, they still conversed through letters. After inquiring about Nhu's health, Can's letter got to the point. He warned Nhu of a growing insurgency in the Central Highlands led by Le Duan. Several of Can's soldiers had been attacked by rebels while out on patrol during the day. This was unusual since the rebels almost always attacked at night. They were getting bolder and growing in numbers. Can also reported a large arms cache that had been lost during transport. Lastly, Can requested that Nhu help his brother Diem understand the dangers of becoming a religious zealot. Diem needed to keep his options open in dealing with the growing insurgency and not be too concerned with sin. In closing, he wished his brother and sister-in-law well and hoped they could come to visit sometime in the near future. Nhu neatly folded the letter and used his cigarette lighter to set it aflame.

Having asked to see Nhu, Major Ly entered the office and saluted his commander. Nhu offered him a seat across from his highly polished teak desk and said, "What is so urgent that you asked to see me this morning, Major Ly?"

"I am sorry to interrupt your day, commander. But last night, we arrested a well-connected gambler after a scuffle in one of the casinos. During the interrogation, we have uncovered further details of the plot against the president," said Ly. "I thought you would want to know as soon as possible."

"These details… what are they?"

"Several of the lower-ranking officers in the garrison at Dalat have been contacted by the opposition concerning their disposition toward the government and President Diem."

"And the names of these officers and conspirators?"

"Unfortunately, the interrogation was cut short when the suspect suffered a fatal heart attack."

"I see. Pity."

"I still thought it important enough to bring to your attention."

"Of course, But this is nothing new, Major. More rumors flittering around our troops and their commanders. I care little what the lieutenants in the field think of our government as long as they carry out their duties."

"But shouldn't we chase down the perpetrators of these rumors before they become something more serious?"

"If we chase down every rumor and punish the creators, we won't have any officers left to command our troops."

"Then you are not concerned?"

"Concerned? Support for the government is strong and getting stronger by the day. Any attempt to overthrow those in power would be squashed like a nat. I assure you, there is nothing to worry about. Rumors only gain significance when they are perpetuated. But I appreciate your bringing this to me. It's always better to be safe than sorry. But perhaps you would find me more responsive if you brought me the names of the instigators. Someone I can sink my teeth into. Then you will have my attention."

"Of course, sir. I'll get on that right away."

"See that you do, Major."

Ly saluted and left Nhu's office. Nhu picked up the phone and dialed, "Captain, I want to see the transcripts of all the interrogations that occurred last night, especially from Dalat. And keep the source of the request quiet," said Nhu.

Wearing a recently pressed Air Force officer's uniform, Lansdale sat in his makeshift office in a large house in downtown Saigon. Marked-up wall maps and a chalkboard for planning missions were the only decorations beyond several framed letters of commendation. Dozens of books on psychology and covert techniques and piles of advertising magazines were stacked around the room like hoodoos forming a paper canyon. It was the way Lansdale liked it… everything at his fingertips.

Unlike his usually focused demeanor, Lansdale seemed distracted and annoyed. He was concerned that Granier and his team had not landed on schedule. He knew that things were often delayed on covert missions, and Granier was one of the best operatives he had ever seen in action. But his scheduled check-in was twenty-four hours overdue. Lansdale despised when things did not proceed according to plan. In this case, there wasn't much he could do about it. The team was in Laos beyond his reach. There was literally nobody he could call to check on them. He couldn't even call the Laotian military because he hadn't notified them of the mission to take down the radio tower.

He thought about the implications if the team was captured. It would embarrass America and put in question their standing in the international community as peacekeepers. President Eisenhower would blow his lid. Lansdale's boss, Allen Dulles, the CIA director, would catch the brunt of the flak. But Lansdale knew that shit always rolled downhill, and he was sure it would eventually roll over him. He was, after all, the man in charge of paramilitary operations in-country. In his mind, that included Laos and Cambodia as long as they didn't get caught. Now, that was a real possibility. He considered sending Lucien Conein, a veteran covert operative with little regard for rules, with a second team to search for Granier's team. But Conein was far from dependable, especially when it came to Granier, who he hated since their botched operation together.

The fact that Tom Coyle was piloting the plane was a comforting thought. He knew Coyle would never abandon Granier and his team during a mission. It wasn't that Coyle liked Granier, who could sometimes be very rigid. It was that it wasn't in Coyle's nature to abandon anyone. Coyle was a bit naïve in Lansdale's opinion. But sometimes, naiveté was what was needed.

Lansdale decided that fretting about it wouldn't help matters. For now, all he could do was wait and hope that Granier was as good as he thought he was.

Countryside, Laos

Granier and the flight crew had led the Viet Minh west for two days. The two enemies were often close enough that Granier could smell the fish sauce on their breath and hear the crunch of dried pinecones under their military-issue tennis shoes. Each time, Granier had been able to escape with the flight crew. But he could tell that the flight crew was exhausted and wouldn't be able to keep ahead of the Viet Minh for much longer.

Coyle's navigator was also a problem. He had been shot in the leg, and while they were able to stop the bleeding, the bullet was still inside the wound. Surgery wasn't an option even if they had suitable instruments, which they didn't. He was running a fever, and that usually meant infection.

After setting out early on the morning of the third day, Coyle asked if they could stop to change the navigator's bandage. Granier agreed, figuring that they had a fifteen-minute lead on the Viet Minh. When Coyle pulled off the bandage, he caught a whiff of the rotten cheese smell that accompanied gangrene. He cleaned the bullet hole out with water and dressed the wound. He was about to toss the bandage into the bushes when Granier reached out and took it from him. "I'll take care of that," said Granier. "Give them all to me each time you dress the wound."

"Why?" said Coyle.

"The Viet Minh can smell just like us."

Granier tucked the bloody bandages into his pants pocket three more times as the day wore on. The wound was not getting better, and the navigator was getting delirious from his fever. He started to shout out at one point, and Coyle covered his mouth to muffle the noise. "He's gonna get us killed, you know?" said Granier.

"I ain't leaving him," said Coyle.

"No, I don't suppose you are. In another day, it won't matter."

"So be it. Until then, he stays with us."

"Alright. But keep him close and keep him quiet."

"Will do."

"Keep everyone here and out of sight. I'll be back in a few minutes."

Granier headed off alone into the forest. He moved through the trees swiftly, keeping an eye out for booby traps. After a few minutes, he came to a small meadow at the edge of the forest. He searched the field and the nearby trees for any sign of the enemy. There was none. He cautiously stepped into the clearing and surveyed the area. After a few moments, he spotted what he was searching for – a red tassel flower. He pulled up the flowery weed until he had a handful. He moved back into the forest the way he came and found Coyle. He handed Coyle the red tassel flower and said, "Grind the flowers up with some rocks and add a little water to make a pumice. Put it on the wound beneath the bandages. I don't make any promises, but it should help with the gangrene."

"Thanks," said Coyle taking the weeds.

They continued westward for another hour until he spotted the terrain he had been hoping for. It was a clearing full of giant ferns densely packed together around a mountain stream in the center of a meadow. "Okay. Listen up," said Granier as the flight crew gathered. "You're gonna hide under these ferns and let the Viet Minh pass. When you are sure they are gone, I want you to head back the way we came and make for that mountain pass above the crash site. It should be clear by now but keep your eyes and ears open."

"What are you gonna do?" said Coyle.

"I'm gonna make sure they don't follow you."

"I'll go with you."

"No, you won't. I travel much faster on my own. Besides, your crew needs you."

"Maybe you're just leaving us to be captured by the Viet Minh," said the co-pilot.

Granier laughed and said, "If I was gonna leave you to the enemy, do you really think I would have waited this long? Get your asses under those ferns and keep your navigator quiet."

"Are you gonna be okay?" said Coyle offering his hand.

"Probably. I'm gonna need your pistol."

Coyle hesitated. It was his only defense. "Don't make me say 'please,'" said Granier.

Coyle handed him the gun. Granier shook his hand and said. "You haul ass no matter what happens, ya hear?"

"I hear."

Coyle and the flight crew spread out. They were careful not to break any of the ferns' delicate branches. Coyle stayed with his navigator. Once everyone was hidden, Granier moved off to the opposite side of the meadow and waited.

When the Viet Minh broke through the tree line, Granier aimed and fired the pistol hitting the lead scout in the chest. He went down, dead. The Viet Minh opened fire at Granier. He disappeared into the forest on the opposite side of the meadow. The Viet Minh picked up their dead comrade and gave chase after Granier.

Coyle and his flight crew waited over an hour before emerging from under the ferns. "You think he made it?" asked the co-pilot feeling guilty.

"I hope so," said Coyle. "Let's get moving."

Coyle and his flight crew backtracked the way they came, heading back toward the crash site and the mountain pass.

It was later that night that the navigator's fever rose even higher. Sweat poured down his face. He was utterly delirious, believing he was back home in his favorite bar, drinking and chasing girls. Coyle wished he had asked Granier more about where to find the tassel flowers. It hadn't helped much, but it was better than nothing.

The navigator never regained consciousness and died two hours later. They buried him beside a huge mangrove tree. There was no grave marker that the Viet Minh could find. They hoped they could find it again and retrieve his body at some point in the future. If not, at least he was at rest. Without his mumbling, they had a good night's rest and started out just before sunrise.

Granier was careful not to get too far ahead of the Viet Minh. It would have been easy. He could move very fast when there was nobody to slow him down. Over the course of the next day, he pulled the reeking bandages from his pocket and dropped them on the ground like breadcrumbs. He knew the Viet Minh would smell them. It was a powerful odor. He continued to lead them away from the flight crew until he ran out of bandages. He waited until he reached a stream in the forest. He ran across it and made sure to make deep imprints on the opposite side. He ran for another hundred yards, then hopped onto the rotting trunk of a fallen tree to erase his tracks. After twenty feet, he leapt off the trunk into the undergrowth and doubled back to the stream. He jumped down into the stream from the top of an embankment, so there were no footprints on the bank. He headed south for a mile stepping on the rocks beneath the flowing water, careful not to leave imprints in the sand and mud. He hid and watched for an hour to ensure the Viet Minh weren't following him. They weren't.

It was decision time. If he went on his own, he was pretty sure he could make it back to South Vietnam in a couple of days. He was tired and hungry. He and the flight crew had been living off bugs and freshwater snails for the last three days. He thought about Coyle and the flight crew. *Did they really need him at this point? Once they were over the pass, it was a straight shot into South Vietnam.* Coyle knew how to read a map well enough. He doubted they would get lost. The only problem was if they ran into a Viet Minh patrol. But he doubted that would happen since everyone had been chasing after him. He started walking.

It was late in the afternoon when Coyle and his flight crew arrived at the wreckage of the C-47. The fires were out, and everything was still. They looked around to make sure they were alone. They were. They rummaged through the wreckage in search of food. They were saddened when they saw the charred bodies of Granier's team. "We should bury them," said Coyle.

"Leave 'em be," said a voice.

Coyle turned to see Granier sitting on the branch of a tree. "The Viet Minh will know where we went if they find the bodies missing. It doesn't matter anyhow. They're dead. Burying them ain't gonna bring them back," said Granier jumping down from the tree.

"You made it," said Coyle with a half-smile.

"Yeah, well… it's downright amazing what I can do when I don't have you dragging my ass down."

"I suppose that's true."

"Did your navigator make it?"

"No. He died."

"Good. He's at peace."

"I suppose."

"Let's go. We still have a couple of hours of daylight."

"What about finding some food?"

"We can be up and over that pass by morning if we walk all night. You can eat then."

"Okay. You're the boss."

"I hate being the boss."

Granier, Coyle, and the flight crew headed east through the mountains. They still had a long way to go, but the worst seemed to be behind them.

Central Highlands, South Vietnam

Long grass swayed in the gentle breeze, stretching across a meadow surrounded by trees. Suong, the Viet Minh bodyguard, paced back and forth beside a road paralleling railway tracks. With his eyes closed, Le Duan, her charge and the Viet Minh commander in Central Vietnam, sat in the grass with his back up against the velocipede they had removed from the rails. "They're late," said Suong irritated.

"Pacing isn't going to get them here any faster," said Le Duan.

"I don't like being in the open like this. We should move into the trees where we can find cover if something happens."

"Nothing is going to happen."

"You don't know that. And it's not your responsibility if it does. It's mine."

"I'm the one they are going to be shooting at."

"I will take a bullet for you, but I won't like it."

"I won't suspect that you would."

"Take a bullet for you?"

"No. Like it. I have no doubt you would take a bullet for me."

Suong grunted. "We should eat while we wait," said Duan reaching into his backpack. "I think we still have some dried fish."

"You eat. I'll keep watch."

"Relax. We're in the middle of nowhere."

"…with no cover."

"We don't need cover if nothing happens."

"It's the 'if' that bothers me. Where the hell are they?"

"It's the countryside. Things happen. Bridges wash out. Potholes flatten tires."

"They should have planned for those things and gotten here early. It's wrong to make you wait. You are their commander. You're important."

"You really think that?"

"Think what?"

"That I'm important?"

"Of course. Ho would never have let me go if you weren't."

"Uncle really liked you, didn't he?"

"He respected my experience."

"As do I."

"Then how come you don't listen to me? We should move to the trees."

"Alright. Fine. We'll move to the trees."

"And here I thought you were stupid."

They gathered their backpacks and walked along the road toward the closest grove of trees. Suong stopped and said, "Listen."

"I don't hear anything," he said.

"That's because you are getting old and deaf."

"I'm not old."

"You're older than me."

"You told me you didn't know when you were born. How can you be so sure you are younger than me?"

"Shut up and listen. Something's coming."

A truck with a driver and passenger appeared on the road through the trees. "It's about time," said Suong.

"I told you nothing was going to happen."

The driver of the truck honked his horn and waved. Hearing the annoying honk, a swarm of tens of thousands of butterflies sprung from the trees and fluttered across the meadow, fleeing the noisy contraption barreling down the road. The cloud of Lepidoptera was migrating to the North now that the monsoons had ceased for the year. The white and orange wings were a strong contrast to the green forest and meadow. As they passed overhead, dozens landed on the arms, heads, and shoulders of Suong and Duan, laughing uncontrollably at the aerial assault. Duan's laugher softened as he looked at Suong covered in butterflies. "What?" she said.

"I don't remember ever seeing you laugh," he said, surprised.

"Don't be ridiculous. I laugh all the time."

"No. You don't."

"Yes, I do. You just don't pay attention."

"I'm paying attention now."

Suong was caught off-guard by Duan's remark. She seemed uncomfortable with his display of affection. She averted her eyes and moved off toward the approaching truck. Feeling spurned and embarrassed, Duan hid his thoughts from the others.

The truck parked next to the velocipede. The driver and the passenger, both young men, hoisted the apparatus into the bed of the truck. Duan climbed into the cab with the driver. Suong climbed in back with the passenger. "There's plenty of room in the cab," said the passenger.

"I like it better back here. It's cooler," said Suong sitting on the side of the truck.

"Suit yourself," said the passenger thumping the roof of the cab, signaling that they were ready. The truck hung a U-turn and traveled back into the forest. Both Suong and Duan rode silently, deep in thought.

Washington DC, USA

After only four years in the House of Representatives, John F. Kennedy made his bid for the senate and defeated Henry Cabot Lodge. One year later, he married Jaqueline Bouvier. Known for his articulate speeches, he was beginning to emerge on the national political scene. Having been one of the few political figures who had actually visited Vietnam, he became a leading expert in the senate.

By most accounts, Senator Kennedy was an ardent anti-communist and pro-interventionist in Southeast Asia. During a speech at a conference luncheon, he said, "We should not attempt to buy the friendship of the Vietnamese. Nor can we win their hearts by making them dependent upon our handouts. What we must offer them is a revolution — a political, economic, and social revolution far superior to anything the Communists can offer — far more peaceful, far more democratic, and far more locally controlled. Such a Revolution will require much from the United States and much from Vietnam. We must supply capital to replace that drained by the centuries of colonial exploitation; technicians to train those handicapped by deliberate policies of illiteracy; guidance to assist a nation taking those first feeble steps toward the complexities of a republican form of government. We must assist the inspiring growth of Vietnamese democracy and economy, including the complete integration of those refugees who gave up their homes and their belongings to seek freedom. We must provide military assistance to rebuild the new Vietnamese army, which every day faces the growing peril of Viet Minh armies across the border."

Kennedy believed, along with many other politicians and government officials, that South Vietnam could only survive the communist expansion pushed by China and the Soviet Union with America's help. He believed there was an opportunity to showcase America's exceptionalism and determination. Now that Vietnam had rejected French colonialism, he thought capitalism coupled with democracy was the clear path for the country to lift itself out of poverty and join the free world. He knew it would be difficult but believed the American people were up for the challenge. To his fellow congressmen, he said, "The Republic of Vietnam represents the cornerstone of the Free World in Southeast Asia, the keystone to the arch, the finger in the dike… If we are not the parents of little Vietnam, then surely, we are the godparents…this is our offspring. We cannot abandon it; we cannot ignore its needs. If Vietnam were to fall because of chaos or poverty or communism, the United States would be held responsible; and our prestige in Asia will sink to a new low." Kennedy fervently believed it was America's destiny and responsibility to save Vietnam from communism… and itself.

Saigon, South Vietnam

President Diem, the leader of South Vietnam, did not want war with North Vietnam. He saw the North as a buffer between South Vietnam and China. He hoped Ho Chi Minh would occupy himself with rebuilding the North after a decade of war with the French and the Japanese. He believed in reunification but was in no hurry to accomplish it. Creating a prosperous nation in the South with America's help was the safest way to reunify the country. When the people of the North saw the failure of Ho Chi Minh's programs and their economy was once again in a shamble, they would naturally want to join the South under Diem's leadership where food, shelter, and, most of all, wealth were plentiful. Refugees from the North would flood across the border, and Ho Chi Minh's regime would collapse. War was an unnecessary waste when reunification could be accomplished through peaceful means.

Diem recognized the power of an ally like America. Its resources seemed inexhaustible. It was only a matter of coaxing money and equipment out of the American leaders. But just because Diem accepted America's help didn't mean he was willing to follow their advice. He believed the Americans to be like spoiled children with too many toys. They were intoxicated with communism and did not know what was best for Vietnam. Only he knew what was best. He was determined to follow his own counsel and that of his brother Nhu.

It was said that if one hundred of his advisors said the truth was one thing and Nhu said it was another, Diem would believe his brother. He had gotten this far listening to Nhu; he would be a fool to march down another path listening to counsel from those he did not trust. At the same time, he knew Nhu and his wife could occasionally be overbearing and needed to be reined in. But that was his responsibility and not for others to interfere in family matters. Above all else, Diem trusted and protected his family.

Now that he was president, Diem needed to expand his political base and consolidate his power.

Brother Nhu was given full responsibility for internal security. Nhu commanded thirteen different security and counterintelligence agencies within the government. He was also the head of Can Lao - a political party that supported Diem and was growing in numbers. When he needed to avoid the government's footprints, Nhu was not above using outside help, especially when it came to blackmail or the assassination of a vocal opponent. Nhu believed in the wisdom of keeping dirty deeds at arm's length.

Known for her harsh and incendiary comments, Madame Nhu was not afraid to point the finger at anyone that opposed the policies of her husband or brother-in-law. In her youth, she was a tomboy who loved ballet and piano and once danced solo at Hanoi's National Theatre. She grew into an attractive and cultured young woman with strong political connections through her family. It was Madame Nhu that had lobbied her cousin, Emperor Bao Dai, to offer her brother-in-law Diem the post of Prime Minister after the end of the Indochina War. She later cast Bao Dai aside and encouraged Diem and Nhu to take control of the government.

Now, she was considered the first lady of South Vietnam and intended to take full advantage of it. Both Diem and Nhu saw her antics as harmless. Her intentions were well-meaning, even if her rhetoric was not. She was, after all, a woman and not to be taken too seriously in their minds. The brothers did not totally ignore her. There were times when her counsel, especially in private, was sound. She had a mischievous mind and was always looking for an angle. To her, things were very black and white – you were either for or against her family. She believed loyalty should be rewarded with promotions and lucrative government contracts. Opposition was to be crushed no matter the cost.

Madame Nhu pushed for the passing of "morality laws" outlawing abortion, adultery, divorce, contraceptives, dance halls, beauty pageants, boxing matches, and animal fighting. She advocated for closing down the brothels and opium dens in Saigon. She was not a politician. She saw herself as a live wire meant to shock common sense into people. Her obsession with power was even greater than her husband's. She was articulate, well-read, and quick-witted. She once said, "Having power is wonderful. Having total power is totally wonderful."

Educated at elite French schools in Hanoi, she was encouraged to be a French lady by her teachers and was taught French history rather than Vietnamese history. Unable to even write in her native language, she had her speeches translated into Vietnamese. She didn't believe in niceties and was willing to offend anyone that stood in her way. Beautiful and intriguing, she believed in manipulation and even practiced it on her husband when necessary.

To ensure continued American support for Diem, Madame Nhu befriended Americans working at the US embassy in Saigon and held lavish parties at the presidential palace to which they were invited. She would later criticize the Americans when it was politically expedient. To her, ethics and honor were matters of convenience.

She was chauffeured in a black Mercedes and wore a diamond-crusted crucifix. Her apparel was often so form-fitting, a French journalist referred to her dress as "molded around her like a dagger in its sheath."

She combined Roman Catholicism with a cult around herself as a modern reincarnation of Vietnam's legendary Trung Sisters, who led a revolt against China and defeated the Han Dynasty Chinese troops in AD 40. She developed her own following and even had public statues erected in her honor within the parks of major cities. Many women saw her as the embodiment of a traditional yet powerful Vietnamese woman. She was truly a "Dragon Lady" like the imperial mistresses of old. A force to be reckoned with. A woman to be feared.

Early one morning, Madame Nhu appeared at the main gate of a military port and demanded to see the commander. Within minutes, she was escorted to his office. "You have a ship carrying American aid that is arriving shortly," she said.

"Yes. Jeeps and trucks," responded the commander.

"You will have every tenth vehicle removed from your inventory and delivered to this address," she said, handing him a slip of paper.

"This is a black market," he said, examining the address.

"That is none of your business. Every tenth vehicle. Do you understand?"

"Of course, every tenth vehicle. What should I write in my report about the missing vehicles?"

"I don't care. Call it a tax if you must."

"A tax on American aid?"

"Yes. Why not?"

He shrugged and left. Before the end of the day, the vehicles were delivered as ordered and sold within a few days to whoever paid the highest price, including the religious militias and criminal gangs. Allegiances mattered little to Madame Nhu when money was involved.

Saigon, South Vietnam

It had been several weeks since Granier, Coyle, and the surviving aircrew had returned to South Vietnam. Granier's report spoke of his team's bravery and the tragedy of their deaths from the crash. He didn't blame anyone except himself, although there was little he could have done to save them. He half expected to be court-marshaled but had to remind himself that he was a civilian now, and the CIA didn't do that sort of thing.

Instead, Lansdale put Granier in for a National Security Medal for having saved the aircrew and completed his mission under dire circumstances. Because of the loss of his team, CIA Director Allen Dulles rejected the request for the medal but did award Granier with a letter of commendation.

During the private ceremony at Lansdale's office with Coyle, the flight crew, and all of the CIA paramilitary unit members present, word came of a film that the North Vietnamese had released to a foreign journalist. The journalist reported that in the film, the North Vietnamese displayed three South Vietnamese survivors along with captured US equipment from a crashed American military plane. The North Vietnamese had claimed the aircraft had crashed in North Vietnam during a covert sabotage mission. It was a lie that nobody would question because the South Vietnamese and the Americans were forbidden from performing covert operations in Laos as part of the Geneva Agreement. Granier was even more shocked when he learned that one of the survivors was Sergeant Dung. "Looks like you misplaced a few of your team members, Granier," said Conein.

"Fuck off, Conein," said Coyle.

"I don't understand how they survived the crash. Everything was burning," said Granier.

"They must have been ejected when the plane split in half," said Coyle. "It's a miracle they're still alive."

"We've got to mount a rescue mission," said Granier.

"A rescue mission? We don't even know where they are being held," said Conein.

"It doesn't matter," said Lansdale. "There won't be any rescue mission."

"What are you talking about? The North Vietnamese will execute them," said Granier.

"I doubt it. They are too valuable as propaganda assets. But even if they do… we cannot acknowledge their existence," said Lansdale.

"Those are our men."

"Technically, they're not. They're part of the South Vietnamese Intelligence group. America had nothing to do with it."

"I was with them. I was their leader."

"You were their advisor, and right now, nobody knows that. So, you will keep your mouths shut and let this thing blow over. Once it has, the South Vietnamese can use diplomatic means to accomplish the return of their men. Maybe a prisoner exchange."

"We can't just sit still and let them be tortured or killed."

"That's exactly what we can and will do. Because that is the job we signed up for. We are covert. That means nobody can know what we are doing."

Frustrated but realizing Lansdale was right, Granier dropped his letter of commendation to the floor and stormed out of the room. Lansdale picked up the letter, studied it for a moment, then set it on fire with his cigarette lighter. "That was unfortunate," he said, dropping the evidence into his trashcan to finish burning.

THE GIRL AND THE WATER BUFFALO

Saigon, South Vietnam

Lansdale and his CIA operatives kept busy tilting the scales in favor of Diem and the South. It was simple. With Diem in power, the South would remain free from communism, and with it… the rest of Southeast Asia. They were playing for all the marbles when it came to Soviet and Chinese expansion. And Lansdale and his men played to win. The more they could disrupt the North's progress and demoralize its people, the safer the South would be.

Having returned from Laos, Coyle and his crew once again became a covert taxi service for Lansdale. Operating under the CAT airline cover, they flew dozens of missions into the North. When possible, they avoided Hanoi because of its strong police presence. The police seemed to be everywhere, setting up roadblocks to check documents and search cargo. It was much safer to use one of the small city or town airfields where airport officials and police could be bribed to look the other way if they even bothered to look in the first place. And when they could not find a safe landing strip, they landed in South Vietnam and crossed the border or circumvented the border through Laos.

Using sea-going vessels was also an option, although the North Vietnamese had well-armed patrol boats and were more than willing to cease valuable cargo and kill a ship's crew. The sharks off the coast grew in number as more and more bodies were tossed overboard.

But Lansdale's two covert teams did not go quietly into the dying light. Although they wanted to avoid attention, they were not above fighting back if they were discovered. As time moved on and the North Vietnamese became more organized, the pathways into the North became more dangerous. When Lansdale planned missions, they became multi-faceted and designed to require the least amount of travel across the border. A team could go out for several weeks and execute five to six missions at the same time. It was exhausting, and with exhaustion, mistakes would be made.

North and South Border, Vietnam

Conein and his team moved through the grasslands that paralleled a dirt road. While on the southern side of the border, they were safe. But they didn't want to be seen by anyone watching from the North, and those in the North were always watching.

Much of the border was separated by the Ben Hai River. However, the river disappeared west near the Laotian border, making it easier to cross undetected. Conein had used that section of the border to crossover many times. The poorly maintained road drew little traffic and was lightly guarded. He stopped and motioned for his team to take cover. He peered through his binoculars and saw the barbed wire fence that divided the North from the South. It wasn't much of a barrier. It was the patrols on both sides that secured the border. He surveyed the surrounding area and spotted a hidden machine gun emplacement manned by a gunner and a loader on one side of the road. He also spotted a few guards milling around under a grove of trees. He imagined they were guarding the small opening in the fence line that allowed local villagers to pass and visit friends and family on the opposite side of the border. Although not encouraged, cross-border visits with locals were allowed since technically, the North and the South were not at war. The troops on both sides were well-armed and experienced. They often clashed, taking potshots at each other, but nobody wanted to start a war… at least not yet.

He and his team hid in the long grass, waiting and watching. They drank from their canteens and munched on salted pork. It had been a long journey from the airfield where they had been dropped off. Conein had insisted that they travel through the bush where they wouldn't be seen. There were spies everywhere near the border, and he didn't want his movements reported to the enemy.

Most commanders would have preferred to cross the border at night under the cover of darkness. But Conein knew that the patrols on the northern side would be increased after sunset. Night crossings were what the North Vietnamese expected. As a general rule, he never did what the enemy expected. He and his team would cross during the day. In the distance, he heard the gentle clanging of a tin bell. He again peered through his binoculars, focusing on the road.

A slender girl wearing an Ao Dai and conical hat rode on the back of a large water buffalo with seven-foot horns. The horns were wrapped with a vine of flowers as if the animal were part of some ceremony. The bell was around the beast's massive neck and clanged with each step. The girl was beautiful and carried a switch in her hand, which she used to control the buffalo's direction and pace. She only needed a light tap for the animal to respond. It was a symbiotic relationship between a master and her pet, each offering friendship and care to the other. As she traveled, she sang quietly to the creature, soothing him and passing the time.

The guards across the border saw her approaching and were intrigued by her beauty. They had seen her before and had enjoyed flirting with her in the past.

Conein had found the young girl several years previous when the Viet Minh had attacked her village. She had become an orphan when both her parents were killed trying to protect her and her little brother. Her brother was killed, and she was raped but survived. The family buffalo had survived too, with only a bullet wound in its shoulder. Now, the two survivors were inseparable. Conein had looked after her, giving her money for food, clothes, and medicine when she was sick. He made sure she attended school and only permitted her to miss class when he needed her for a diversion.

Conein watched her for a few moments thinking about what a lovely young woman she had become. Next year, she would graduate high school, and he wondered if she would marry. He knew he would be envious of her suitor but wanted the best for her. He tucked his binoculars in his pack and readied his team to move.

The girl approached the crossing and smiled at the guards like she always had. They quickly surrounded her and began their flirtations. Her buffalo bellowed from too many strangers, and they all laughed. She scratched his ears and whispered gently to him. He calmed.

With the guards distracted by the girl, Conein and his team reached the fence unseen. He had given his men strict instructions not to damage the fence, which could reveal their passing. Instead, he guided them to a fence post that he had previously loosened. One of his men lifted the post while the others slid under the wire. Everything was going well until the wooden post slipped through the soldier's hands, sending larger slivers into his palm. He dropped the post on the last man crawling under it. The barbed wire caught on the man's shirt, and he struggled to free himself. "Fuck," said Conein in a hushed voice.

The guards heard the commotion and went to investigate. The girl tried to distract them again, but they weren't having it. The machine gunner swung his gun around, pointing in the direction of Conein and his team.

Although the high grass hid the team from the guards' view, there was no cover if a firefight should break out. Conein eyed the tree line, a hundred meters away. If they could reach that before the guards discovered them, they would be safe or at least protected if a brawl broke out. After ordering the rest of the team to move toward the tree line, Conein ran back to the soldier on the ground and used his knife to rip his shirt open where it was caught on the barbed wire. He pulled the man up to his feet and pushed toward the tree line. Conein looked back toward the approaching guards and could see that his men would not make it to cover before they were discovered. Kneeling in the grass, Conein would buy them the time they would need. He waited until the first guard appeared in the long grass and fired a burst from his Thompson machine gun into the man's chest. He fell dead. Conein continued to fire, sweeping the barrel of his gun back and forth at what he hoped was the enemy's midsection.

The guards returned fire, and the machine gunner opened up, sending a barrage in Conein's direction.

Conein hit the dirt and started crawling toward the tree line. It was far off. He knew his chances of surviving were slim.

The girl watched as the firefight unfolded. She was frightened for a moment but then calmed. She climbed off her buffalo and ran toward the machine gun. She pulled off her hat as Conein had trained her and pulled the pin on a hidden grenade. She flung the hat into the machine gun emplacement and hit the ground, covering her head with her arms. The grenade exploded, sending hot shrapnel into the gunner and loader. The machine gun went silent as both fell dead.

Frightened by the explosion, her buffalo bolted. The girl climbed to her feet and called after the fleeing animal.

The leader of guards heard the explosion and turned back to see the smoldering remains of the machine gun emplacement and the girl running away.

Hearing her voice, the buffalo slowed, then stopped. When a few feet away, she called her pet's name again. The animal turned its head to see her as a barrage of bullets from the guard leader's rifle ripped through the slender girl and into the buffalo. The girl fought the pain and stumbled toward the buffalo, bellowing with fear and agony. She reached out and touched her friend one last time as she collapsed to the ground. The buffalo licked her hand, then wandered off into the trees where he died several hours later.

Conein was halfway to the tree line when his team sprang from cover and charged the three remaining guards and their leader. Conein shouted for them to stop, but it was too late. His men made short order of the enemy killing all four with a broadside of machine guns. "God dammit," said Conein climbing to his feet.

Conein knew that he was going to catch hell from Lansdale for botching the crossing. But the good thing about Lansdale was that he didn't like to make waves either. He would berate Conein but would bury the action report. The South Vietnamese army or a local militia would be blamed for the skirmish. Still, Conein hated it when things did not go according to plan.

Recognizing that the damage had already been done, Conein walked back to where the girl had fallen and gently turned her over. Her beautiful eyes were lifeless. She was gone. He surprised himself when tears welled up in his eyes then flowed down his cheeks. He had fought back his feeling for so long, trying not to love anyone or anything. He had lost that battle and wept.

Allowing himself a few minutes to collect his thoughts and right his mind for the mission at hand, Conein gathered his team of five Americans and eighteen 5th Bureau operatives and crossed the border. Lansdale had given him six sabotage targets and expected them all to be destroyed. It was a tall order, especially since he had been given scant intelligence on the targets and the North Vietnamese forces protecting them. Not to mention, the whole thing felt rushed.

He and his team had no time for training. Even worse, the plan was to split the team into six parts, with one American leading three 5th Bureau operatives on one of the assigned missions. Conein was going to complain, but he knew Lansdale would reassign the missions to Granier, and the thought that Granier and his men might succeed turned his stomach. It was not a friendly competition between the two teams and their commanders. Far from it. Lansdale often thought Granier and Conein might very well kill each other if given a chance. He wanted his teams and their leaders to be aggressive. He needed that pent-up energy to be unleashed on the enemy. He saw them as two pit bulls barking at each other from across a yard. As their commander, his job was to keep them far enough apart that a showdown never took place. The best way to do that was to keep them both busy in separate parts of the country. When one team was expected to return to Saigon's CIA base, he sent the other team out on a mission. An ongoing game of musical chairs with only one chair left.

Each group of sabotage missions had a core theme. The current sabotage theme was the North Vietnamese train system. By sabotaging the trains, transportation of raw materials production and distribution of weapons and supplies would grind to a halt. Troop transport would also be curtailed. It was a "juicy target," as Lansdale put it when issuing the orders. While Lansdale gave Conein a list of targets, he did not define the methods to be used. He left that to Conein.

Blowing up trains was nothing new to Conein, who had broad experience sabotaging German supply lines and troop transportation during WWII. He quickly came up with a plan that was both simple and effective. Conein believed in redundancy, especially when it came to sabotage. He fully expected that some of their tinkerings would be discovered by the North Vietnamese before it could be executed. For this reason, Conein designed two methods of destruction for each target. If one of the sabotage schemes was discovered, there was a good chance that the second scheme would remain undetected and succeed in accomplishing the mission.

For the trains, Conein chose to use hidden explosive devices to destroy the locomotives as the team's primary method. The secondary method would be the destruction of the bearings in the wheels of the train cars. Both methods would be effective but destroying the locomotives would have a longer-lasting effect since North Vietnam had no factories that could manufacture locomotives, and importing the engines would use up their limited financial resources.

The C4 that was to be used in the explosive devices would not ignite on its own, even when set on fire. It required a detonator that created a shockwave. The C4 was made of a white, pliable material similar to clay that could easily be molded into just about any shape. It was also very stable, considering its powerful punch. When properly applied, one block of C4 could rip a 14-inch steel girder in half. The explosive devices would make shorter order of the locomotives' fireboxes and boilers, rendering the engines useless without significant repairs.

Conein wanted to destroy the locomotives while they were moving to ensure that not only the engine was destroyed, but the train itself was heavily damaged. This meant that he couldn't use electric detonators or even timed detonators because he never knew when the train would get underway. Instead, he and his team needed a technique that would trigger the explosion while the train was moving. Hiding the explosive device within the coal that would be fed into the engine's firebox was the solution. They would plant the coal holding the C4 in the train's coal tender. Placing it near the top of the pile of coal ensured that the explosive device did not enter the firebox too early before the journey began. It was an ingenious method that Conein had learned for the Corsican mob during WWII.

Not all the train engines were powered by coal. Most of the locomotives were now run by diesel which was far more efficient and needed less maintenance. Most of the coal-burning engines were used on supply trains operating at slower speeds. This made them an attractive target. Lansdale did not want his teams to kill North Vietnamese civilians if it was possible to avoid it. He wanted to disrupt the supply chains supporting the army and industry. His main goal was to destroy the North Vietnamese economy, and in so doing, discredit Ho Chi Minh and the politburo. If communism could not support the people, it was an ineffective political system and should be abandoned. Even incapacitating the rail line between Haiphong Harbor and Hanoi would have a detrimental effect on the economy. Damaging the rail line from Dong Dang to Hanoi would cut off weapon and ammunition shipments from China. Both of these rail lines used coal locomotives.

The biggest problem facing Conein was that he had no idea where the coal locomotives were located. The intelligence from the undercover 5th Bureau operatives working in and around Hanoi was over a week old, and the trains were constantly on the move. So, the plan was for each of the six sub-teams to find a nice spot overlooking their assigned train depots and wait until a coal locomotive was spotted, then sabotage it. It was a lousy plan, and Conein knew it. North Vietnamese patrols could stumble across the mini-teams, causing the mission to fail and the team members to be captured or killed. But there wasn't much he could do. He had his orders. He considered sending recon squads out to search for the locomotives, but he quickly realized that strategy was even more dangerous and would take more time than his sit-and-watch strategy. Everyone was just going to have to do the best they could under the circumstances.

The little time available before the mission was used gathering the required material and demonstrating how to build the hidden explosives. C4 was new, and most of the men had no experience with it. It was also deceptively simple in form. Conein decided he needed a demonstration to convince his men of the white clay's explosive potential. He had his men dig a hole five feet deep, then had them place a blacksmith's anvil at the bottom of the hole. Next, he placed a half-block of C4 with a long pyrotechnic fuse attached to a blasting cap. Finally, he stacked three truck tires with their rims on top of the C4. He lit the fuse with a long Chinese match for fireworks and ran for cover behind a stack of sandbags. His men laughed, thinking it was one of Conein's jokes until the C4 exploded with a deafening boom. The three tires and their rims were launched fifty feet in the air. A few moments later, it rained tires, and Conein's men ran for cover. One of the tires came down and bounced so hard it landed on the roof of a supply hutch.

When his men pulled the anvil out of the hole, they found the steel head had been flattened with a wide crack down the center. Conein's purpose was achieved, and his men had a new appreciation for the plastic explosive.

Once across the border, Conein and his team maneuvered to a rendezvous point. Six lumber trucks driven by undercover 5th Bureau operatives were waiting on a nearby road. Under the lumber on each truck was a hidden space where Conein's team could travel unseen. They had used this technique before, and it worked well when they encountered North Vietnamese patrols or checkpoints. It would take almost two days to wind their way out of the foothills and into Hanoi's suburbs. The roads were poorly maintained, with potholes the size of a water buffalo. It was a bumpy ride, and the bed of the truck was hard. Conein was grateful he had chosen C4. There was no guarantee dynamite or some other explosive material would have survived the trip.

After a long and grueling trip, Conein and his men arrived at the abandoned sawmill they would use as a base of operations outside Hanoi. They took a few hours to catch some shuteye since it had been impossible to sleep in the trucks. A large pile of coal had been recently dumped outside the sawmill's main building. Conein and his men spent an entire day selecting and carefully hollowing out large pieces of coal. Most of the pieces broke in two before they were completed and had to be discarded. Conein had decided to use two camouflaged explosive devices for each locomotive; that way, if one got damaged or failed to go off for any reason, a backup device could complete the mission. That meant producing twice as many devices and the hollowed-out coal covers that would disguise them.

When they finally had enough hollowed-out coal covers, they inserted a block of C4 plastic explosive along with a pyrotechnic fuse connected to a blasting cap. And an additional layer of C4 was molded over the detonation device and made to resemble the contours and texture of the coal. When completed, the C4 was painted brownish-black to match the coal.

Before leaving to their assigned targets, Conein had each team member gather a small bag of sawdust from the mill. The sawdust was to be used against targets of opportunity, such as diesel engines or fuel storage tanks. Although it was unlikely that the sawdust would make it all the way into an engine, it would gum up the fuel filters and force the train to stop for repairs. Fuel storage tanks would need to be emptied, cleaned, and refilled. A slowdown in rail shipments was not as good as destroying a train, but it would make a difference.

Conein went over the details of the mission one last time before the team divided. If they could not find coal locomotives after four days, the operatives were to use their explosives to destroy the depots' fuel storage tanks and hopefully start a larger fire that would engulf the depot.

The team split up into six new groups and headed off. Conein was the leader of one of the new teams that included three 5th Bureau operatives. They were loaded down with as much gear and supplies as they could carry. His team would take on the most challenging target – Hanoi's rail hub. It would have more trains than any other depot within the rail system. A very juicy target. It wasn't that Conein didn't trust his other team members; he just trusted himself more than anyone. He was determined to do major damage to Hanoi's rail system no matter the cost.

Conein and his team were smuggled past the checkpoints and into the heart of Hanoi using a firetruck their undercover operatives had highjacked a day earlier. The truck's water tank was emptied halfway, and a rubber raft was lowered inside to hold their supplies while the men stood on the bottom of the tank with water up to their waists. The supplies were wrapped with rubber tarps to keep them dry. If the guards at the checkpoints became curious, the driver would open one of the hose couplings on the truck's side, and water would gush out, demonstrating that the tank was full. It was risky but so was just about any mode of transportation. The water sloshed over Conein and his men whenever the truck stopped suddenly, which was often with city traffic. Several times during the three-hour journey, they were knocked off their feet. Several of the men suffered from motion sickness and befouled the water making the trip even more unpleasant. However, it did work as expected, and they arrived at their destination undetected.

Conein and his team took up a position inside the loft of a rice warehouse next to the train hub. It gave them a good view of the trains moving in and out of the hub. The terminal was bustling with activity. By the end of the day, they had identified three coal locomotives. Conein knew that the engines would not stay idle for long, but he and his team could do little before nightfall. It was too risky to attack in daylight. Just before sunset, he watched in frustration as one of the coal engines hooked up to a train and pulled it out of the hub. An opportunity lost.

There was no moon that night. It was one of the reasons the mission was executed so quickly. The rail hub was still busy late into the evening with trains dropping off cars and picking up new ones. Floodlights and train headlights cast hard shadows but still left plenty of places where light would not reach. Conein and his team leapfrogged from shadow to shadow as they hunted down their targets.

The first engine they found already had its coal tender car attached. It was full of coal which is what they wanted. While his men kept guard, Conein climbed up onto the coal stack. He removed two of the camouflaged explosives and placed them on opposite sides of the tender just below the surface of coal. He predicted it would take a half-day before one of the bombs reached the locomotive's firebox. There was no way to ensure the engine was underway with a full load when the explosive detonated, but the odds were in his favor. He would settle for good odds. Satisfied that the bombs were well-hidden, Conein climbed down from the tender. He found it a little strange that no guards had passed nearby. That was a mistake that he and his men would take advantage of.

They used a grease gun filled with pumice-infused grease to inject the train's wheel bearings in several spots. The pumice would grind down the bearings over time until they failed. Even after the train crashed when the locomotive exploded, the train's cars would eventually be hoisted back on the track and re-enter service. The cars would mostly be shuffled off to other trains. The pumice-filled bearings would travel through the rail system like a virus until they ground to a halt and locked the wheels. The secondary sabotage would cause a significant delay even after the primary method had destroyed the locomotive.

Once they had sabotaged several wheels on the first target train, Conein and his men searched for the second locomotive. It didn't take long. The coal tender was not yet hooked up to the engine, which meant there was no place to hide the explosives. They spent their time greasing the wheels of a nearby train with the pumice-infused grease gun.

When they returned, the coal tender was still missing from the engine. Most of the night was already gone. Time was slipping away before sunrise and the end of their mission. Conein and his men went in search of a fuel storage tank. They found it on the far side of the yard. They took the sawdust bags they had brought and dumped them into the tank. Clogging fuel injectors in multiple diesel locomotives was a far cry from completely destroying an engine, but it would slow the rail system.

When they returned the second time to the coal locomotive, it was gone. Conein cursed to himself, "Another fucking target lost."

Just as they were about to leave, the second locomotive with its coal tender backed up to couple with a long line of train cars. They watched from the shadows as the engineer jumped down from the locomotive to check in with the operation center and fill his thermos with hot tea for the journey ahead. As soon as he disappeared, Conein and his men crossed the tracks. Conein climbed into the tender and placed the explosives under the top layer of coal. He dropped down, and the team worked its way out of the hub sticking to the shadows. Conein took the lead.

When he came to the end of the last parked train, a maintenance man rounded the last car's corner and almost walked into Conein. Conein drew his knife as he pushed his free hand over the man's mouth to keep him from shouting out. The knife plunged deep into the man's abdomen. Conein kept driving forward, pushing the man until he fell backward. Conein landed on top of him, changed his grip on the knife, and pulled downward, disemboweling the man. He would bleed out and die in less than a minute. Conein could feel the struggle leaving the man's body until it became still.

The successful mission suddenly turned to shit. Even if Conein and his men carried the maintenance man's corpse with them, he would be missed. After a quick search of the hub by his fellow workers, the military would be alerted. Suspecting possible sabotage, the soldiers would do a more thorough investigation. Conein was sure he and his men had covered their tracks well and that the bombs were well hidden, but he was also sure that the army would perform an exhaustive search. If the bombs hidden in the coal were found, a warning would be sent to the other depots and hubs to look out for similar sabotage. The incident could put the entire mission and his teams in jeopardy.

Conein's mind was racing as he and his men pulled the maintenance man's body behind a building. "What do we do, boss?" said one of the operatives that spoke a little English.

Conein knew that his team wanted to pull out now before the North Vietnamese discovered the maintenance worker's body. There was no benefit in getting captured, and if they left now, there was a good chance they could escape. But Conein had grown accustomed to winning. He valued his reputation as a man that succeeded where others failed. Giving up after they had come so far just didn't seem right to him. He didn't want to risk his life any more than the other men on his team, but risk was part of the job. He knew it, and they knew it. He couldn't just let the mission fail without at least trying to make things right. Conein took another moment and said, "We burn it to the ground."

"Burn what?"

"Everything. The entire hub."

"How?"

"Let me worry about that. You and your men make your way back to the engines we sabotaged and remove the bombs from the coal tenders. We cannot let them be found. They will endanger the other missions. When you are done, head for the rendezvous point."

"Without you?"

"I'll be along."

The three operatives took off into the night and disappeared. Conein made his way back to the diesel storage tank. He climbed up the supports and opened the valve. Diesel fuel poured out onto the ground, pooling up between the tracks then seeping out and spilling over. Before long, the liquid was spreading toward the trains. He didn't have much time before the guards or maintenance men noticed the smell and discovered his sabotage.

His biggest problem was igniting the fuel. Diesel had to be preheated to forty-three degrees Celsius before it would ignite. Because of its high flash point temperature, the diesel could not be easily set afire with a match or lighter like gasoline. Plus, he needed it to look like an accident. There were half-burned matches and cigarette butts littered throughout the yard. They were enough evidence of how a small fire might have started. He found a rag lying on the ground. It had been used to clean excess grease off the bearings. He lit the rag on fire and set it in the path of the diesel. He stepped back and watched as the fuel flowed across the ground and surrounded the rag soaking it thoroughly. Overwhelmed with liquid, the flame on the rag went out. Conein cursed.

He thought for a moment. He needed more heat. He pulled out his pistol, ejected the magazine, and removed three bullets. He used his knife to remove the bullet heads and poured the propellant from the cartridges into a small pile next to the end of a railroad tie. He pocketed the bullet heads and empty cartridges, then grabbed some old twigs and dried leaves at the base of a fence and placed them over the propellant. He used his knife to scratch a little trench in the ground to divert the fuel to his mini campfire. He was careful not to make the trench in a straight line, so it was undetectable. When the fuel reached the trench, it flowed toward twigs and leaves. Conein waited until it made contact with the little campfire. He used his lighter to ignite the propellant. It flashed and burned hot, setting the leaves and twigs on fire. It even set the end of the railroad tie aflame. The fuel flowed underneath the burning pile of twigs and leaves, heating up as it moved. It only took a few seconds for it to reach the ignition point and catch fire. It was a slow burn, hesitating at first, then gradually spreading across the shallow stream of fuel.

Satisfied, Conein moved off to the shadows of a building and continued to watch as the fire spread. He was sure the guards and maintenance workers would spot the fire in the next two or three minutes. He hoped it would be too late. The stream of burning diesel fuel spread under the first train car – an empty boxcar with the doors opened. Through the opening, Conein could see the next train. It was loaded with fuel tankers. He couldn't tell, but he expected at least some of them held gasoline instead of diesel. If the flames reached them before the crews could extinguish the fire, the mission was guaranteed to be a success. The fire spread to the undercarriage, and before long, the boxcar was engulfed in flames. Crew members ran toward the flames.

Conein needed to buy more time for the fire to spread. He spotted a hydrant sticking out of the ground and an emergency box next to it. He moved toward it, keeping low and sticking to the shadows. He opened the emergency box and found an axe and a long coil of hose. He used the axe to break off the hydrant's handle, but he realized that it wouldn't take the fire crew long to remove the broken handle and turn the hydrant on using a wrench. He thought about cutting the hose with his knife, so it was useless but was concerned with leaving evidence of his sabotage. Instead, he picked up the hose, threw it over his shoulder, and stole it. Sometimes the simplest solution was the best.

He took one last look around the yard and saw the fire spreading toward the fuel tankers. He had done his best, and it was time to leave. He moved off into the shadows and headed for the rendezvous point.

Ten minutes later, a massive series of explosions rocked the city. Conein smiled to himself. He had snatched defeat from the hand of fate and turned it into success. He hoped his other teams had done as well. They had.

In all, they had destroyed fourteen locomotives and severely damaged over a hundred freight cars and tankers. The slowdown in North Vietnam's economy was noticeable. The damage to their rail systems set them back almost six months and used up most of the government's financial reserves to repair and replace the lost engines and cars, not to mention the rail hub Conein and his team burned to the ground.

HANOI CARPETBAGGERS

Countryside, South Vietnam

Most, including the Americans, believed that land reform in the South was the key to building popular support for the Diem government. One of the Viet Minh's biggest attractions during the French Indochina war was that they redistributed the land that came under their control to the peasants. They simply confiscated the land from the French plantation owners and wealthy Vietnamese and gave it to the locals.

When Diem came to power, he rescinded the Viet Minh land reform program and returned the land to the original owners. While it strengthened his support with the wealthy landowners, it was a very unpopular move outside of Saigon and caused many peasant farmers to reject the new government.

Lansdale designed a program to confiscate and redistribute the land in hopes of once again winning back support from the countryside for Diem. It was called Ordinance 57.

The new law forbade ownership by an individual of more than 250 acres of rice land. The excess land that the government confiscated was transferred to poor farmers and landless peasants. The redistributed land comprised ten percent of the 7.5 million acres of cultivated land in South Vietnam.

One of the program's most significant problems was that Diem assigned Catholics and refugees with the responsibility of distributing the land. The Catholic church was the largest landowner in all of The Republic of Vietnam. As a devote Catholic, Diem dedicated the entire country to the Virgin Mary. Under Diem, the Catholic Church's property was exempt from land reform, and the church was given special privileges in acquiring the new land.

As a result, the farmers and peasants in the countryside did not trust the Catholics and saw the refugees from the North as carpetbaggers. The program was riddled with corruption and administered poorly. The revised land reform program ended up taking land given to farmers and gave it back to the landlords so that seventy-five percent of the land was owned by fifteen percent of the people. As was expected, the villagers in the countryside rebelled against the government. It was this type of bureaucratic stumbling in what should have been a popular program that continually fed the ranks of the Viet Minh.

Vietnamese children often played in the irrigation ditches between the fields of rice, corn, sugar, peanuts, and potatoes. Five or six boys and girls would sit one behind the other in a ditch blocking the water. When the built-up pressure was enough, the water would push the children down the ditch like a little human train. Tiny boats made out of coconut husks and banana leaves were also a favorite toy in the canals. And there was always time for a water fight.

That was the one thing the Vietnamese didn't need to worry about… water. It rained constantly in the wet season, which lasted five months. The ground became saturated, filling the wells to the brim and turning the mountain streams into rivers. Reservoirs and lakes were often overflowing, flooding surrounding flatlands and occasionally villages. Rain covered the rice in the fields, cooled the water buffalo, and cleaned thatched-roof huts of dust. Rain swept the debris from the streets and cleaned the bird shit off the park statues and neighborhood rooftops. There were times it was too much, but that wasn't often.

Rain created mud so deep and thick it could suck a man's shoe or sandal off, never to be seen again. In the mountains, the rain made driving impossible, with roads being washed away in flash floods and mountainsides collapsing under their weight as they became saturated. Rain gave life and sometimes took it, but it was always God-sent.

In the dry season, there were occasional thunderstorms to cool things down and keep the abundant vegetation growing. Even the poorest of peasants had a conical hat made of grass or bamboo to keep the top of the head dry in the monsoons and cool from the sun.

Rain was what made Vietnam special. It allowed rice to be harvested three times a year instead of the single harvests experienced by its neighboring countries.

To combat the growing insurgency in the South, the American advisors came up with the idea of an agroville. While most villages were made up of twenty to thirty hamlets, an agroville was its own subdivision containing six thousand preconstructed huts, a hospital, and a school. All within a bamboo-walled compound and patrolled by the local militia. The idea was to keep all the families in the area within one compound. The government could better protect them and ensure that the rebels didn't recruit them.

To build each agroville, Diem conscripted twenty thousand farmers pulling them away from their fields to dig a twenty-foot-wide moat lined with hundreds of thousands of punji sticks and surrounded by a twelve-foot-high bamboo wall that encircled the entire compound. The huts inside were lined up against straight pathways that led to a perfectly straight main street stretching from one end of the agroville to the other. Each super complex was magnificent, and the people hated them. Of the twenty thousand workers forced to build the agroville over six weeks, only twelve thousand would be given huts within the newly constructed agroville. The others were thanked for performing their "civic duty" and returned to their villages. They were the lucky ones.

Forced to give up their family farms and tend the fields around the agroville, the Vietnamese felt their freedom and culture were being taken away. One recently completed agroville mysteriously caught fire the night before the villagers had been assigned to move in. Without anyone to put out the fires, the entire agroville burned to the ground. The following day, the farmers were informed of the disaster and asked to return to their villages until repairs could be made. Everyone cheered.

The more agrovilles the government made, the more the Viet Minh ranks swelled, and the stiffer resistance developed. Again, Diem and the American advisors had missed the mark. It was a common theme. The more they tried to control the South Vietnam population, the more the proud Vietnamese rebelled, especially the farmers that had grown accustomed to living without government help or interference over the decades.

The Viet Minh had their own problems. The local cadres in the South were growing impatient, waiting for the war they knew was impossible to avoid. Many complained of intolerable boredom from the slow-moving political actions they were forced to perform. Even with their efforts, government reform was sluggish, with two steps forward and one back. They felt they were dying a slow death as Brother Nhu's secret police closed in and arrested the communists one by one as they handed out pamphlets or in groups during demonstrations.

Forced to spend more time in the North with the Politburo, Le Duan felt that the army of followers he had worked so hard to build in the South was being whittled down to nothing. The leaders of the Viet Minh in South Vietnam took their cues from the politburo in Hanoi. Even after hearing the testimony of dozens of witnesses describing Saigon's "cruel terrorism," the politburo members refused to authorize the escalation to full-scale warfare with the South Vietnamese government.

Ho Chi Minh was adamant that North Vietnam was not ready to sustain an ongoing war in the South. The northern economy was still suffering from the extensive infrastructure damage left by the French Indochina War. Money was flowing in from China and the Soviet Union, but it wasn't enough. The people in the North were struggling. Many were hungry and sick from malnourishment. The land reforms that the government had implemented had not worked as expected. In fact, they had the opposite effect, and rice production had shrunk even further.

It seemed that the North and South had decided to leave each other alone for the time being. Both were trying to stabilize their governments and improve their economies. Neither government wanted to leave things as they were with Vietnam split in two, but all-out war was being put off until a later time when they were better prepared. The Americans, Chinese, and Soviets agreed with this strategy. None of the major powers wanted war in Southeast Asia… not yet anyway. While not ideal, the status quo was acceptable.

But all of this wishful thinking did nothing to pacify the southern cadres. They wanted action now. There was a growing feeling that if they just attacked the South Vietnamese Army, the people would join their just cause, and Diem's government would fall apart. At the very least, the cadres and their local leaders felt they could capture the entire countryside and leave the government and its supporters to starve in the big cities until they were overthrown or capitulated. The biggest problem with that theory was the Americans could prop up the Diem government by purchasing food and supplies from neighboring countries. The big cities in the South were all located along the eastern coast and had shipping ports that allowed them to receive U.S. aid indefinitely.

But nobody wanted to go against Ho Chi Minh. Despite his age and conservative approach to the new phase of the revolution, everyone in the North and most in the South saw Uncle Ho as a national hero. After all, he had driven out the French from the North and freed his people from over a century of western imperialism. It was considered unpatriotic and political suicide to go against Uncle Ho.

But even Ho could not withstand the winds of change. Moves behind the scenes were being made to unseat him as party leader. Ho realized that younger leaders with new ideas were desperately needed in the politburo if the revolution was to survive. It was he that would finally arrange his own overthrow despite his loyal followers.

Western Mountains, South Vietnam

A young Viet Minh fighter watched a mountain road from his perch on a rock outcropping. He was armed with a pre-WWI musket and a small bag of ammunition, including nine lead balls. His job was to report any enemy activity, such as troop or supply convoys. He didn't have a radio. If an urgent message needed to be sent, he was allowed to travel to a local village and hire a messenger. Once finished, he had orders to immediately return to his post on the outcropping and continue his watch.

There was nobody visible within miles. He was alone. The only sound was the wind and an occasional wild animal call which he welcomed. Anything to break the silence. He had been at his post for seven months. His commander sent a bi-monthly supply shipment of rice, fish sauce, six mangos, four cans of plums, two dozen dried squid, two bottles of rice wine, and a local newspaper.

One night, he thought he heard the voices of his parents. Both had passed away during the last famine. Their voices died with the wind. The thought that he was going crazy saddened him. He was a patriot and wanted desperately to serve his country, but the loneliness and boredom were too much. He knew that his fellow communists would take away his weapon if they found out he was insane. It made sense. He was resigned. He thought about shooting himself in the head but decided that would be a waste of ammunition needed to fight in the coming war. Instead, he simply stood up and walked off the end of the outcropping. He landed headfirst on the rocks below and died after a few minutes. His boredom and loneliness were finally gone.

Nguyen Gia Kien was the area commander for the Viet Minh. He was saddened by the report of the young scout's death. The report said it was an accident, but Kien knew better. His troops were demoralized. This was not his unit's first suicide. In fact, they were becoming more frequent. Kien did not understand why the Central Office had not issued orders to attack the South Vietnamese. He did not believe his commanders were cowards. He knew them to be patriots. But that just made their inaction all the more confusing. What were they waiting for? Surely, they understood that war was inevitable. If the North Vietnamese army would not give them weapons, then his troops would find their own by raiding enemy convoys and supply depots.

He wondered if the politburo thought he and his men were not up to the task of defeating the South Vietnamese soldiers. Nothing could be farther from the truth. Even after all that had happened or not happened, his troops still had a deep-seated desire to free their country by overthrowing Diem's government. *Perhaps the solution to the North dragging their feet was to show them what he and his followers could do*, he thought. He knew any violence against the Diem government would be frowned upon, but at that point, he didn't care. Let the politburo strip him of his command. *"I'd rather die than live like this. The armed struggle must begin now,"* he thought.

At least he would be doing something to boost his troops' morale and show Diem and his family that their oppression would not stand without a fight. He would once again be able to look at himself in the mirror and be proud that he was a man of action.

Kien took personal charge of a platoon of his best fighters. He didn't want the lieutenant commanding the platoon to be blamed for his decision to defy the politburo's orders. If Kien commanded the platoon directly, he alone would shoulder the blame.

He and his men created an ambush on Highway 4 in the Mekong Delta. A civilian bus approached. The Viet Minh sprang from their hidden positions and forced the driver to stop by threatening to shoot him through the windshield. The civilians on board were terrified as the rebels entered the bus. The passengers were forced out onto the road. Many believed they would be shot when they were ordered to kneel and put their hands on their heads. Before the highjacking, Kien had given his troops strict instructions that no civilians were to be hurt unless he alone gave the order. No one was hurt. The entire platoon climbed aboard the bus, and Kien ordered the driver to take them to a South Vietnamese fortified outpost in a nearby town.

As the bus pulled up to the fortified post, Kien was surprised to see the gates open with people and troops walking in and out the stronghold. It was market day, and local vendors were allowed into the post to sell their goods to soldiers and officers inside. Kien ordered the driver to continue inside the post, then ordered his men to keep their weapons out of sight.

As he expected, the guards at the gate didn't give the bus a second look and waved it inside the perimeter walls. When the bus finally stopped, the Viet Minh piled out of the bus and spread out through the compound. Most of the South Vietnamese soldiers within the fortress were unarmed. Their commander had ordered that their weapons be kept under guard to prevent theft while the villagers were inside the compound. Only the guards protecting the front gate and patrolling the walls were armed.

There was a short but violent firefight between the rebels and the post guards. The Viet Minh quickly overwhelmed the guards killing several. The rest of the South Vietnamese troops surrendered without a fight. Even though they were vastly outnumbered, Kien and his rebels captured the South Vietnamese company protecting the post.

Kien was unsure of what to do now that he had control of the stronghold. He never thought he and his men would get as far as they had. He took all the South Vietnamese soldiers and their officers prisoner. He made them kneel with their hands on their heads. They too thought they would be shot in their backs. Some pissed themselves.

Kien ordered his men to search the compound and find the company's weapons. It didn't take long. They were all leaning against a wall inside the supply warehouse. The rebels loaded the weapons and ammunition into the bus. They also loaded as much food, support gear, and medical supplies as the bus could carry. It was a massive haul for the Viet Minh.

When Kien was satisfied that everything of value was in the bus, he ordered the village chieftain, who was inside the compound visiting the commander, to be taken to the front gates. The chieftain was forced to kneel as his people watched. Kien ordered the bus and his troops to leave the compound.

As the bus passed through the gate, Kien shot the chieftain in the back of the head. He fell dead. Kien shouted to the villagers that their chieftain was killed as an example because he collaborated with the South Vietnamese army. Lastly, he told them that the Viet Minh were now in charge of the area and they should stop paying taxes to the South Vietnamese government. Kien climbed aboard the bus, and the Viet Minh left.

The raid on the Mekong Delta post was the first time the Viet Minh had captured a South Vietnamese fortified position. It was evidence that the Viet Minh were up to the task of overthrowing Diem's government.

Hanoi, North Vietnam

When the news of the raid reached the members of the politburo, it made a strong impression and forced many to reconsider their position.

General Giap wanted the belligerent major who led the raid to be imprisoned. Ho Chi Minh stopped him. He explained to Giap that he didn't want to draw attention to the major's disobedience. Instead, he requested the politburo issue a letter of commendation to the major for his selfless act of bravery. He would be a hero, not a martyr. Ho was a wise politician that knew when the tide had turned. The realities of North Vietnam's resources to fight a protracted war in the South had not changed. But Ho would bide his time and wait until the politics of the major's raid had calmed down before returning to his call to tow-the-line of caution and hope for a peaceful solution.

Saigon, South Vietnam

When Diem heard about the Viet Minh raid on the fortified outpost, he was furious. Rarely had he shown his temper as he did on that day. Not even Lansdale could calm him. The fact that an entire company of ARVN soldiers surrendered to a platoon of Viet Minh was an embarrassment. He was concerned about how it would look to the Americans. There was little doubt the North Vietnamese government would be emboldened, not to mention the rebels in the South.

Outspoken and over the top in her criticism, Madame Nhu wanted to behead the fortress commander for his incompetence. Lansdale suggested restraint for fear of demoralizing the ARVN troops further. Brother Nhu kept silent, hoping to avoid becoming the target of his brother's rage. The damage had already been done, and the South Vietnamese Army's reputation had been tarnished. Nhu would use the fiasco as evidence that the army needed reform and that leaders loyal to the family should replace those currently in power.

Central Highlands, South Vietnam

It was late in the afternoon, and the sky was clear—no rain in sight. A traveling vendor weighed down by two large baskets stuffed with brooms pedaled his bicycle down a country road. The brooms were handmade by his wife and children while he went from village to village, pedaling the family's wares. It was a good living. The broom handles were made of bamboo that he cut down from the embankment of a nearby lake. They cost him nothing. The broom bristles were made from two kinds of material - coconut tree leaves and fishtail grass. The coconut leaf brooms were stiff and robust, ideal for use in the canals and rice paddies to move water or sweep up fallen leaves to keep them from clogging the gateways. The fishtail grass brooms were soft and used indoors to sweep up fallen food scraps and dirt tracked in from outside. The broom heads were handsewn by his wife and were high quality. The villagers in the surrounding area loved his brooms which could last for months and waited for his visits.

As he pedaled, he looked out across the rice paddies and could see the sun's reflection in the muddy water. It was getting late, and he was still far from home. Distracted by the beauty of the setting sun, he failed to notice a pothole in the road. When his front wheel hit, the bike stopped immediately, and he went flying over the handlebars landing in the road. The bike fell sideways, and his broom inventory toppled out of the baskets. He wasn't hurt beyond a few cuts and scrapes that his wife was sure to clean up as soon as he arrived home. His brooms were dusty from the road dirt. He would need to clean them before going out again tomorrow. But the real problem he didn't notice until he climbed back on the bicycle – his front tire was flat.

Fortunately, he carried a spare inner tube and repair tools with him on the bicycle. He took another look at the sun low on the horizon. There wasn't much daylight left. He went to work repairing the tire. The rim was slightly bent. He used a pair of pliers to tighten the spokes, eyeballing the straightness of the rim. It would have to do until he could get back to his village where his neighbor was experienced at fixing bicycles.

Forty-five minutes later, he was back on his way, pedaling down the road with his broom inventory back in the two baskets. Although not happy, he was satisfied. It could have been much worse. The surrounding countryside was cast in a reddish-orange hue. A serene setting. Picturesque.

When the sunset and darkness overtook the road and rice paddies, he was still a few miles from his village. He had known this area all his life. He was born there. He had married there. And he had raised his children there. He had the same friends from his childhood. Very little changed from generation to generation in his village. It was a good life. A peasant's life. He never heard the gunshot that delivered a bullet into the side of his head. It was a clean shot and killed him instantly. No suffering. Just death. He didn't even feel the ground as he and his bicycle once again toppled to the road, his precious broom inventory spilling out.

The Viet Minh sniper was a young man accompanied by his best friend. He had borrowed a musket and three lead balls from an elder in his village. He had not asked the elder for permission to take the weapon. But he felt he would be forgiven when word of his deed reached his village. The broom vendor's death sent a clear message to the villages in the area. It was the Viet Minh that controlled the roads, not the Diem government. The sniper and his friend each took a broom as a trophy and headed back to their village, where the girls were sure to swoon over their exploits.

As more and more amateur snipers performed their patriotic duty with random assassinations, transportation of goods between cities slowed to a trickle, as did all travel. The country was grinding to a halt, and there wasn't much Diem and his family could do about it.

Two out of three peasants backed the communists or the government out of fear. Having a son that joined the ARVN or the Viet Minh could be a death sentence to the parents depending on which side was currently in power in the area.

However, the revolution did offer some peasants a sense of belonging to something bigger than themselves. It gave pride to the humble peasants that they could not find in their lives of day-to-day survival. It gave them a sense of purpose. There was a growing belief in the countryside that Ho was the future and Diem was the past.

But while some peasants truly believed in the revolution, most just wanted to live their lives in peace and raise their families. Neither the Viet Minh nor Diem's government troops gave the villagers the option of staying neutral. The peasants in the countryside were forced to choose.

But the choice was usually relatively easy – whomever currently controlled the area was the faction of choice. Loyalty would continue until the opposing faction kicked out the current faction. Then the villagers simply changed their banners and rhetoric to support the new boss.

Of course, some holdouts stood by their principles and continued to support the ousted faction. They didn't last long. Their village elders would deal with the troublemakers by either kicking them out or waiting until dark and silencing them forever with a machete. It was the elders' job to keep the peace and continue prosperity in their villages. Survival in South Vietnam was dependent on practical decisions and actions. It was not wise to make waves.

The Viet Minh's main objective was to demonstrate to the enemy and the people that they could strike at will. "The tiger has awaked," was the saying painted on banners and shouted in the streets during gatherings.

Almost all of the villagers paid secret taxes to the Viet Minh even if they didn't believe in their cause.

It was safer to pay the communist tax collector when he visited the village than to stoke their ire. During their visits, the cadres collecting the taxes often cited proverbs, like "Better the head of a rat than the tail of an elephant" or "No matter how hard you try to shed your horns, you will always remain a water buffalo." They would stage rallies accompanied by a cacophony of megaphones, whistles, gongs, and "wooden fish" – the clackers of temple bells. Trees and huts around the village would be plastered with posters and slogans. Any government flags or proclamations would be torn down and urinated on.

Rumors spread the Viet Minh's magical powers: their enchanted rice cookers, inflatable boats in their backpacks, "sky horses", and guns that could kill fifty soldiers in one shot. The uneducated peasants embraced such myths, and supporters repeated them as evidence of the Viet Minh's superiority. Many knew the rumors were false but repeated them anyway, wanting to show their loyalty to the vicious Viet Minh.

The government troops were no better and used similar tactics of intimidation. Killing an accused Viet Minh with a machete in broad daylight was a powerful demonstration of the government's dominance. The army commanders knew how to make an impression and were not above using torture and violence to get their point across. Fear was met with fear, and the peasants were caught in between.

Most of the younger peasants were trapped in a relentless cycle of boredom and agrarian toil on the family farm. They had little hope of ever visiting a big city like Saigon or Hue even once in their lives, let alone another country. They were imprisoned in poverty with little hope of a prosperous future. When the Indochina War veterans living in the villages would talk of their heroic deeds and those of their comrades, the young men would get excited perhaps for the first time in their lives. Joining an army, any army, was the one opportunity in a teenager's life that might result in glory. It was a chance to make their lives mean something beyond another rice harvest. And so, the war machine was once again fed the youth of Vietnam. Many of the teenagers would desert after a few months and return to their villages demoralized and homesick. They were usually hunted down and made an example by either being brought back in chains or executed on the spot. The South Vietnamese army used a portable guillotine leftover from the French. They hauled it from village to village to make a lasting impression on the civilians that harbored the deserters.

Nothing seemed to stop the Viet Minh. They accepted setbacks in stride. After the Diem government had abandoned the promised elections, the Viet Minh decided to play the long game toward reunification. They would keep continual pressure on South Vietnamese forces, whittling them down. The rebels forced the government to use their precious resources and manpower to chase down the saboteurs who just vanished back into the population whenever they wished. And when the South Vietnamese soldiers took out their frustration on the villagers in the countryside, the Viet Minh would grow in number from the farmers and peasants seeking revenge that joined their ranks.

SIAMESE CROCODILES

Cua Song Bay, South Vietnam

Government patrol boats with 50-Cal machine guns mounted on their decks patrolled the estuary leading into the Cua Song Bay on the Southern tip of South Vietnam. Gunrunners from Cambodia were the main problem. In addition, there were always a few pirates and contraband smugglers that needed rounding up.

Leading into Cua Song Bay, the estuary with its saltwater and freshwater mix was the perfect breeding ground for shrimp. Dozens of sampans crowded the waters every morning a few hours before dawn when the shrimp were feeding and active.

Some fishermen waded into the estuary up to their waists and flung large round nets with weights on the ends into the dark waters. A small rope in the center retrieved the net and closed the bottom, trapping the shrimp inside. On a good day, each throw would catch three or four pounds of shrimp of various sizes.

It didn't take more than three or four hours before an experienced fisherman had more than he could carry to market.

If a fisherman was lucky enough to own a motor-scooter, he could fish a little longer and beat the other fisherman to market. Once his catch was sold, he could use the motor-scooter as a family station wagon. Most Vietnamese were slender and didn't weigh much, so a patriarch could carry himself and five or six of his family members plus a couple of live chickens and a basket of eggs on his motor-scooter. Loading up a scooter with one's family was a common sight around the countryside and even in some cities. In the country, people rarely traveled beyond the villages in the surrounding area. A visit to a big city by one of its citizens would become the gossip of a village for weeks on end and was always looked upon as a cautious event.

There were, of course, dangers in the estuaries – Siamese crocodiles, poisonous snakes, and the occasional shark that wandered from the bay into the shallows. Every month or so, a fisherman would fail to return to his village, and a bodiless funeral would be held in his honor. Life was hard in Vietnam. Danger was everywhere. But no matter the risk, it was a man's responsibility to feed his family.

There was no social safety net in Vietnam like those that were being developed in more advanced countries in Europe and North America. Children were the only reliable safety nets in Southeast Asia. Parents would do whatever was necessary to raise their families. When the children became adults and the parents grew old, it became the siblings' shared responsibility to support their parents. The more children the parents had, the better their life would be once they could work no more. The parents' responsibilities did not stop with old age but merely shifted. The old raised the young while the new parents went off to work and provided money for the entire family. If a man or woman's parents were found wanting, the man or woman would be shamed by both young and old in the local community. Cultural compliance was strong throughout Southeast Asia. It was an endless cycle.

If a child went off to fight in a war, the parents would be forced to do without and continued to work well beyond reason until the war was over. The Vietnamese had been fighting for decades and the older generation, while patriotic, grew weary of the conflict that took away their children and retirement. Both North and South paid their professional soldiers, but it was a low wage incapable of supporting a large family, especially in the North. War was merciless on the young and old of Vietnam, no matter which side one pledged their allegiance to.

A few minutes past midnight, a lone saboteur, his face and hands smeared with black grease and wearing black pajamas, waded into the reeds along the eastern shore of the estuary. He moved like a shadow across the shallows, barely visible. He carried an oil drum, a coil of twin wire intertwined with a heavy fishing line with lead weights attached a foot apart all along the line. He had already tied one end of the fishline securely to the drum's handle. In addition, two wires had been fastened to an electrical detonator attached to a canister of Soviet TNT inside the drum. The twin wires exited the drum through an opening sealed with a thick layer of candle wax to prevent water from entering the drum.

The saboteur found a log half-buried in the mud within the reeds and placed the drum on top of the rotting wood. The drum and log were surrounded by a wall of reeds, making them undetectable from the river or shore. He fed the wires and fishing line through the reeds and into the open water. He slowly swam across the estuary, meting out the twin wires and fishing line as he traveled to the opposite shore. As the coil of twin wires and fishing line fell into the water, it sank, and the lead weights carried it to the muddy bottom of the estuary.

It took over an hour to reach the opposite shore. The saboteur, once again, entered the reeds, letting the last of the wire and fishing line sink into the mud. He climbed up onto the embankment and made his way to a tree. Under the tree sat a car battery and a backpack. He took out his knife and stripped the plastic and paper off the ends of two wires, exposing the copper wire inside of each. He took one strand of the twin wires and attached it to one of the car battery's poles. The other strand he left beside the battery. Hungry, he ate a dried fish and a handful of sticky rice from his backpack. He laid down and fell asleep under the tree. He was exhausted. It had been a long night.

The next morning, the saboteur awoke to the sound of a boat engine. He looked out at the estuary and saw a South Vietnamese patrol boat stopping and searching sampans that had entered the river before sunrise. As the patrol boat maneuvered its way deeper into the estuary, the saboteur took up the remains of the fishing line in his hands. He waited until the patrol boat was less than fifty feet from where the underwater fishing line and twin wires stretched across the estuary. Estimating when the boat would cross the unseen wires and line, he pulled the fishing line hand over hand until it became taught. He gave the line a strong jerk.

On the opposite shore, the drum toppled off the log and into the water. As it began its journey across the water, it tangled in the reeds.

The saboteur felt the resistance in the fishing line and cursed. He looked out at the boat. It was getting closer. There wasn't much time. He jerked the fishing line, careful not to break it. The resistance remained. He knew the drum was snagged. He picked up the twin wires and eliminated the slack. With the twin wires and fishing line in his hands, he tugged as hard as he thought the wire and line could withstand without breaking. He knew it was possible that one of the wires inside the plastic coating could fracture and break. If either wire fractured, the mission would have been over, and he would have failed. It didn't matter. At that point, he had to risk it. He tugged harder.

The drum stayed stuck in the reeds, then suddenly wiggled free and entered the open water. The drum skimmed across the top of the water, heading toward the opposite shore and the intersection of the approaching boat.

The crew on the boat saw the strange object approaching. The captain of the boat, a lieutenant, realized what it was and shouted, "Torpedo!"

The machine gunner swung his weapon around and opened fire. It was too late, and the angle was bad, making him miss his target. The drum hit the side of the boat… and nothing happened.

The crew laughed, relieved. The lieutenant did not. He grabbed a rifle from one of his crew and panned the gun's sight across the opposite shore, searching for the trigger man he knew was there. He spotted the saboteur under the tree and opened fire.

The saboteur was undeterred by the bullets whizzing beside him and over his head. He took the end of the loose wire in his hand and pressed onto the unoccupied battery pole. There was a small spark - evidence he had made a good connection and that the twin wires leading to the drum were still operational.

A moment later, the drum exploded, sending a cascade of water into the air and punching a hole the size of a basketball in the side of the boat. The boat lurched hard, and the crew fell to the deck. Water flooded into the hole, and the boat immediately began to sink. Mad as a rooster in a cockfight, the lieutenant ordered the helmsman to run the vessel ashore near the saboteur. The helmsman climbed to his feet, cranked the wheel, and gunned the engine.

The saboteur watched as the sinking boat turned and sailed straight toward him. He stood for a long moment, waiting, giving the boat crew and their commander a good look at their prey. When the boat was within fifty feet of shore, he took off running toward the nearby jungle. He disappeared into the tree just as the boat ran aground and came to an abrupt stop. The crew, once again, tumbled to the deck. They climbed back on their feet, grabbed their weapons, and jumped off the boat. Led by the lieutenant, they ran toward the tree line where they last saw the saboteur.

When the South Vietnamese troops chased the saboteur into the jungle, a small unit of Viet Minh was waiting. Several empty tin cans had been lashed to trees next to a pathway through the forest.

The undergrowth was heavy, making it difficult, if not impossible, to travel off the trail. But the saboteur had no intention of leading his pursuers off the path, nor of being caught. He made sure to keep ahead of the boat crew just enough so they couldn't shoot him but close enough that they believed they could capture him. He knew he would be tortured before being killed if caught.

As he came close to the area where his comrades were waiting, he sprinted ahead of his pursuers, creating a two-minute distance between them. It was all that was needed. Completely exhausted, he ran past his comrades. There would be time for greetings later. His comrades pulled the pins on multiple grenades but did not release the spoons. Instead, they tied wires to the spoons and slid the grenades into the empty cans on the trees so that the spoons kept the grenades from exploding. The wires were stretched across the trail, a few inches above the footpath, then tied to another grenade in a can attached to a tree on the opposite side. More grenades and wires had been previously rigged off the trail. The process was well-rehearsed and took only a minute to set up. Satisfied that their traps were set, the Viet Minh and the winded saboteur moved off into the jungle and waited.

It didn't take long. Believing that they may have lost their prey, the boat crew had picked up their pace.

While the point man missed tripping over the wire across the trail, the next in line did not. He tripped the wire, pulling the two grenades free from their cans. The spoons flipped away, and the grenades, set to detonate immediately, exploded, sending shrapnel into the crew and the lieutenant. Whenever under attack, the South Vietnamese troops instinctively spread out and formed a defensive line. When they stepped off the trail to form their line, they tripped over more wires, and those grenades were pulled from their cans and exploded. The lieutenant was shredded and fell to the ground dead. With the boat crew in chaos and without their leader, the Viet Minh attacked. The entire crew was wiped out in less than a minute with no losses to the Viet Minh. It was a great victory and a warning to Diem and his troops to stay out of the rivers and jungles – now the property of the Viet Minh.

Saigon, South Vietnam

As the Viet Minh attacks grew in number, Diem saw them as a security issue. The village chieftains were failing to control their citizens. Some were even encouraging the attacks. Diem knew that if he could not control the countryside, it was only a matter of time until the Viet Minh and possibly the North Vietnamese would be emboldened to the point where they would attack his army in the cities. That worried him. Except for the Catholic refugees he had given land to, he cared little about the peasant farmers that hated him and his family. But the citizens in the cities were a different story. He had learned from experience that they held the power that controlled the country. As long as the city dwellers stayed loyal, he and his family would remain in power.

Diem's solution to the rising number of assaults was to tighten his grip on the reins of power by once again rewarding those loyal to him and his family and punishing any opposition. He started by dismissing forty-one province chieftains throughout South Vietnam. They were replaced with Catholic refugees and loyal military officers that were willing to crack down on the rebels. Many innocent villagers were arrested, and some were tortured until they revealed the names of co-conspirators or Viet Minh living in the area. It was a never-ending circle of violence, with more and more citizens being imprisoned. And more and more villagers were turning to the Viet Minh for justice against the government, which in turn allowed the Viet Minh to carry out more raids on government facilities and troops.

The new chieftains were hated by the people they governed. So much so that the chieftains were forced to live in fortified compounds surrounded by barbed wire and protected by heavily armed blockhouses. They only ventured out of their fortresses when they could be surrounded by their troops and accompanied by American advisors. They often traveled in armored cars to discourage assassination attempts.

The South Vietnamese peasants and farmers saw the Catholic interlopers as opportunistic thugs willing to use whatever means necessary, including confiscation of farms and businesses to squeeze money from the villagers in the provinces. The Diem government protected the Catholic leaders and turned a blind eye to their harsh methods as long as they restored order in the regions they controlled.

Diem never accepted the argument that the people's defiance came from his policies and nepotism. He saw the farmers and villagers as uneducated peasants that were incapable of expressing constructive criticism. It was simpler to silence them and punish them like children when they misbehaved.

American aid poured into South Vietnam like a spring melt over Niagara Falls. Much of it was in the form of government requests, while some were what the Americans thought the South Vietnamese needed. There were planes, tanks, trucks, jeeps, rifles, machine guns, pistols, hand grenades, bazookas, bulldozers, excavators, steamrollers, saws, picks, shovels, hammers, and nails. The list went on and on.

It was an order of barbed wire that caught the American officer's eyes in charge of requisitions. It wasn't a request for a dozen or so spools. It was 150-tons of the stuff. That was a lot of barbed wire, even for an army. But that wasn't even what caught his eye. It was that the request came from Diem's brother Nhu. He wasn't part of the army. He was internal security. When the officer looked at the box on the form for the requested materials and saw that it was blank, his curiosity was piqued. He phoned the palace and asked to speak to his South Vietnamese counterpart about the requisition. He was surprised when Brother Nhu got on the phone and said, "What is the problem?"

"There is no problem, sir. I just need to know how the barbed wire is going to be used," said the American officer.

"Why does that matter?"

"It's part of the form. You left it blank."

"So, fill it in with whatever you wish."

"It doesn't work that way. You need a legitimate purpose for any aid request. And well… it's a lot of barbed wire."

"I see. What might be a legitimate purpose for that much barbed wire?"

"Oh, ah… I don't know. I suppose it could be used for protecting government facilities."

"That's it. Write that down on the form," said Nhu and hung up.

The officer thought for a moment, then filled in the blank spot on the form.

It took almost a month for the cargo ship carrying the barbed wire to arrive. The order had been divided into two parts – 100 tons of wire went to the port in Saigon, and the other 50 tons went to the port in Hue. It took an entire day to unload it and stack it in warehouses.

Two dozen trucks showed up the next day and hauled the barbed wire away. Nobody knew where it went until several weeks later when the South Vietnamese Army Corps of Engineers built dozens of detention centers around the outskirts of Saigon and Hue. The assumption, of course, was that they were to be used as prisons for captured Viet Minh. But there weren't enough Viet Minh in the entire country to fill that many detention centers. A few weeks later, everyone got their answer…

Saigon, South Vietnam

Diem enacted Order 46, which permitted "Individuals considered dangerous to the national defense and common security to be confined by executive order to a concentration camp." Brother Nhu carried it out using his newly-formed Special Forces unit that wore white helmets. The program was called "Denunciation of the Communists." Its goal was to root out and destroy the Viet Minh cadre and their sympathizers wherever they were in South Vietnam.

Tens of thousands of communists were rounded up in the cities, towns, and villages. But Nhu did not stop there. He also used the mandate to detain anyone who criticized Diem or his government, including journalists, university professors, politicians, and former government administrators. By the end of the year, 50,000 Vietnamese were being held in the detention centers.

Nhu used the detention of young family members of outspoken political opponents to silence their criticism of Diem. Many agreed to support Diem in exchange for the release of their children and relatives, who Nhu had threatened to interrogate and even torture.

While Diem's program denied the Vietnamese free speech and other human rights, it also worked to curb the Viet Minh movement... at least in the beginning. The people were afraid to join or openly support the Viet Minh, most of which had been rounded up and were now in the detention centers. Terrorism and military attacks dropped significantly, and for a while, it looked like the Viet Minh would be wiped out from South Vietnam.

Most Americans in-country disapproved of Diem's draconian methods but did little to stop them. It was well understood that South Vietnam was not America. It had its own culture and ways of dealing with its citizens. America wanted Diem to take control of the country so he could defend it against the communists in the North.

In the Ambassador's office deep within the American embassy, Lansdale sat with Ambassador Reinhardt and Lieutenant General Samuel "Hanging Sam" Williams, a veteran of WWII and Korea and the newly assigned head of MAAG. Technically, Williams was Lansdale's boss, but when Lansdale first accepted his assignment in Vietnam, he was told to report directly to Allen Dulles, the head of the CIA. He didn't feel obliged to accept William's request for a meeting but accepted anyway. While not a politician, Lansdale understood the importance of keeping the embassy staff and military advisors happy. He occasionally needed their help, but more importantly, liked to keep tabs on the Americans in-country.

On the other hand, Reinhardt and Williams knew that Lansdale had Diem's ear and could influence the unpredictable leader if he so chose. They needed Lansdale more than Lansdale needed them. "President Eisenhower has been chewing my ass on Diem's denunciation program. It seems it is all the press wants to talk about and not in a good way," said Reinhardt.

"We can't really blame him," said Williams. "It's an embarrassment to democracy."

"I hardly think the Republic of Vietnam is a democracy. But Diem is our ally, and he should behave as such. It may be time to apply pressure by cutting aid."

"Gentlemen, I think you are looking at this the wrong way," said Lansdale. "This is basically a public relations issue."

"Fifty thousand civilians in concentration camps is a public relations problem?" said Williams.

"From America's point of view… yes. You can't deny that Diem is getting results. Most of the people he has locked up are either Viet Minh or their supporters. That's what we wanted him to do… take control of the country."

"Yes, but concentration camps?" said Reinhardt.

"That's just the label the press has given them. We could also call them 'detention centers' or even 'suburban shelters' if we want. We just need to do a better job labeling them."

"Labeling doesn't mitigate the fact that he's holding and interrogating students, schoolteachers, and political opponents."

"It's true, Diem's brother Nhu cast a very wide net in the initial round-up. I am sure some innocents have been detained along with the bad apples. But they are the minority, and it takes time to sort them out."

"It's been two months," said Williams.

"And President Diem assures me that a large number of civilians are about to be released, which should quell much of the people's anger."

"And the others?" said Reinhardt.

"They will continue to be held and interrogated. Now that we've got the agitators, it would be unwise to release them back into society where they can make trouble. Diem has informed me that military tribunals are being set up to deal with the ringleaders. They will be tried and executed if found guilty."

"Great. Then we'll have a country full of martyrs."

"I have considered that. I think the solution is to change the story."

"What do you mean?"

"This is not all bad. There are success stories out there that need to be reported. It's safe, once again, for civilians to walk the streets of Hue and Saigon without worrying about a drive-by shooting from the back of a motor scooter. Business owners no longer need to worry about a terrorist's grenade rolling into their bar or restaurant to target their patrons. Journalists need to be encouraged to write these stories."

"You want to manipulate the press?" said Reinhardt.

"Giving a journalist that prints a positive story an interview with a high-ranking official is hardly manipulation."

"That's exactly what it is," said Williams.

"Potaytoe, potahtoe," said Lansdale. "We need to change the story, especially those written by the foreign journalists."

"We need to get Diem to back off and stop arresting his citizens for no good reason."

"He's not going to do that," said Lansdale.

"Why not?" said Reinhardt.

"Because he thinks he's right. It's hard to imagine the pressure he's under. Every day, he stands on the precipice of war with the North and revolution in the South. Threatening with aid cuts is not going to improve the situation."

"And what will?" said Williams.

"Locking up the communists as he has done. At least for now, he's preventing them from spreading their propaganda. Viet Minh recruitment of students and farmers is down almost ninety percent. That's a real improvement we should celebrate. We should be encouraging him, not punishing him. We said we wanted a guy that would take a tough stand against communist expansion. Well, Diem is it, and he's all we have. Nobody else comes close. We should accept that and move forward."

"Do you think you can control him and his family?" said Reinhardt.

Lansdale laughed, "Diem, maybe. His family, never."

"So, we just let them run amok?" said Williams.

"It's their country. We don't have much of a choice," said Lansdale. "Until we're willing to commit troops, we're just along for the ride."

"And paying for the gas," said Williams.

"And paying for the gas," said Lansdale with a slight nod.

"Alright. I'll inform the president what we talked about. Just try to keep Diem from doing anything foolish, will ya?" said Reinhardt.

"Of course. I'll do my best," said Lansdale.

Williams was not reassured by Lansdale's commitment. Many officers that had worked with him reported that Lansdale was brilliant. Williams was beginning to wonder. He didn't know Lansdale well, but he was sure he could never completely trust him. He was a spook, and spooks always had their own agenda. Assuming the meeting was over, Lansdale rose to leave. "One last thing," said Reinhardt.

"Yes?" said Lansdale.

"Diem has been requesting a face-to-face meeting with President Eisenhower. Up until now, the president has thought it a bad idea that Diem should leave Vietnam for any amount of time. But with the detention of the Viet Minh, the president has reconsidered and would like to invite President Diem for a **P.R.** tour of the United States early next year. An official invitation will follow, but you can tell your boy he's gonna get his meeting."

"That's good news. I'm sure he'll be pleased."

"We understand that your job is not easy, Colonel. It's a fine line you must walk to keep Diem's confidence while serving your country," said Williams. "Just don't get lost during the journey."

Lansdale nodded, then saluted and left the office.

Central Highlands, South Vietnam

A convoy of jeeps and trucks raced through the countryside on a dirt road. Even with large units, the South Vietnamese troops didn't like to dilly-dally when traveling outside the cities. It was unusual for the Viet Minh to attack a major convoy. They were too large a target and well-armed. Instead, the Viet Minh would rely on snipers hidden in the long grass or up in the trees to place well-aimed shots into a truck's radiator or front tire. If that failed to stop the convoy, the sniper could always attempt to take out the trucks' or jeeps' drivers. Identifying and killing the commander of a convoy was also a good option and sure to cause chaos.

On that particular day, there was a surprising lack of sniper fire. The convoy came to a bridge and stopped long enough for its scouts to inspect the bridge supports for damage or explosives. There were none. Satisfied, the commander ordered his vehicles across one by one.

Nearby a farmer weeding his field with a hoe watched as the last vehicle crossed the bridge and the convoy disappeared over a hill. He raised his hoe in the air to signal the Viet Minh commander waiting in the tree line. Eight Viet Minh and a water buffalo ridden by a boy, the farmer's son, emerged from the forest.

The rebel commander ordered his men to go to work. The soldiers used picks and shovels to loosen the soil around each of the bridge supports. Once loosened, the Viet Minh tied a thick rope around a cross beam and attached the opposite end of the rope to the water buffalo's yoke. The water buffalo pulled on the cross beam. With the support columns compromised, the bridge collapsed. But the Viet Minh didn't stop with just toppling the bridge. They pulled all the supports out of the ground, then stacked all the wood used to construct the bridge into a huge pile beside the river. A dosing of kerosene with a match and the woodpile turned in a blazing fire destroying the wooden pylons permanently.

It wouldn't be an easy matter for the South Vietnamese engineers to reconstruct the bridge. They would need to cut new pylons and cross beams from the nearby forest. A repair that should have taken a few days would now require a major construction effort.

The Viet Minh saboteurs would destroy seven more bridges in the area, making it impossible for ARVN convoys to resupply their troops in the area. The commander would have no choice but to pull back his forces until the bridges could be rebuilt. The Viet Minh commanders knew that they did not need to confront the better-armed ARVN troops when a team of saboteurs could prevent them from controlling an area.

Saigon, South Vietnam

South Vietnam was considered a challenging but important post for any American diplomat. The energy required to deal with the avalanche of problems caused by Diem and his family was exhausting. This was especially true for the Ambassadors. Ambassador Elbridge Dubrow replaced Reinhardt as America's Ambassador for the Republic of Vietnam. Now that it had been decided that Diem was America's only real hope of stopping the communist expansion into Southeast Asia, Eisenhower wanted someone with new energy and ideas to boost Diem's confidence in America's support. To Eisenhower, a proactive leader by nature, it was never enough to let things stand. He wasn't afraid to try new people in significant positions in hopes they would find the key to solving America's problems.

Dubrow was thought to be that key. While Reinhardt was a career diplomat with vast experience, Dubrow was more of a policy wonk and had served as Chief of Station in the embassies of many Cold War countries. He had spent time as an advisor to the National War College, making Eisenhower more comfortable with his military assessments in Vietnam. Like most of the Ambassadors that served during the era, Dubrow started out liking Diem and believing he was the right man for the job. Over time, his opinion would change…

BIGGEST LITTLE MAN IN ASIA

May 8, 1957 – Washington D.C., USA

Hundreds of reporters and politicians gathered on the tarmac watched as the plane carrying President Diem, a C-121 Silver Constellation aircraft, landed at Washington National Airport and taxied off the runway. Sitting in a limousine with dual American flags mounted on the hood, President Eisenhower and Secretary of State John Foster Dulles waited until the aircraft stairway was rolled into place before emerging from the vehicle.

When President Diem climbed to the bottom of the stairway, he was greeted with the American president's hearty handshake and a big smile. Dozens of camera bulbs flashed, capturing photos for the evening headlines. America's guest was given a 21-gun salute. It was a big deal, especially for Diem, who would use it to demonstrate his power through his warm relationship with President Eisenhower, the leader of the free world.

Diem had come to secure more financial aid from Eisenhower and the American Congressmen who held the purse strings. It wasn't difficult. Diem was extremely popular, and it seemed like everyone, including the congressmen, wanted a photo with him to hang on their office walls. Over 50,000 Americans lined the streets of Washington D.C. taken by the Vietnamese president's motorcade. That evening, the New York Times editorialized that "President Diem is a substantial partner in a going enterprise on behalf of free men in his country and ours. We honor him and make him doubly welcome on that account."

The next day when Diem addressed a joint session of Congress, he said, "We affirm that the sole legitimate object of the state is to protect the fundamental rights of human beings to existence, to the free development of his intellectual, moral, and spiritual life. We affirm that democracy is neither material happiness nor the supremacy of numbers. Democracy is essentially a permanent effort to find the right political means in order to assure to all citizens the right of free development and the maximum initiative, responsibility, and spiritual life."

Although most of the congressmen and Vice President Nixon were confused by the statement, especially the odd definition of democracy, they smiled and applauded anyway. They had all heard the rumors that the South Vietnam President was peculiar, and his speech confirmed it. No matter. He was the hero of the day. Nobody wanted to be accused of rocking the boat, especially when it came to Vietnam.

At a state dinner that evening, President Eisenhower toasted Diem for demonstrating "how much moral values and the concept of human dignity could count for in the minds of men."

Reader's Digest saw Diem as the "Biggest Little Man in Asia," while Life magazine hailed him as "The Tough Miracle Man of Vietnam."

The organization American Friends of Vietnam engaged in a campaign to encourage U.S. media companies to write only positive stories about Diem's visit. They even hired a writer to review Diem's speeches and correct any cultural blunders. In addition to Washington D.C., Diem visited New York, Boston, and Michigan, where he once lived during his exile. He took time to speak privately with Senators Mansfield and Kennedy, both considered experts in Southeast Asia and strong Diem supporters.

After a solid week of meetings, receptions, and speeches, Diem's final stop was in Hawaii, where he was a guest of Admiral Felix Stump, the United States Pacific Fleet commander. Diem was concerned with America's reaction if South Vietnam came under communist attack. Reiterating Washington's policies, Stump reassured Diem that nuclear weapons would be used to defend any anti-communist country that was attacked by communists and that America would do so by dropping nuclear weapons on communist China. Diem left satisfied.

All in all, Diem's visit to America was a success. He was given assurances from Eisenhower that the

Republic of Vietnam would receive the additional financial and military aid he had requested. With America's help, he could continue the economic miracle that would outshine Ho Chi Minh and one day reunite North and South under Diem's leadership. It seemed he could do no wrong.

Central Highlands, South Vietnam

The sun peaked over a nearby hillside. Grey smoke rose from a village surrounded by rice paddies filled with vibrant green sprouts and muddy water. It was lake water that traveled to the fields through a canal system that the villagers had built.

Each field had a two-foot dirt dike around it to keep the water from escaping. The canal ran down the center of the fields and had a footpath on one side of its berms. The canal was dry most of the time, and the mud on the bottom was cracked from the heat of the day. When water was needed, a wooden gate by the lake was opened, and water would rush down the canal. Individual gates on each of the paddies were opened to flood the farmers' fields. Multiple paddies were connected so that when one field was flooded, the next would fill. The canal fed hundreds of paddies. Having access to a lake made the farmers in the village wealthy compared to villages without a lake. Lake water meant that the farmers did not need to wait for the monsoons to plant their crops. They planted and harvested three times a year and had plenty of water. Water was life to the farmers.

The rice plants were young, with luminous green leaves rising from the two-inch deep brown water. When first planted, the rice seeds were sown into a seedbed on a slightly acidic clay. Once sprouted, the young plants were transplanted by hand into a larger field. Replanting was time-consuming and backbreaking work but was more likely to yield a good crop than simply sowing the seeds directly into the field.

Everyone in a family participated in planting, replanting, tending, and harvesting rice. From the age of eight, children were taught how to farm the family's fields. But even younger children were given the responsibility of keeping the water buffalos out of the fields while they grazed. It was not uncommon to see a five-year-old herding three or four of the giant beasts along a road. The young children often talked or sang to the family's water buffalo to keep them calm and break the boredom.

When the children reached the age to work in the fields, they were given a conical hat made from palm leaves or bamboo to keep the sun off their faces and necks and to shed the rain during monsoon season. The hat was a source of pride, symbolizing a right of passage for the young boys and girls. A well-crafted conical hat could be handed down through generations as the children outgrew them and passed them on to their siblings. As they aged, they yellowed, and when broken, the hats were repaired with new palm leaves or strips of bamboo, giving them a quilted look.

After the hard work of sowing, then replanting, the rice paddies needed little care beyond occasional weeding, fertilizing, and flooding. The farmer's lifestyle was surprisingly relaxed, with time to socialize and discuss the day's news. Drinking was also popular. During their downtime, the farmers made liquor from fermented rice and fruit. Similar to American moonshine, the clear-colored liquor was called "ruou", meaning alcohol. When distilled properly, ruou was surprisingly smooth like vodka, but when not given the proper amount of time, it burned the throat when swallowed.

After the evening meal, neighbors often visited, bringing a bottle or jug of ruou with them. It was a friendly competition to see which family could make the finest liquor. Both men and women drank, but rarely together. They had different interests. The men were likely to discuss hunting or politics, while the women discussed children and cooking. Gossip was always a popular subject of discussion by both genders.

As the liquor was consumed and inhibitions were laid low, singing and dancing would commence. The children would always join in trying to copy the movements of their parents and older siblings. Men smoked hand-rolled cigarettes, and the women chewed beetle nut staining their teeth and gums red. They spit the red juice like camels into a communal bucket.

Farmers did not earn much money from their crops. They often traded a bag of rice and a bottle of ruou for ten coconuts and a basket of fish to avoid taxes. Money was rarely exchanged within the villages, except for good-quality knives and tools sold from a traveling vendor's cart.

With the village near a lake, the huts were built on stilts to prevent flooding during the monsoon season and give livestock a place to rest out of the sun during the hot season. The elders gathered in the village dinh – a communal house with a Buddhist pagoda and pond in front and a shade tree in the back.

On that day, they discussed the upcoming festival honoring the village Thang Hoang – the spirit of an ancient hero that protected the people in their village. They were not expecting South Vietnamese troops and the foreigners with guns that came to their village.

Granier led his team of American CIA officers and a new team of 5th Bureau operatives into the village. The air was thick with smoke which cut down on the mosquitos and stench from human and animal waste. Having lived in Vietnam for a number of years, Granier was not surprised by the villagers' lifestyle. Neighbors lived in harmony with the occasional burst of anger and violence. Roaming freely, pigs ate the family's garbage. Roosters fought constantly, ganging up, pecking viciously at the youngest male, and humping hens whenever they could catch one. Children played in the dirt, sometimes urinating in the open, making mud.

The women in the village cooked outside on rock-stacked stoves to contain the fire. When not cooking, they slept, gossiped with neighbors while chewing beetle nuts, or spun silk to clothe their families and sell at the local market. The men were gathered in social groups of three or four. Some drank ruou and smoked hand-rolled cigarettes as they eyed the foreigners entering their village. Giant earthen urns in front of each hut caught the rain for drinking water, washing dishes, and giving baths to toddlers that had defecated on themselves. Flies swarmed the air. A half-dozen dogs barked at the strangers until a villager threw a couple of rocks to silence them. Village life was relaxed, natural, and primitive.

The Viet Minh were active in the area. While Granier and his team met with the elders, 5th Bureau guards were posted around the village's perimeter and watched the surrounding forest and rice paddies for any unusual movement.

Lansdale had assigned Granier to light duty after the fiasco in Laos. Granier had succeeded at accomplishing his mission in Laos but at a great cost. The team commander had a rough couple of weeks in the mountains, not to mention the emotional rollercoaster of losing a good portion of his team.

Lansdale knew it was never easy losing team members. He had lost plenty himself during his time as a team commander in the Philippines in WWII. It wasn't that Lansdale felt sorry for Granier. He didn't. Losing soldiers under his command was part of the job. But he needed Granier to be 100% effective before sending him out again on a difficult operation. In the meantime, Conein would lead all paramilitary operations in both the North and the South.

Lansdale had sent Granier to the village to encourage the elders to accept the government's help in fortifying their village's defenses. The elders would not trust the foreigners, but they would respect them. Foreigners were wealthy, and money meant power.

The Americans' appearance would give credibility to the proposal.

Granier allowed the 5th Bureau unit commander, a lieutenant, to make their pitch. The proposal was straightforward. The government would pay to have the village fortified, and in exchange, the village would provide four young men to join the ARVN ranks. The South Vietnamese wanted more soldiers that grew up in the villages and knew the local culture. Seeing a familiar face put the people in the villages at ease and helped sway the villagers away from the Viet Minh propaganda.

The village elders objected, saying the Viet Minh would punish them if they accepted the government's help. They feared the Viet Minh more than they feared displeasing the government soldiers.

Granier jumped in with his translator's help and explained that during construction, the ARVN would garrison a squad of soldiers to protect the village against the Viet Minh. When construction was completed, the soldiers would train the local militia and give them weapons to protect the village on their own. When the elders still seemed hesitant, Granier offered them a monthly stipend as long as they stayed loyal to the government's fortification program.

The elders liked the money and discussed the proposition among themselves. As part of the negotiation, the elders asked for the government to dig a well in the village so the children could have clean water. Granier agreed, and the deal was done.

Granier purchased a pig from one of the villagers and gave it to the village for a celebration. The elders were pleased by the gesture. Granier had also brought several bottles of whiskey with him. He knew the elders would decline the whiskey as they were unaccustomed to the taste and preferred their ruou. That was fine with Granier. He and his men would drink the whiskey.

The pig was slaughtered and roasted over a fire in the center of the village. Pots of rice were cooked, releasing a starch aroma. Piles of vegetables were placed on straw platters for everyone to share. The villagers didn't use utensils or bowls, preferring to pick up the pieces of roasted pig with a clump of rice or vegetable leaf then dipping the bundle into a spicy sauce before popping it into their mouths. Granier and his men followed their example and ate with their fingers. As the drinking commenced, it didn't take long before the singing and dancing began. Granier ordered his men to participate. Bonding with the villagers was important. It built trust.

The soldiers stayed the night in the village. The villagers offered to share their huts, but Granier declined, saying his men preferred to sleep outside under the stars. It was a lie, especially when it started to rain. But Granier did not wholly trust the villagers. For all he knew, they could have already made a deal with the Viet Minh and would send a messenger informing them of the soldiers' presence. If an ambush occurred and a firefight broke out, Granier wanted all his men nearby. They stood a much better chance fighting as a unit than as individuals. He made sure his men did not drink too much, and the guards were rotated during the night so that they stayed vigilant. He rose several times that night to check on his men and personally patrol the perimeter. If the Viet Minh were out there, they chose not to attack. The night passed without incident.

When Granier woke the next morning, he could smell the fish the villagers were cooking for their guests. He watched a woman bathing her toddler next to her hut. He was startled when she, unashamed, removed her pajama top and used a rag to wash her breasts and underarms. She was young, and the water glistened off her dark skin. Granier felt guilty for watching, but he couldn't take his eyes away. It had been a long time since he had been with a woman.

After breakfast, he and his men said their goodbyes and left. The soldiers that Granier had promised the elders would show up in a week along with the money and the supplies needed to fortify the village and dig the well. The villagers would be paid for their labor and would work under a South Vietnamese engineer's supervision. That was something the Americans were good at – throwing money at projects. Labor was cheap in the countryside, and the men, having built their own huts, were surprisingly experienced at carpentry. Diem's government prevented another village from falling into the hands of the Viet Minh, and it cost them nothing… the Americans picked up the tab.

As he and his men hiked down the road leading to the nearest town, Granier felt satisfied. The clouds overhead threatened rain, but he didn't care. It would cool him and his men off if it came. His mind drifted to the young woman washing herself, then to his time in the jungle with Spitting Woman, now known as Suong, the only woman he had truly loved.

New York, United States

The United Nations building in New York looked more like a book standing upright than the headquarters of the world's diplomats. Next to the office tower was the conference center where the world leaders argued their cases to the assembly. Both iconic buildings had a nice view of the East River.

The Soviet team of delegates and their assistants arrived early in their black limousines. It was an important day, and they wanted to be ready for their presentation. They knew from experience that they needed all their ducks in a row if they were going to embarrass the United States. Their proposal was designed to do just that.

When the Soviet Ambassador to the United Nations, Andrei Gromyko, stepped to the podium, the assembly quieted from a low rumble to whispers. When the superpowers spoke, the delegates listened. In the West, Gromyko was nicknamed "Mr. Nyet" because of his frequent use of the Soviet's veto power in the U.N. Security Council. He was born in Belarus and had worked his way up to be one of the most powerful men in the world. He was a master of political strategy and often laid traps for his opponents to stumble into at just the right moment. His proposal that day was just such a trap designed for his principal opponent – The United States of America.

Addressing the assembly, Gromyko proposed that the delegates admit both North and South Vietnam as separate nations into the United Nations. He hoped that the newly admitted nations could negotiate a peaceful reunification of their country and avoid civil war. The trap was set, and the audience of delegates exploded with applause. If the proposal were accepted as was expected, the United States would be recognizing a communist country, something the U.S. Ambassadors had refused to do up until that moment. Furthermore, it would be seen as a betrayal of their ally – South Vietnam – and would give the communists an official foothold in Southeast Asia.

The United States Ambassador, Henry Cabot Lodge Jr., had been outmaneuvered by Gromyko, and he knew it. It did not sit well with him as he had grown unaccustomed to losing. When the proposal passed, Lodge had no choice but to use the United States veto in the Security Council to squash Gromyko's bid for Vietnam. While the Soviet Union was hailed as a peacemaker, the United States appeared to be a warmonger to the rest of the world. It seemed the last exit to avoid conflict had been closed by the American Ambassador, and Vietnam was destined for war. Gromyko could not have been happier.

Hanoi, North Vietnam

Le Duan had a wife and seven children. He had married when he was twenty-two years old, and his wife was nineteen. She, too, believed in the revolution and was willing to die for the cause if required. His family lived in Hanoi, but he rarely spent time with them. They were always happy to see him and he them, but he was often tired from a long journey and the endless meetings held by the politburo. They did not travel with him when he went South. It was a lonely existence with no companionship – another sacrifice for the revolution. He loved his wife and children but missed them greatly. At times, it seemed almost too much to endure.

Le Duan saw Suong as she was, his bodyguard. She would lay down her life for him if required. She was also the most stubborn and ornery woman he had ever met. She said what was on her mind even when not invited. It was a trait Duan both loathed and admired. Duan was her superior and felt she should respect him and obey his orders. But Suong didn't see it that way. She had been ordered by Ho Chi Minh to protect Duan. Ho was her commander, not Duan. Keeping her mouth shut, as Duan demanded on many occasions, was not part of Ho's orders and she did not feel obliged to obey Duan's requests. She simply ignored him and spoke her mind. Duan had thought about asking for a replacement, but he knew that Suong was the best bodyguard available, and he felt safe with her protecting him. Besides, having someone play the devil's advocate was not a bad idea. Command was not an easy task. It was not possible to see all things. As much as he hated to admit it, Suong was another set of eyes. Seeing a situation different than he saw it was not a bad thing as long as she understood who was boss. It was that last part that caused most of the friction between the two.

She did not like her job but understood the necessity of being Le Duan's bodyguard. He had many enemies, and not all were in the South. She had to keep constant watch and drew her pistol many times, most of which were false alarms. She didn't care. The ninety-nine times she was wrong was not critical when compared to the one time she was right. It was difficult to always stay alert, especially when Duan was in meetings and she was stuck guarding the door. She focused on potential threats and how she would defeat them. If they didn't develop into real danger, at least they kept her awake.

Suong believed Le Duan to be hard but fair. She liked how he commanded respect from those under his control. He was not a handsome man, and his body was too thin even for a Vietnamese. He was intelligent and well-educated considering his beginnings. He was a self-made man. Duan was someone she could appreciate, perhaps even admire. But she knew better than to reveal her feelings. She did not want to give him leverage over her. She would allow no man to control her, except for Ho. Her allegiance was to the man everyone called Uncle.

After a long day of meetings with the politburo, Duan emerged mumbling to himself like a hermit.

"What's wrong?" Suong said as she fell in next to him, scanning for threats as they moved.

"Nothing," said Duan.

"You're lying."

"Where do you get off calling me a liar?"

"Where do you get off lying?"

"It's just… never mind."

"Maybe I could help."

"I doubt it."

"Try me."

"Fine. Ho and the others want me to join the politburo full time here in Hanoi."

"And that's a bad thing?"

"Yes. It's a bad thing. They are taking away my command of the Central Office. I worked my ass off to build an army to take on Diem's government, and now they are just going to hand it over to someone else."

"You believe you are the only one that can command?"

"No. Of course not. But this is different. Our followers in the South are under siege. We are losing more soldiers than we're gaining. I don't see how turning the command over to someone with less experience is going to help matters."

"That's a good point. But a new commander will have fresh ideas that may solve the problem."

"Are you saying I have bad ideas?"

"No. Of course not. It's just that some of your ideas are stale like leftover rice."

Duan didn't know what to say. He wondered if she even knew she had insulted him. "You know, this is your problem too," he said.

"How is that?" said Suong.

"If I am relocated to Hanoi, you will be reassigned. There is no need for me to have a bodyguard once we leave the South."

"A change could do me good. Maybe I could get back in the field."

"Really? You wouldn't miss me?"

"What's to miss? Look at the bright side… you will finally get to spend more time with your family."

"I doubt it. The politburo will load me down with reports and meetings."

"It's better than getting shot at."

"You have an answer for everything, don't you?"

"You need good counsel."

"I didn't say your counsel was good."

"Ouch."

Angry and frustrated, Duan marched off. Suong followed.

When Le Duan returned to his headquarters, he was informed of the villagers' cooperation with the Diem government and that their village would soon be fortified. He was furious upon finding that no action had been taken against the village while he was gone. Construction on the fortifications had already begun making any assault more difficult and potentially more costly in lives.

Le Duan stood in front of his unit commanders. A well-worn blackboard borrowed from a local school displayed his plan of attack. "It is unfortunate that many of our brothers and sisters in the South have chosen to cooperate with Diem's government and build fortified hamlets," said Le Duan. "It is important for the movement that we send a clear signal as to the consequences of such actions. They feel protected behind their punji trenches, barbed wire, and bamboo walls. We shall teach them they are not. The deaths of a few dozen peasants and their village elders shall save the lives of thousands."

"Such violence will turn the people against us," said one of the commanders as others grunted their agreement to his comment.

"Some, yes. But if we wish the people to shun Diem's bribes and protection, they must fear us more than they fear his troops. They must understand that it is the Viet Minh that controls the countryside, not the government. Not Diem and his family."

Captain Bui was placed in charge of the company that would perform the mission against the village. Le Duan wanted to make sure his orders were carried out correctly. A propaganda assault on a village was never an easy task, and the Viet Minh tended to get caught up in the bloodlust unless supervised by a strong leader. Duan knew he could trust Bui. He had personally trained Bui and had watched him rise through the ranks. Bui would keep his men under control and obey Duan's orders. To deter resistance, an overwhelming force of 150 men was to be used. They did not take heavy arms with them. They wouldn't need them. The villagers were untrained in combat. Resistance would be foolish, and if it occurred, his men would need nothing more than their rifles to wipe out the village.

Construction in the village had already begun. The men were digging a moat around the village's perimeter, and the women were busy carving punji sticks out of bamboo stocks. Even the well near the village center was already six feet deep, with mounds of dirt piled around it. The engineer had been pleased with the progress and hoped to hit the water table once the villagers dug beyond twelve feet.

The Viet Minh slept in the nearby jungle and waited until sunrise to approach the village. They fixed their bayonets at the ends of their rifle barrels, then surrounded the village, some through the jungle and most through the rice paddies.

Seeing the vast number of Viet Minh approaching, the squad of ARVN guards tossed down their weapons and threw up their hands to surrender. Bravery would not have made a difference. The Viet Minh were determined, and the guards would have easily been overwhelmed. The Viet Minh took them prisoners. The engineer climbed into the tree behind the dinh, hoping not to be discovered. The villagers did not resist the Viet Minh. They knew better. They were rounded up at the points of bayonets and herded like cattle to the center of the village in front of the dinh. Children and mothers cried. The men stood defiant.

Bui spoke directly to the elders as the villagers watched. "After many warnings as to the consequences of collaborating with the enemy, you have chosen to side with Diem and his government," said Bui. "The Viet Minh believe in justice. We will have a trial at which you may speak in your defense.

If found guilty, you will be punished. Do you have a table and chairs?"

The villagers looked at each other then shook their heads, indicating that no table or chairs were available. "Very well. We shall stand. Let the trial begin. I shall stand as judge," said Bui. "You are accused of collaboration with the enemy. How do you plead?"

The villagers exchanged glances, not knowing what to say. Bui could see their confusion and clarified his question making it similar, "Did you agree to let the government fortify your village?"

"We had no choice in the matter. The government soldiers came and threatened us with their rifles. They brought foreigners with them. They had weapons too," said one of the elders.

"So, you accepted their help like cowards?"

"We are farmers. We don't know how to fight. We have no weapons."

"Good. That makes things easier. You are guilty of collaboration with the enemy. You are traitors. My judgment will be swift and fair. Your livestock is forfeit."

Bui ordered his men to kill the livestock. Pigs, chickens, even the water buffalo used to plow their fields were shot dead. The village dogs were also killed. "Your rice is forfeit."

The soldier hauled rice bags from each family's storage room in their huts into the center of the village. The bags were split open with the points of bayonets. The Viet Minh urinated on the rice mounds on the ground. The village watched in horror as two cans of kerosene were dumped on the rice until it was well saturated, then set afire. "Your elders are forfeit," said Bui.

Bui ordered his men to put the elders in the unfinished well. The elders were ordered to jump into the six-foot deep hole. They hesitated. Bui's men used their bayonets, stabbing the old men in the ass until they jumped into the hole. Bui ordered the remaining men in the village to fill in the hole. They hesitated. The children were lined up next to the hole. The villagers were told that the children would join the elders unless the hole was filled immediately. The women wept uncontrollably. A woman ran forward, picked up a shovel, and threw dirt into the pit on top of the elders pleading for their lives. The men joined her shoveling soil. The children wailed as the elders, all grandfathers, were buried alive. The old men coughed and sputtered as the level of dirt rose to their heads.

One elder put his hands above his head as if they might give him more time. They didn't. As the last of the soil was shoveled into the hole, only the elder's two hands were still visible. His fingers clawed at the dirt, then slowed until they only twitched. Finally, they stopped moving entirely. The elders were dead. The villagers wept. "Tell the other villages what you saw here today. This is what happens when traitors accept the government's help. Viet Minh justice is swift, certain, and severe. Long live the revolution and long live Ho Chi Minh," said Bui thrusting his fist in the air.

His men followed their commander thrusting their fists in the air and shouting his slogan, "Long live the revolution and long live Ho Chi Minh."

"Burn it to the ground," said Bui as he turned and left the village.

The villagers watched helplessly as the Viet Minh torched their huts and set the dinh aflame. The engineer died of smoke inhalation before the fire spread to the tree and consumed his body. The heat was intense as the fire spread, the dried thatched roofs providing plenty of fuel. The villagers moved out of the village and watched from a distance as their homes were engulfed in flames. The Viet Minh set fire to the last hut and left the village. Their mission was a success. Black smoke rose, signaling for miles the calamity that befell the village.

As a final act of retribution, the Viet Minh used axes and picks to break the slash boards and destroy the sluice gates that controlled the canals that fed their villagers' fields. The nearby reservoir emptied. The precious water gushed down the canals flooding some fields to the point that their dikes collapsed and leaving the sprouts of rice in other fields dry. Exposed to the sun, the young plants would wilt and die within a few days. Without water, the villagers' crops would be limited to rainfall which was sporadic during the hot season. Even if they repaired the sluice gates, the damage was done. The water was gone until the next wet season, and their annual harvests would be cut by two-thirds destroying the villagers' income. The villagers watched in disbelief as their only hope of rebuilding their lives was systematically demolished by the Viet Minh.

With no livestock, no rice, and their fields left in ruin, the villagers would starve. Even their tools to plant and harvest their precious rice were burned in the flames. They had nothing. Many would starve to death, others would die of disease from their weakened bodies, and others would commit suicide from the distress of seeing their lives ruined.

The government did little to help them. Word spread of Diem's indifference toward the broken villagers. The one thing Le Duan could always count on was that Diem would react the wrong way, and more recruits would join the Viet Minh.

Saigon, South Vietnam

When Lansdale received word of the massacre, he decided to keep the news from Granier. The team commander had suffered enough and didn't need another blow to his conscious. He went himself to survey the damage to the village. Conein and his team escorted him.

Countryside, South Vietnam

The ground in the village was still smoldering from the intense heat. ARVN soldiers were pulling the elders' bodies out of the village well when Lansdale and his team arrived. Additional ARVN troops dug through the charred rubble that was once the village. Three villagers had been killed by the flames when they tried to save their homes. The corpses of bloated pigs, their skin split from the heat, were everywhere. The smell of smoke and charred flesh was powerful and sickening when the source was considered.

Lansdale used an interpreter to interview a few of the survivors. Their story was the same. There was no mystery as to what had happened. Usually a model of self-control, Lansdale was angry. He knew the Viet Minh would use the massacre as propaganda against the government. The fortification program was his idea and now a bust. He would look like a fool to Diem and his family. But most of all, he would look incompetent to Allen Dulles, the head of the CIA and his boss. Frustrated, he called Conein over and said, "I want you to hunt him down."

"Who?" said Conein.

"Le Duan. I want you to hunt him down and bring me his head."

"Do you really want his head?"

"Shut the fuck up and listen. No, I don't want his head. Yes, I want him dead."

"Got it."

"I don't want any excuses. Anything you need, just ask. I will see that you get it. You will receive no other assignments until this mission is completed. Be quick about it. We have other work to do."

"Alright. What are my limitations?"

"Only two… keep your activities quiet and don't get caught. Everything else is on the table."

"I can deal with that."

"Go now. I'll find my way back with the ARVN. Good hunting."

Conein nodded, signaled his men, and moved off. Finding Le Duan would not be easy, and Conein knew it. He had been trying for years, and except for a brief encounter that went sideways, he had come up dry. This time, Lansdale made it sound more probable – no limitations except keeping it quiet and not getting caught. Conein wondered how far he could push it. In the past, his commanders often made outlandish statements of allowing untethered action only to back off a few days later when they realized the consequences of their words. He decided the best way to avoid that from happening was simply not to inform Lansdale what he was up to. Lansdale would want progress reports. Conein would be vague. If pressed, he would say that it is better if Lansdale does not know. Lansdale would be annoyed at his insubordination, but the hint of foul play would soothe Lansdale's curiosity. It would be Conein's way of saying that extreme measures would be used to find Le Duan, so extreme that not even Lansdale should ask. Lansdale wanted action, and Conein was going to give it to him.

Saigon, South Vietnam

Conein's first stop was the 5th Bureau interrogation unit in Saigon. Lansdale had supervised the training of the 5th Bureau and even brought in advisors with enhanced interrogation techniques from the Philippines and France to train the special unit.

Conein spent days pouring over the list of prisoners and intelligence reports that had come in from military units around the South. He knew that most of the enemy that had been captured would be of little use in finding Le Duan. He needed someone with a connection to the mysterious Viet Minh leader.

AMERICAN EXCEPTIONALISM

Saigon, South Vietnam

Along with the hundreds of millions of dollars in financial and military aid, thousands of American aid workers and advisors flooded into the country. Their intentions were pure – rebuild The Republic of Vietnam into a model Southeast Asian society.

New roads and bridges connecting the countryside were designed and built by American engineers and equipment. American-built flood control canals prevented the rising water that occurred every monsoon season from wiping out the villages and roads. Hospitals and clinics staffed with American and Philippine doctors and nurses saved hundreds of thousands of Vietnamese lives. Medical field teams inoculated millions of children from deadly diseases and offered rudimentary healthcare to villagers. Health workers taught villagers hygiene and nutrition. Scientists taught farmers new methods of farming that increased their harvests and protected their fields from pests. Thousands of miles of irrigation ditches and windmills to power water pumps ensured a bountiful rice supply, the staple in the Vietnamese diet. And they even placed stoplights on Saigon's streets to handle the growing number of vehicles, motorbikes, and cyclos.

American college students took sabbaticals from their education to serve in aid organizations in Vietnam. Students became schoolteachers of Vietnam's youth, teaching reading, writing, math, and in some cases English. Wells were dug to supply villagers with a steady supply of clean water. Warehouses with concrete floors and sheet metal roofs were constructed to prevent crops from rotting while waiting to be distributed. The Americans built homes, community centers, health clinics, schools, and anything else that might help the Vietnamese people.

It was an enormous effort by well-meaning aid organizations backed by American money and technological know-how. But instead of becoming self-sufficient as was the goal, the South Vietnamese became dependent on American aid. Instead of building a diverse economy, the South Vietnamese built an economy supported by American aid and serving in-country American aid workers and advisors. While much good was accomplished, the nation's economy became an illusion, a false hope.

American aid also created the unforeseen consequence that Diem no longer needed to listen to the people he ruled. With so much financial assistance pouring in from America, he was no longer reliant on the taxes his government collected. He skimmed off what the government needed, and he used the rest to create popular programs to win broad support. He could afford to reward more politicians if they fell in line and supported him.

It worked. The Republic of Vietnam became more stable over time. Business owners were especially grateful to Diem for securing so much American aid on which they depended. Unemployment throughout the country declined as citizens were hired to build roads, bridges, hospitals, schools, and flood canals. While the people were far from rich, they could feed their families and maintain their homes. At times, there was even money left over for luxuries like a new bicycle or a radio. Inflation increased drastically as more people had more money and wanted more consumer items.

With American advisors helping businesses increase exports, the price of basic necessities like rice rose, putting the old and poor in danger of starvation even with the new abundant harvests. Corruption increased dramatically. Everyone wanted their piece of the American pie. It started at the ports when equipment was delivered and "taxed" by government officials. The corruption continued as the equipment was distributed throughout the country to local governments demanding their fair share. Local army commanders and police demanded protection payments to safeguard the equipment from being vandalized or stolen by the enemy. The more aid that came in, the more creative the methods to siphon it off. The people did receive benefits but only a fraction of what was initially intended.

It didn't help that rumors of the Americans cutting off aid periodically circulated through the government and the population. A hoarding mentality developed, and people wanted whatever they could get now. They saved their newfound wealth for a rainy day, which caused the economy to contract as consumer spending was minimized. The economy in the South became a see-saw tipping back and forth between expansion and contraction. Business owners were hard-pressed to predict their customer's needs and keep a stabilized inventory. Abundance turned to scarcity, then back to plenty within a monthly cycle.

The military relied on American technology and weapons more and more. Field commanders ordered their soldiers to stay undercover during battles while waiting for artillery, armor, or air support to pound the enemy before attacking or counterattacking. Why risk the lives of their men when a 105mm artillery shell could kill their opponent just as well? It was safer for the soldiers to flatten a village than go in and root out an enemy sniper. Civilian casualties climbed. It was all well-meaning and becoming a potential disaster if the aid ever went away or even decreased. The Republic of Vietnam and Diem's government were utterly dependent on the Americans.

Hanoi, North Vietnam

While Diem used his aid money to create programs that would generate popular support, Ho Chi Minh took a different tactic. His nation was starving and broke. The North Vietnamese used Chinese and

Soviet aid to rebuild their infrastructure and economy. The North had suffered the devastations of the French war far more than the South. American bombs and artillery given to the French military had destroyed many of the bridges and roads. Villages that had supported or even sympathized with the Viet Minh had been burned to the ground by the French, and all livestock slaughtered and left to rot.

And when the French finally left, they took everything of value with them. The factories were emptied; all the machines and raw materials were gone or destroyed. Business owners acted like spoiled children who were picking up their toys and going home. The plantations were burned, and orchards cut down. All of the medical equipment and supplies in the hospitals had been removed and sent back to France. Government facilities such as power plants and water treatment plants were left without fuel, tools, or spare parts to keep the monitoring equipment and heavy machines working. They even destroyed a large number of dikes, causing rice production to plummet. If the French could not have Northern Indochina, then nobody would have it. The economy and infrastructure of North Vietnam were wrecked.

The North Vietnamese government was stingy about what they paid their workers to rebuild their country. They made every Rubel or Yuan count. There was corruption, both national and local, that siphoned off some aid, but it was a fraction of what was happening in the South. Just as the South was dependent on foreign aid, the North badly needed the influx of capital. The difference was that as the aid flowed into the North, Ho Chi Minh and his followers became less dependent on their sponsors, while Diem and the people of the South became more and more dependent on aid as time wore on.

Life in the North and South was far from easy for the average citizen, but the Northerners seemed more prepared to sacrifice for their new nation while Southerners became greedier. Though Ho Chi Minh's land reform programs were far from perfect, by the mid-'50s, over fifty percent of the families in the North became landowners. Uncle Ho was their hero, and their support of his policies was devoted.

Saigon, South Vietnam

Lieutenant General Williams had accepted the assignment to create an up-to-date South Vietnamese army of 150,000 soldiers trained and equipped to hold the line against a full-scale assault from the North Vietnamese. The idea was to hold back the red tide until the Americans could arrive with reinforcements as they had done in Korea. It was no small task. To help him, 342 American advisers working for the U.S. Military Assistance and Advisory Group were flown in. None knew the Vietnamese language, and only a few understood the country or the culture.

Fortunately, Ho Chi Minh and his followers were too busy rebuilding their country to plan a conventional invasion of the South. Neither China nor the Soviets were interested in sponsoring another war. The Chinese had lost over a million soldiers in

Korea, and the Soviets had their hands full with NATO. Nobody was in the mood for World War III. The undermining of Diem's government would be left to the Viet Minh in the South and their leader, Le Duan. Communist cadres in the South believed that Duan understood their anguish. Diem's government had imprisoned or executed ninety percent of the communist forces in the South. Those that remained desperately wanted to rise in total rebellion but needed the support of the North. Duan took their arguments to the North and Ho Chi Minh.

Duan's position was simple. The politburo could approve military operations against the Diem government, or the Viet Minh would act unilaterally without their permission. It was a bold statement bordering on treason. Duan explained that it was not he that would lead the Viet Minh in their attacks against the South. They would need to find a new leader. Duan had vowed never to betray the communist party, and he would not cross it now. But that would not stop the Viet Minh. The only way the politburo could control the upcoming war was to supply arms and unleash the Viet Minh.

The news was not a surprise to Ho Chi Minh and the other members of the politburo. They had expected as much and were surprised that the cadre in the South had waited so long. But now, they were faced with a decision. Things had not changed. North Vietnam was not ready to fight a protracted war with the South. But that didn't seem to matter. War was coming in the South, whether they wanted it or not.

During a break in the discussions, Giap approached Ho and said, "Le is forcing our hand."

"Yes," said Ho. "But he speaks the truth. Our troops in the South are dwindling in number. I fear that if we do not support them, the army will vanish within the year."

"We can always build a new army in the South, Uncle. It is the Northern army that must concern us. We still have much to do in organization and supplies."

"I understand. Le is not asking for troops from the North, only arms and supplies. Surely, we can provide him and his followers what they require to begin the fight."

"We should never start a war we do not know we can win. Besides, we need those weapons and supplies for our troops in the North should the South choose to attack. I fear we will be stretched too thin."

"I have been considering such a situation. It occurs to me that the Chinese and the Soviets are in the same position as we are in the North. They too will need to choose if they will support the revolution in the South."

"And will they?"

"I think they will have no choice. They know as we do that revolutions are wild things. You cannot predict when they will come and what will happen when they arrive. But one thing is certain, you cannot let them slip from your hands, or you may never see them again."

"I doubt that, Uncle. There will always be those in the South that are willing to fight the government."

"Perhaps, but the opportunity to achieve our dream of reunification is before us like never before. I do not have many years left. I know it is selfish, but I would like to see it happen before I die."

"As would I, Uncle. As would I."

Mekong Delta, South Vietnam

Each day at sunrise, the fishermen from surrounding villages waded into the shallows of the Mekong Delta and checked their nets for damage. The enormous square nets were suspended by taut ropes mounted on four bamboo poles buried deep in the mud below the waterline. The nets' height was controlled by a foot-powered wooden wench onshore that tightened or loosened the ropes. Fishing began by lowering a net below the surface of the river. The fisherman operating the winch would observe the water. When he sensed movement, he cranked the winch raising the net and hopefully trapping a school of fish. A second fisherman in a sampan or round boat, usually a son or apprentice, would paddle under the suspended net and herd the captured fish into a hole in the center of the net where they would drop into the bottom of the boat. This process was repeated a dozen times or until the boat was full. It was a simple life. For centuries, the fisherman's only real fear was the Siamese crocodiles always lurking. The war between the Viet Minh and the government troops changed all that, and patrol boats became the most significant danger.

The Mekong Delta south of Saigon was not only the nation's largest rice-growing area, but it was also a major waterway for trade. It was also the easiest path to smuggle Viet Minh troops and weapons into the South. The 2,700 miles long Mekong River started in China, flowed through Laos, Cambodia, and finally Vietnam, where it branched into a delta and emptied into the South China Sea.

There was no simple method to determine if someone in a boat was a civilian or Viet Minh. Scars from battles were often the only evidence needed to convict a person of being the enemy. The South Vietnamese Army patrols' thinking was that it was better to imprison or kill five or six innocent civilians rather than let one Viet Minh escape detection. Confessions were coerced out of suspects through torture. But the government soldiers often didn't even bother. If nobody was looking, a single bullet or razor-sharp bayonet quickly solved the issue of a suspect's allegiance, and the crocodiles in the Mekong disposed of the evidence. The soldiers were then free to scavenge through the sampan for anything of value that would fit in their pockets or backpacks.

Reports of pirates attacking villages along the river's shore brought a harsh response from the South Vietnamese commander in the delta. He ordered four of his patrol boats armed with 50-Cal machine guns on their forward decks to hunt down the pirates.

The patrol boats swept upriver, checking every boat heading downriver like a long net strung across the water. They thought they spotted their prey when a motor-driven sampan made a swift U-turn upon spotting the patrol boats. All four boats chased the smaller sampan. With the bigger boats quickly catching up, the sampan's pilot turned into the mouth of a tributary surrounded by tall reeds and mangrove trees. The deck gunners opened fire. It was too late. The sampan disappeared into the tributary. Undeterred, the four patrol boats continued their hunt and entered the mouth of the tributary. They did not notice the old junk abandoned on a rickety pier near the mouth of the channel.

As the army boats proceeded up the tributary, they came to a fork in the smaller river. They split their force in two and continued down each fork. When they encountered a second set of forks, they again split up to cover both rivers. There was no sign of the sampan.

The old junk was not abandoned. The Viet Minh crew, hidden below deck, emerged, cast off the lines, and sailed the junk into the tributary's mouth. Inside the junk's cargo hold, four Viet Minh used axes to punch holes in the ship's hull. The wood was old and rotten. It splintered easily. As water rushed into the hold, the Viet Minh climbed out and jumped into a waiting sampan. The junk sank, its masks and rigging sticking out of the water blocked the tributary entrance.

The crews of the separated patrol boats kept a keen eye out as they weaved their way through the mangroves. They continued their search until the trees closed in, and they could go no further. They turned back. It wasn't easy maneuvering their boats in a confined space.

On their way back down the tributary, each patrol boat encountered an abandoned sampan stretched across the waterway, blocking their path. The sampans had chains on both ends, tying them to the trunks of mangrove trees. As expected, the chiefs of patrol boats sent several crew members to board the sampans to release the chains. When the chains were removed, ropes hidden beneath the waterline were pulled taught by unseen water buffalos driven by Viet Minh handlers downriver. The sampans were rapidly pulled away from the patrol boats separating the crew members on the sampans from the crew members on the patrol boat. The Viet Minh had split up the crews of the entire flotilla of patrol boats, making them easy pickings.

As soon as the crews were separated, the rebel soldiers opened fire from within hidden positions in the mangroves. The crews on the remaining patrol boats could hear the distant gunfire and knew what was coming.

Within a few seconds, the government soldiers in the sampans having no cover were torn apart by the enemy barrages. The crews in the patrol boats faired only slightly better. Without their entire crew and trapped in a confined area of the river, the chiefs were unable to maneuver the boats effectively. An additional chain stretching the length of the channel had been hidden beneath the water. The chain was raised to a level that would allow the patrol boat to pass over, then pulled tight to foul the boat's propeller preventing the government troops' escape. The boat gunners were able to return fire with their 50-Cals. The large-caliber bullets ripped into the mangroves, tearing them apart. It was dark beneath the canopy of leaves and difficult to identify enemy targets hidden among the trees. The patrol boat gunners used the flashes from the enemy's weapons to focus their aim, but the Viet Minh kept moving from position to position behind the mangroves' trunks. One by one, the gunners were killed until the boats became defenseless. The captains and any remaining crew members were quickly picked off.

One patrol boat managed to escape the Viet Minh trap. It barreled down the waterway and turned hard down the tributary. As it reached the mouth, it was forced to stop to avoid colliding with the sunken junk's masts and rigging. Hidden Viet Minh along the shore opened fire from both sides. There was nowhere to run and nowhere to hide. The patrol boat's captain and his remaining crew died like the others, overpowered and torn apart by the enemy volleys.

Word of the Viet Minh victory traveled fast through the surrounding villages. When the Viet Minh tax collectors made their rounds, few villagers failed to pay their share. It was now the Viet Minh that ruled the Mekong Delta, not the government.

July 1957 - Nha Trang, South Vietnam

With rain pouring down, a C-47 landed at Nha Trang airfield in South Vietnam. After taxing off the runway, eight U.S. Special Forces advisors departed the aircraft with their gear. Members of the 1st Special Forces Group had flown from their forward operating base in Okinawa.

While they were not the first Special Force operators in Vietnam, their role would be vital in developing the South Vietnamese Army's abilities to fight against the guerrilla tactics used by the Viet Minh. Their mission was to train fifty-seven of the country's best and brightest soldiers into South Vietnam's first Special Forces unit. Not only would the SF operators learn to fight using guerrilla tactics, they would learn to train others, especially the indigenous tribesmen of the Central Highlands – the Montagnard. It was a tall order.

With a population of almost one million, the Montagnard were made up of thirty different tribes speaking three different languages – Katuic, Bahnaric, and Chamic. The Montagnard did not share the same culture as the Vietnamese and therefore did not trust them. Over the centuries, they had often come into conflict, especially when the Vietnamese decided to confiscate some of the Montagnard's best land for coffee plantations.

Over half of the Montagnard were Christians, converted by early French and American missionaries. The communist party was suspicious of the Montagnard. However, both North and South Vietnam wanted to recruit the tribesmen to join their cause. Because of their quiet resolve and tracking skills, the South went to great lengths to enlist the Montagnard in their campaigns to cut off the Viet Minh supply trail near the Montagnard villages.

Except for a few young men, the Montagnard as a whole stayed neutral during much of the early conflict. The Montagnard even established the own organization known as "BAJARAKA" to unite the tribes against the Vietnamese. It was only when the American Special Forces became directly involved in recruiting and training the tribesmen that the Montagnard became one of the great fighting forces in Vietnam, Cambodia, and Laos. The Montagnard did not know the Americans and therefore had no reason not to trust them. They liked the money and the weapons the Americans gave them. With the Americans' help, they could defend their land, and their people prospered. And in exchange, the Montagnard were asked to track and kill communists, something they excelled at and enjoyed.

January 1959 - Hanoi, North Vietnam

Duan spoke passionately before the members of the politburo, "Political resistance in the South is useless. Diem and his illegitimate government grow stronger as the people's army in the South grows weaker. The North has been focused on rebuilding their new nation while letting their brothers and sisters in the South suffer under Diem's whip. Nowhere is safe. Brother Nhu's security forces care nothing about the laws or rights of its citizens. They are cruel and deceptive beyond measure. They turn father and son against each other. Soon, his prisons will be filled with what remains of our members, and it could be too late. The party must act now if it is to save South

154

Vietnam. Our people are like mounds of straw waiting to be ignited. Ready to join the fight, they just need the means to do so. The time has come to reunite our country under Hanoi's leadership. The military must support our efforts to topple Diem's government and take over the South. Only cowards would turn away from this moral obligation."

The members mumbled their objections to Duan's harsh words, but many knew they were true. "A man that recognizes danger and exercises caution is not a coward, but prudent," said General Giap. "You make it seem so simple. I assure you… it is not. Our soldiers are now well-trained and ready to fight, but we still lack the weapons and supplies needed for a sustained conflict. All we have gained after years of hardship and sacrifice could be lost by striking before we are truly ready."

"I have heard your arguments before, General. It seems you always have a reason for not fighting these days. One might begin to think; you have lost your nerve."

"I have lost nothing of the kind and stand ready to obey the committee's commands. But I do not wish to sacrifice our soldiers' blood for a fruitless cause."

"And yet, you are willing to sacrifice the blood of those in the South by doing nothing to aid them."

"If blood is sacrificed in the South, it is only through the stupidity of those that lead with their hearts and ignore their minds. Success in war requires both courage and strategy. It was the great General Sun Tzu that said, '"He will win who knows when to fight and when not to fight."

"Leave it to a general to quote another general when avoiding criticism for his cowardice."

Giap's expression sharpened as he rose and walked over to Duan. For a moment, it seemed he would thrash Duan until Ho Chi Minh intervened. "It is good that passions run high when we talk of revolution. But we must remember to whom our anger should be focused. I assure you; they are not in this room."

Hearing the meaning of Ho's words, Giap backed off and sat back down. "We should never question our brothers' motives in public," said Ho. "Such words will poison our deliberations and destroy the very purpose of our brotherhood."

In the afternoon, when the meeting was on a break, Giap approached Ho and said, "Why do you put up with his impudence?"

"Because Le is the future," said Ho.

"And I am not?"

"You are the people's general."

"But not their leader?"

"Do not sully your celebrated deeds with politics. You will go down in history as the man that brought the French to their knees at Dien Bien Phu. Isn't that enough?"

"I only wish to serve the revolution."

"And you will… when your time comes. In the meantime, let Le lead our rebels in the South. Help him when you can. You have far more experience in military matters, but he has the people's hearts."

"No, Uncle. You have the people's hearts."

"My time is passing. Too quickly, I feel. But passing nonetheless. We need younger leaders that young men and women can follow."

"He will get them killed."

"Perhaps. But don't underestimate him or our people. He is right; they have a strong will to fight. We should let them."

"Then you will vote to support the overthrow of Diem's government."

"With everything short of declaring war. We do not want to anger the Americans to the point they will enter the conflict. Once they start, it may be impossible to stop them."

"I think you fear the Americans too much."

"I have seen their factories. They are endless and can produce enough bombs and artillery shells to crush our forces if they wish. I do not want to bring that onto our people if we can avoid it."

"And if we can't… avoid it?"

"Then we shall do our duty. We cannot leave our country divided. The thought is too painful to comprehend."

The vote later that evening was carried in Le Duan's favor. The North would support the South in their revolution against Diem's government but would not commit regular troops to the fighting unless the government troops or aircraft crossed into the North. "For the liberation of our compatriots in the South," one politburo member wrote, "a situation of boiling oil and burning fire is necessary."

In groups of fifty, hundreds of communist cadres carried their new supply of weapons and ammunition as they recrossed the border and entered the South. They used a network of footpaths that wound their way through Laos and Cambodia, crossing dozens of rivers and mountains. It took two to six months to walk from North Vietnam to South Vietnam, during which time they ate the rice they could carry and leaves from the trees. Occasionally, someone would kill a wild animal or bird. They would share the treasure with their comrades giving them the strength to continue their long journey.

Finally, given the military support from the North they had longed for, Viet Minh attacks steadily increased until at least one government official or soldier was killed every day in the South. It was welcome progress for the Viet Minh leaders but had little effect on the government in Saigon. Diem wrote it off as communist agitation and not a real threat to the stability of his government.

Duan needed to make a strong statement to the politburo and the world that his rebel force was ready and willing to overthrow the illegitimate government in the South and reunite his country. He sent word out to his spy network throughout the South to search for targets of opportunity. He found what he was looking for at a military base in Bien Hoa, twenty miles northeast of Saigon. It was the perfect target to send a message to the leaders in Saigon and Washington D.C. that nobody was safe and that the Viet Minh could strike whenever and wherever they wanted. Duan also knew that Ho Chi Minh would be angered by the assault he was planning. In Duan's mind, the North's leaders had to get over their fear if the revolution was to succeed. He determined it was a gamble worth taking.

THE TATTERED DRESS

July 8, 1959 – Bien Hoa, South Vietnam

Walking across the South Vietnamese military base, thirty-seven-year-old Major Dale Buis from Imperial Beach, California, picked up the sixteen-millimeter movie reels delivered along with the mail from Saigon. Typically, he had one of the enlisted men under his command pick up the mail and deliveries, but he had just finished a letter to his wife and wanted to ensure it made it on the next postal flight back to the U.S.

He did not carry his sidearm when inside the base's well-guarded perimeter. Like the seven other MAAG advisors stationed on the base, he felt safe. In the four years MAAG had been operating in South Vietnam, no American advisor had been killed or even severely wounded by the enemy. The most significant risk was snipers, but the South Vietnamese Army kept the vegetation around the perimeter cleared for over one hundred yards, and he was nowhere near the perimeter. It would be one hell of a shot if a sniper's bullet even came close to him, and the Viet Minh were not known for their aim at distance.

The base was the home of the South Vietnamese elite 7th Division. Its 10,000 well-armed soldiers were a strong deterrent against any enemy attack. Constant patrols in the surrounding jungle also kept the enemy at bay. The living quarters for the American MAAG advisor group were situated in the middle of the compound. It was a two-story structure with sleeping quarters and the head on the second floor. The first floor held the kitchen, a mess hall, a storage room, a small toilet, and a reading room. The facility was much larger than the eight Americans needed, but they weren't complaining. The extra space was welcome and allowed more privacy than usual. Like Buis, the other advisors rarely carried their weapons while on base, especially not in their quarters. Their weapons were stored beside their bunks on the second floor within easy reach if there was ever an assault at night which is when the Viet Minh preferred to attack.

When Buis returned with the mail, the Vietnamese cook and his eight-year-old son were already preparing the evening meal. It was movie night, and that meant hamburgers and fries with all the fixings. Tonight was a double feature that would require a snack at intermission – popcorn and a bowl of mango slices. The cook usually prepared meals for much larger groups than the eight Americans and needed to remind himself not to waste food.

Americans had big appetites, but even they had limits.

Master Sergeant Chester Ovnand from Copperas Cove, Texas, sat on the couch in the reading room finishing a novel his wife had sent him – *On the Beach* by Nevil Shute. It was a cautionary, post-apocalyptic story of the survivors of nuclear war as they await the arrival of deadly radiation spreading towards them— a dark tale for a dark time in world history. The ending sent a shiver through his spine, and he questioned whether he should have read the book. It made him miss his wife even more than usual. He saw Buis walk past the doorway and said, "Any mail for me?"

"Not today, Sergeant," said Buis.

The American advisors were casual about saluting. Salutes attracted snipers. Besides, officers lived with the enlisted men, most of which were veteran sergeants. It was just too much trouble to be snapping to attention and saluting all the time. At ease was the order of the day unless there was a visit from a high-ranking officer from Saigon. Then, it was business as usual. Buis was the commanding officer and the newest member of the group. He had arrived two days earlier and was still learning the ropes. Fortunately, everything was running smoothly before he arrived, and he only needed to keep from mucking it up.

The group's mission was to advise and train the commanders and soldiers of the 7th Division. The Vietnamese were skeptical of the American strategy and tactics. The Americans were teaching the Vietnamese how to fight a full-scale holding action.

The idea was that if the North invaded in strength, the South Vietnamese Army would hold the line until the American Army arrived and could push back the invasion as they had done in Korea. But the Vietnamese commanders didn't see the conflict unfolding as such. They believed their troops would be fighting a guerrilla war in the jungles and mountains. Both were right... and wrong. Still, the training was welcomed. The Americans used up-to-date training methods and had a clear understanding of how to fight with the modern weapons they were supplying the South Vietnamese through military aid. The South Vietnamese had been using antiquated weapons given to them by the French and hand-me-downs from WWII. The American advisors were all veterans of at least one war and were highly experienced.

Captain Howard Boston, a thirty-seven-year-old WWII veteran and the group's artillery advisor, sat at a mess hall table cleaning his sidearm when Buis walked in and handed him a letter from his wife. "Thanks, Major," said Boston. "What are the movies?"

It occurred to Buis that he hadn't bothered to look at the labels on the canisters when he picked them up. His mind had been elsewhere. "Oh, ah... *The Tattered Dress* and *The Searchers*," said Buis reading the labels. "*The Searchers* is pretty good. I haven't seen *The Tattered Dress*."

"I haven't seen either. But it wouldn't matter anyhow. Watching a movie you've already seen is better than staring at the wall."

"I guess."

"How are you settling in?"

"Pretty good. You guys seem to have things running smoothly. That always makes it easier."

"Yeah. Your predecessor, Major Weaver, was a stickler for organization."

"I'll give him my compliments if I ever meet him. Enjoy your letter. I've got a few things to take care of before supper," said Buis moving off.

On the edge of the jungle, Major Duc Van Tien sat high in a tree watching the South Vietnamese compound. The guards patrolling the perimeter were of particular interest. He made a mental note of their weapons and their intervals between each pass in front of his location. It was a job for an experienced scout, but Tien insisted on performing his own reconnaissance. It was the only way he could know the situation for sure. He had been chosen personally by Le Duan to lead the team that would breach the compound. Duan had told him it would be the most important mission of his life and, if successful, would strike a blow at the heart of the Saigon government. Tien believed him and was determined not to disappoint his commander.

Tien was a veteran of WWII and the Indochina War. He had fought at Dien Bien Phu and participated in the assault on the French trenches of strongpoint Gabrielle. After taking the hill, the French counterattacked. Tien and his men fought off the French paratroopers and secured the hill once and for all. Because of its position overlooking the airfield, the strong point's capture was considered a major blow to the French garrison. Like most, Tien did not ask for and was not given a medal for actions during the siege. His desire was only to serve the revolution and kick the French out of his country. Now, it was the Americans' turn.

Once satisfied that he understood the guard's schedule for the day, Tien returned to his men deeper in the jungle. It was a small team of twenty soldiers. They were the best of the best; most were veterans like himself. They were men he trusted. He went over the final assignments and schedule. He made sure everyone knew their position and when to move. He had split the team in two – half to enter the compound to assault the American quarters and half to protect their escape route with covering fire. Tien expected that some of his team would die this night. He reminded them that their names would not be forgotten and that their sacrifices would prepare the way for their country's reunification. He allowed each man to take ten minutes to prepare himself so he could focus on the mission once they started.

As dark descended on the base, the team moved into position in the jungle next to the compound. On Tien's signal, two sappers belly-crawled one hundred yards over open ground to the edge of the fence. Their uniforms' camouflage had been painted to match the ground, making them all but invisible. They waited until the guards passed.

The second half of the team took up firing positions in the jungle to protect the escape route when the mission was completed or if, for any reason, the mission was abandoned and the team needed to fall back.

Although the sappers had wire cutters that would easily cut through the barbed wire, Tien had ordered them not to use them. He did not want the guards to spot the break in the fence line when they passed again. Instead, one of the sappers used a trenching tool to dig an eighteen-inch-deep trench under the wire. It was just enough room to crawl under the fence. The other sapper kept watch and signaled the team in the jungle when the trench was near completion. The eight remaining members of the assault team belly-crawled to the fence just as the sapper completed the trench and crawled under. The team members followed the sapper under the fence and moved to hide in the shadows of the buildings inside the compound. When the second sapper crawled under the fence, the two sappers pushed the loose soil back into the trench and smoothed it over, so no evidence of the hole remained. They, too, moved into the shadows of the buildings to join the others.

They leapfrogged forward, using the shadows to mask their movements as they advanced toward their target. When the American advisors' quarters were finally in view, they could hear the movie playing through the open windows. The only lights on were upstairs in the sleeping area and in the kitchen toward the back of the building. Tien gave his final commands using hand signals to indicate who was to go where. They advanced surrounding the house.

There was a slight fear of the unknown tugging at the team members. Most in the team had never fought against the Americans before but had heard of their exploits in Korea and WWII. Tien knew the

Americans. They had fought by his side when the Viet Minh attacked the Japanese during WWII. He knew them to be brave and skilled fighters, but he also knew they were not invincible. There was a tinge of sadness in his heart that he must now kill those that he once counted as his allies. *They had chosen their path to aid the South Vietnamese. They had chosen to become his enemy,* he told himself. *They are to blame for their fate.*

There were three open windows on the right side of the building. Two gunmen for each window moved into the shadows. The sound of the movie covered their footsteps. One of the soldiers at the windows carried a homemade satchel charge that would be used to set the building on fire to cover the Viet Minh's escape and kill any Americans that might be hiding.

Tien and three more soldiers moved to the back of the building and approached the kitchen door. The plan of attack was simple and straightforward. Tien did not want his men caught in their own crossfire. The Viet Minh at the windows would wait for Tien's signal before opening fire. The three soldiers at the kitchen door would wait until their comrades at the windows finished their magazines before entering the building through the kitchen to finish off any survivors. The satchel charge would be thrown through the window after all the Viet Minh were accounted for and headed back to the fence line. Tien hoped that any South Vietnamese troops that arrived before their escape was complete would be more worried about saving any survivors from the fire than chasing the perpetrators. It was a good plan if everything happened as he anticipated. But this was war where few things happen as expected. The

Viet Minh slipped the barrels of weapons through the open windows. Tien checked the doorknob on the kitchen door. It was unlocked. He could hear the cook shaking the pan as he finished the popcorn for intermission. The cook had given his son the job of cutting the mangos into bite-sized pieces and placing them in three bowls.

The Americans were watching the end of *The Tattered Dress.* Ovnand was operating the projector. As "The End" flashed up on the screen, Ovnand switched on the lights in preparation for changing the reel to the new movie, *The Searchers*. The Americans had no weapons downstairs.

Outside the window, the Viet Minh were caught off guard by the light now shining through the windows. They panicked and opened fire, sprayed the interior with bullets.

Ovnand was the only man standing and was a clear target for the gunmen who had to stand on their toes to see through the windows. He was hit seven times but was still able to flip off the lights and attempt to climb the stairs to retrieve his weapon. He died before reaching the top.

Barrel flashes lit up the room, creating a bizarre strobe effect as the Americans hit the deck using whatever they could as cover.

The Viet Minh could not see them but continued to fire until their weapons clicked empty. There was silence as they reloaded in preparation for their escape and to provide covering fire for the comrades inside if required.

Hearing the end of the gunfire, Tien opened the backdoor and entered the kitchen. Seeing the door open, the cook flipped off the room lights and whispered to his son to get down on the floor. Still holding the knife he used to cut the mangos, the boy stood up from the chair he had been sitting on and turned toward the back door.

Hearing the gunmen reloading outside the windows and realizing that the assault was not over, Boston crawled across the room to the stairs, stood up, and flipped the switch to the outside floodlights.

Inside the kitchen, the boy was silhouetted by the light from the mess hall. As Tien entered, he saw the silhouette of a man holding a knife and fired a burst from his machine gun. The boy was killed instantly as his bullet-riddled body dropped to the floor.

Hearing the gunshots and realizing that there were gunmen in the kitchen, Buis rose to his feet and ran into the hallway connecting the two rooms. He was unarmed, but it didn't seem to matter. He was going to stop them. Tien had moved forward to look at the dead boy on the floor and realized his mistake. When Buis entered the hallway, Tien looked up and hesitated for a moment. Buis charged straight at him, hoping to close the distance before the assassin in the kitchen could fire his weapon. He didn't make it. Tien raised his machine gun and sprayed Buis with a long burst of gunfire. Buis fell dead next to the boy. Their blood mingled together on the floor.

Seeing his son dead on the floor, the cook stood up and wailed as only a heartbroken father could lament. Tien swung his machine gun around but did not fire. It didn't seem fair to kill the man, having lost what Tien imagined was his son.

Outside the windows, the gunmen were startled by the floodlights. The shadows no longer offered refuge. They ran back the way they had come. The man carrying the satchel charge realized he had not done his duty as ordered and ran back to the open windows. He pulled the detonation cord on the satchel charge and pushed the canvas case into the window opening. It was too big to make through the opening. He moved to the next window, and it still didn't fit no matter how hard he pushed. Time ran out, and the satchel charge exploded, blowing the man into chunks of bone and flesh.

Inside the mess hall, the explosion ripped open the wall where Boston was standing. He was pelted with sharp wooden shards, and flames set his uniform on fire. Knocked unconscious from the blast, he fell. The room filled with smoke. Several of his comrades crawled over, patted out the flames on his uniform with their bare hands, and tended to his wounds to keep him from bleeding out.

Rocked by the explosion, Tien and the other gunmen retreated out the backdoor. They moved around the building to see the severed feet in the tennis shoes of their comrade carrying the satchel charge. They ran across the compound toward the fence and rejoined their other comrades waiting in the shadows of another building. Tien signaled the rest of the team outside the compound. They opened fire, laying down a barrage to cover the retreat. Two South Vietnamese soldiers were sprayed with bullets and fell to the ground dead.

The Viet Minh sapper with wire cutters ran forward and snipped the barbed wire creating a man-sized opening. The assault team ran through the fence opening at full speed and entered the jungle. Tien was the last to escape. The death of the boy would haunt him for many years to come.

The White House was infuriated at the attack on the base and the deaths of the two advisors. The shit rolled downhill from there. It seemed the Americans at the Saigon embassy had been caught with their pants down from a complete intelligence failure. The South Vietnamese Army was responsible for the American advisors' safety. If 10,000 of Diem's best troops couldn't keep out a small band of sappers and assassins, what hope was there that they could stop the North from invading. There was more talk of cutting off aid, packing up everything, and leaving the country.

Diem and his family shed the blame for the attack like a duck sheds water. The commander of the base received the bulk of the accusations and was stripped of his command. The officers and soldiers assigned to guard the Americans were quickly dealt with by Brother Nhu and his security forces. Some were accused of being traitors and quietly executed with photographic evidence being sent to the Americans, who found it distasteful.

Lansdale and the CIA head of station at the embassy both caught flak. They had been given a large amount of resources and yet were unable to unearth the attack before it happened. Lansdale, in particular, was criticized for not keeping Diem focused on the Americans' security needs. It was unfair, but that didn't matter. The colonel was taken down a few notches in the eyes of his superiors because of the incident. Lansdale knew he would need to do something notable in retaliation to regain their confidence.

Deep down, Eisenhower knew it was only a matter of time until the American advisors in Vietnam were attacked. They were a juicy propaganda target, and as much as he hated to admit it, they were spread out across the country, and nobody could protect them if the enemy were determined. It was the reality of the simmering covert war that the Americans were now fighting against the communists. With the embassy marine guards as the only American troops on the ground in Vietnam, there wasn't much hope in preventing further attacks. But he also knew that if America suspended military support, it was only a matter of time until South Vietnam fell, and the communists obtained the foothold in Southeast Asia they longed for. Even if things were slowly getting worse, at least the situation in the South was somewhat stable, and the bulk of the communist forces was being held at bay. It was a small consolation, but at this point, he would take whatever he could get. Besides, he was nearing the end of his second term as president, and soon Vietnam would be the next guy's problem. For now, he just needed to keep the whole thing from falling apart.

Captain Boston had been airlifted to an Okinawa military hospital and survived his wounds. Upon leaving the hospital, he was reunited with his family. Decades later, he visited "The Wall" at the Vietnam Memorial in Washington D.C. There, he walked to the panel marked "1959" and saw the top two names etched in black stone – Dale M. Buis and Chester R. Ovnand – the first American soldiers killed in the Vietnam War. Like so many, he wept for his fallen brethren.

TRUONG SON ROAD

Duan had been correct in his prediction. Ho was furious when he learned about the assassination of the American soldiers in Bien Hoa. He felt betrayed by Duan. He had supported Duan in his plea for assistance from North Vietnam. Now, Duan had stabbed him in the back with the one thing Ho wanted to avoid above all else – pissing off the Americans. Duan's insolence was not the only problem facing Ho and the politburo. Things were heating up quickly in Laos.

France had given the Kingdom of Laos its independence within the French Union in 1953. Several years later, the Geneva Conference established Laotian neutrality. This meant that no other country was allowed to interfere with Laotian politics or government, and no foreign soldiers were allowed in Laos. From the start, everyone seemed to ignore the agreement.

North Vietnam continued to command a significant armed force in Northern and Southern Laos. Hanoi and the People's Army of Vietnam (PAVN) had no intention of withdrawing from the country or abandoning their Laotian communist allies – the Pathet Lao. The Royal Lao Army had made several attempts to push the North Vietnamese out of Laos with little success.

The Royal Lao Government had good relations with the Americans, which gave the country covert financial and military aid to assist in their struggle against the Pathet Lao and the North Vietnamese Communist movement. While the Americans were unwilling to offer direct military involvement in Laos, they were willing to provide substantial covert assistance. In 1957, America provided more financial and military assistance to Laos than any other country in Southeast Asia. The United States paid 100% of the Royal Lao Army military budget.

Originally named "Truong Son Road" by the North Vietnamese, the supply trail leading through Laos and Cambodia had been recognized as the key to victory in the South. Vietnam's geography was shaped like a Picassoesque hourglass with two large landmasses on the northern and southern ends. In the middle of the country, the territory thinned to a narrow strip only thirty miles wide. The demilitarized zone that divided North and South Vietnam was in that narrow strip of land.

To transport weapons, ammunition, and supplies to the Viet Minh in the South, communist smugglers had three possible routes. The first was by the South China Sea, which ran along Vietnam's coastline. The sea route was by far the fastest route between the North and South. It was dangerous, with dozens of heavily armed South Vietnamese patrol boats traversing the waters and checking even the smallest sampan. The second path was the route through the demilitarized zone. Tens of thousands of South Vietnamese troops and dozens of outposts protected the border between North and South making passage almost impossible. Every vehicle, cart, and bicycle was thoroughly searched for weapons, ammunition, and supplies. Bribes would sometimes work to circumvent the guards at the border crossings but traveling near the border was still risky. Even if their contraband made it past the border, the smugglers would be harassed by multiple patrols and checkpoints on the main highway and surrounding roads as they moved farther South. The third and final route was the Truong Son Road through Laos and Cambodia. The road began in North Vietnam in a gorge called "Heaven's Gate."

Until 1959, the Truong Son was made up of hundreds of pathways that wound their way through the Ammonite Range of mountains in Western Laos and Northern Cambodia. The road was a 16,000 km long mishmash of truck routes, footpaths, and waterways. Along the way were a series of mountain passes that could be used to access South Vietnam at different points depending on the covert shipment's final destination.

Group 559 was established to maintain and upgrade the road through Laos and Cambodia. Originally just a few thousand men and women with a few reinforced bicycles, the group grew to over 24,000 soldiers and included hundreds of trucks and anti-aircraft guns. Considered by many to be the greatest engineering feat of the twentieth century, the road was renamed "The Ho Chi Minh Trail" by the Americans after the notorious communist leader.

Tons of weapons, ammunition, and supplies were carried on trucks, horses, rafts, reinforced bicycles, and handcarts. Some cargo was even carried by thousands of peasants with backpacks. A civilian carrying cargo rarely traveled the entire road. Instead, the most efficient transportation mode was used for a designated stretch of the trail, then unloaded and picked up by another type of transportation for the next leg of the journey. Storage depots were built along the road to keep cargo dry from the rain and cool from the sun. Rest areas with hammocks and mess halls were also built and included recreation areas where singers and actors would often perform to boost morale. Maintenance depots with inventories of spare parts would repair vehicles and bicycles. Fuel depots provided gas for trucks. All of it was heavily camouflaged, and guards were posted twenty-four hours a day along the road to protect the workers. When the Americans began bombing campaigns to destroy the road, the Vietnamese installed anti-aircraft installations, especially near bridges and critical pathways.

When the road was damaged, a detour was quickly created to keep the cargo flowing while crews of workers repaired the damage using picks and shovels. Repairs rarely lasted more than a day before the original path was ready to transport cargo once again. Its rustic nature and redundancy were what made it near impossible to destroy. Most of the materials to repair the road were found in the surrounding jungle. There was no need to wait for a load of cement or steel when bamboo and hardwood would do the job. Compressed soil was the main ingredient for most of the trail. But the most significant advantage was that the trail was not a single trail at any given point but dozens of different pathways all heading in the same direction. The Ho Chi Minh Trail was more of a supply corridor than a single road or path. When one pathway failed, another popped up in a matter of hours.

As time wore on, more and more of the road was upgraded. Footpaths became bicycle trails, then roadways for trucks. Monkey bridges were converted to vehicle bridges capable of bearing tons of cargo in multiple trucks. And with each upgrade, the flow of weapons, ammunition, and supplies increased. It was an unstoppable river of cargo, flexible and resilient.

The relationship that the North Vietnamese communists had built with Pathet Lao rebels made the trail possible. While strong and brave fighters, the Pathet Lao were poorly trained and lacked modern weapons. The North Vietnamese supported the Lao insurgents in their quest to overthrow the U.S.-supported Royal Lao government located in the capital city of Vientiane. Many of the Pathet Lao recruits were sent to North Vietnam for training by veteran Vietnamese troops. By supplying weapons, ammunition, supplies, and training, the North Vietnamese were not only helping their communist comrades in Laos, but they were also creating a buffer between the Pathet Lao and the Royal Lao Army. Forced to deal with multiple raids from the Pathet Lao, the Royal Lao Army had little time to search and destroy the Ho Chi Minh Trail and its builders.

The United States supported the Royal Lao Army. The Lao soldiers were less experienced at warfare than the soldiers in the North Vietnamese Army. Many of their weapons were WWII hand-me-downs and in need of repair. The Americans were willing to resupply the Lao with modern weapons but lacked supply routes leading into the country. Laos was land-locked, preventing any shipping by sea. On top of the lack of ports, Laos, a mountainous country with dense jungles, had few well-maintained roads crossing its borders. When the rains arrived each year, many of the roads were washed out, making them unpassable.

The Americans were flying new weapons into Laos through CAT, the CIA's covert airline, but it was a slow process. Artillery was especially difficult because of the size and weight. Beyond the major cities, the Lao airfields were lacking, with many only capable of landing smaller aircraft. There was a bottleneck of weapons and ammunition stored in

Vientiane warehouses waiting for delivery to the soldiers in the field.

July 28, 1959 - Laos

Another problem cropped up when the American diplomats and CIA officers realized that the weapons they were giving the Royal Lao Army might one day be used against them. During negotiations at Geneva to end the Indochina War, the Laotian government had agreed to free elections and absorb the Pathet Lao soldiers into the Royal Lao Army units to avoid further bloodshed. The Americans were concerned that the Pathet rebels were being repatriated in the Royal Lao Army without background checks or reeducation. For all the Americans knew, the insurgents would infiltrate the government army units and convince the government soldiers to join a coup against their government leaders and commanders. It sounded preposterous and was rejected by the Royal Lao commanders until one night in late July…

After the elections, on the night before they were to join the government forces, two of the Pathet Lao battalions near Luang Prabang disappeared into the surrounding mountains taking their newly received American weapons and ammunition with them. They had reneged on the agreement. It was the doing of the North Vietnamese. They had convinced the Pathet Lao battalion leaders that with North Vietnam's and China's help, the rebels could overthrow the government by force. There was no need to kowtow to the Royal Lao Army commanders. The civil war in Laos had begun again, just as Ho and his commanders had planned.

As part of the Geneva agreement, Ho and the Viet Minh had agreed not to interfere in Laos. The French had made the same agreement. Now, the French were gone, and Ho no longer felt the obligation to keep his hands off Laos. However, he also saw the need to keep the international community's eyes off of any North Vietnamese incursions into Laos. He did not want to draw any more attention to North Vietnam's use of the Truong Son Road.

Ho's commanders saw the problem with the Pathet Lao rebels. While they were good at defending a position, they could not coordinate their units into an effective assault against the enemy. Their solution was to use North Vietnamese troops to perform the initial attack on a village or military installation. Once the enemy position was captured, the North Vietnamese would turn the prisoners and defensive positions over to the rebels to hold. It worked beautifully, and the Pathet Lao, with the North Vietnamese troops' help, advanced through the countryside rolling up one government unit after another. Before long, the scales of war had been tipped to the rebels' advantage as more and more territory came under their control.

In the meantime, the North Vietnamese took advantage of the absence of enemy opposition to expand their supply routes through the mountains. Redundancy was seen to be just as crucial as travel speed. It was redundancy that was the guarantee of success against the South. Ho and his commanders wanted more. They wanted to expand and upgrade the tail end of the trail, so it reached all the way to the Southern end of Laos and even into the flatlands of Cambodia. This would allow the Viet Minh a much closer entry point to Saigon and the Mekong Delta area, where the majority of government troops and facilities were located.

The continuation of the Civil War in Laos was a disaster to the Americans who understood that while courage and tactics won battles, it was logistics that won wars. Convincing the South Vietnamese commanders of the danger was another matter. They had never been good at logistics because they were always lacking in supplies and weapons. There was no need to transport or store what you don't have. As far as the civil war was concerned, the South Vietnamese government didn't see what all the fuss was about. Laos was a poor country with few roads. The French had chosen to mostly ignore Laos for a good reason – it had little to offer in the way of exports and little infrastructure to take advantage of the few raw materials it could sell abroad. Laos was landlocked and didn't even have a shipping port. Laos was nothing compared to the rich rice fields and rubber plantations of Vietnam.

But the Americans knew that if the Ho Chi Minh Trail was left to operate without disruption, the Viet Minh in the South would eventually become well-armed and supplied. What was now no more than a mob could quickly become a real threat to the South Vietnamese government and Army.

As a counterbalance against North Vietnamese troops and the Pathet Lao protecting the Ho Chi Minh Trail, the American CIA sent a force of covert advisors to train and support an indigenous, guerrilla army of 30,000 anti-communist tribespeople, mainly from the hill communities of the Hmong, Mien, and Khmu. The tribesman also raided the North Vietnamese supply convoys headed South, disrupting the flow of arms and ammunition to the Viet Minh. The CIA's covert advisors included 149 U.S. soldiers from the 77th Special Forces Group on temporary duty. Technically they were employees of the American Programs Evaluation Office and wore civilian clothes to further protect their identities. They operated under the codename "Hotfoot." In addition to the Green Berets, 103 Filipino military veterans worked for a newly formed front company named Eastern Construction Company. CAT provided air transportation between South Vietnam and Laos.

Through the guerrilla tribesmen and the Royal Lao Army, the anti-communists were able to keep pressure on the Pathet Lao and the North Vietnamese forces in Laos. More importantly to the Americans, continual raids on the Ho Chi Minh Trail slowed the delivery of weapons, supplies, and replacement troops to the Viet Minh in the South.

Tooj was excited. It was his first mission as a sapper after being trained by the CIA officer during Operation Momentum. He wore a traditional dark blue tunic minus the bright red waistcloth. He was a Blue Hmong, part of the 30,000 tribesmen that made up the anti-communist guerrilla force in Northeastern Laos. The Americans had given him a rifle, the first gun anyone in his village had ever owed. The weapon was leaning against a tree, close, in case he needed it. His unit commander had also given him the two grenades, wire, and the wire cutters he was using to construct booby traps along an overgrown footpath.

The footpath was part of the Ho Chi Minh Trail. It was one of six alternative paths paralleling the main road a half-mile to the West. A company of Hmong guerrillas was hidden along the main road waiting to ambush a North Vietnamese supply convoy. Once the ambush was executed, the North Vietnamese would reroute their supplies to one of the alternative pathways, all of which were being booby trapped by the Hmong sapper unit. Tooj hoped it was his footpath that was chosen by the North Vietnamese. He hated the Vietnamese soldiers.

There were two booby traps that he was building. The first was a tripwire on the downhill side of a slope. He had strung the wire across the path just below the top of the downhill side so the convoy leader would have little time to see the wire as he crested the hill. One end of the wire was wrapped around a large rock just off the path, while the other end of the wire was attached to the safety ring on a grenade tied to a tree trunk on the opposite side of the trail. With the wire stretched two inches above the compressed soil that formed the top layer of the footpath, Tooj needed to be careful. The booby trap was live. He pulled out a small tin container from his waistband and opened the lid. Inside was a dark brown oil given to him by his instructor. He carefully coated the entire wire with the oil and then sprinkled dirt on the oil, making the camouflaged wire almost invisible. Finished, he inspected his work to ensure that the booby trap was well hidden from view. It was.

He moved to the location of the second booby trap just off the right side of the trail. The idea was that once the first booby trap exploded, the survivors would dive off the trail into the cover of the surrounding vegetation where the second booby trap would be waiting. It, too, was a tripwire design stretched between the base of a bush and a boulder. The wire holding the second grenade was wrapped around the boulder. He hoped that the boulder would deflect most of the explosion toward the survivors. If he was lucky, he might kill or seriously wound five or six North Vietnamese. He would be a hero in his village, making his wife and aging parents proud.

He was almost done with the second booby trap when he felt a thud against the middle of his back. Feeling a slight twinge of pain, he looked down to see the head of an arrow sticking out of his chest. The arrow had pierced his heart. He fell forward, setting off the booby trap and exploding the grenade. His body was pelted with shrapnel. It didn't matter. He was already dead.

A Pathet Lao fire team, one soldier carrying a bow, emerged from the jungle. They were armed with Chinese weapons in addition to the bow. The rebel bowman walked over to the corpse to check his handiwork. It was a clean shot. Silent, if not for the grenade. He saw the rifle leaning against the tree and picked it up. Chinese weapons were good, American weapons were better. He would keep it as a trophy for killing a Hmong. He hated the Hmong.

The grenade explosion had warned the approaching North Vietnamese supply convoy that something was amiss. They slowed and sent more patrols forward to survey the road ahead.

After hearing the explosion, Granier knew that the ambush was blown and that the company of Hmong guerrillas he had been advising would soon be in deep shit.

He and his team had been sent to Laos as a stopgap. The Green Beret advisors would be arriving soon but, in the meantime, he and his team had the responsibility of training and advising the first battalion of Hmong guerrillas. The South Vietnamese Army needed to cut off the flow of arms to the Viet Minh in the South. The Royal Lao Army had their hands full, keeping control of their cities as the Pathet Lao pressed their assaults. The Hmong guerrillas were seen as the solution. They would not only put pressure on the Pathet Lao, but they would also be able to disrupt the North Vietnamese supply lines through Laos.

Training didn't take long. Granier was a firm believer of in-the-field training. The Hmong already had good survival and tracking skills. They quickly learned how to operate and maintain their weapons. Hand-to-hand combat came naturally to the

Hmong. Explosives were a bit more of a challenge since most of the Hmong had never dealt with chemical or electrical reactions. Santana had been put in charge of training the sappers. He kept things simple. The Green Beret could continue with more advanced training once they arrived and got organized. Grenades and simple explosive devices were the initial training Santana taught the Hmong.

The team of Americans soon learned that the Hmong, who fought in units based on their villages, were fiercely loyal to one another and had tight unit cohesion. This was great when defending a position or assaulting the enemy. It was not so great when trying to retreat. Like the American Marines, the Hmong would not leave a wounded or dead comrade on the battlefield. They were willing to die trying to save their wounded or retrieve the bodies of their dead. While this was a great morale booster, it was also a bad way to lose a lot of Hmong.

The other team members had been advising their own companies of Hmong. Granier's team was the first to go out on a major ambush mission. Now, he was wondering if that was such a great idea. The fact that he only spoke a few words of Hmong didn't help matters. He had a Hmong to Vietnamese translator, but his English was not good. He found that hand gestures and drawing in the dirt worked best as the fastest method of communicating with the Hmong.

Granier told his translator to tell the Hmong company commander that they needed to pull back ASAP. ASAP was confusing to the translator, and precious time was wasted for Granier to explain further. When the message finally got through, the

Hmong commander nodded that he understood and ordered his men to fall back. Two minutes later, the North Vietnamese patrols made contact, and a firefight broke out between the two sides.

At first, it seemed like a somewhat even match with the Hmong forming a defensive line and holding their ground as they were taught. After a few minutes of fighting, Granier told the Hmong commander to continue his retreat. As the Hmong leapfrogged backward, taking up new firing positions and covering their comrades as they fell back, gunfire erupted on their uphill flank. It was a company of Pathet Lao. The Hmong were now outnumbered two to one and were starting to panic.

Granier feared panic more than he feared the enemy. If the Hmong broke, they would be slaughtered as they ran from the battlefield. He needed to do something quick… anything. He broke a small branch from a nearby bush and grabbed the Hmong commander. He kicked away the grass and rocks from a small area on the ground. He drew a line and pointed to the North Vietnamese line. The commander nodded. He drew an intersecting line and pointed to the Pathet Lao flanking their position. Another nod. He drew a box signifying the Hmong position and pointed to the commander and his men. A third nod. He put his hands together and then pulled them apart. He motioned with one hand toward the commander and the other pointing to himself, meaning he wanted to split the company into two – half staying with Granier and the other half falling back with the commander. He drew a "J" on the ground, signifying that the commander's half of the company would fallback, then turn uphill once they had cleared the Pathet Lao flanking line. Granier and his half would hold the defensive position until the commander had completed his move. The commander would then attack Pathet Lao's flank on the hillside as Granier pulled back to form a new defensive line with the commander's men as they continued their attack on the Pathet Lao. The Pathet Lao would need to reorganize their position into a defensive line facing the Hmong or risk being wiped out. The commander nodded that he understood. It was a dangerous move dividing his company as Granier was advising, but the commander had learned much from the American and trusted him.

In truth, Granier had no idea if the commander understood everything he had just proposed. Still, Granier figured it was better to do something rather than risk the Hmong's defensive lines breaking. Action gave men hope.

The commander gave orders to his platoon commanders and began his withdrawal with half the company. Granier joined his half of the company, keeping his translator with him. Technically, Granier was not allowed to fire or even carry a weapon while in Laos. He thought it a stupid order but had obeyed it up and until that moment. He picked up a rifle from a dead Hmong soldier and opened fire. He fired in three-bullet bursts, rising from the long grass, firing, ducking down, moving to his next position, rising again. He never popped up in the same place. He never gave the enemy a chance to kill him. His target acquisition was fast. He wasted no time swinging his barrel from side to side. He lined up the direction of his shots before he rose, then executed once up, shooting the first thing that appeared in his sights. Disciplined. Efficient. Whenever he spotted an enemy unit commander, he did his best to take his head off. He killed one enemy commander and severely wounded a second. The Hmong watched the American in awe as he picked off the enemy each time he rose. It gave them courage that a true warrior was leading them. The Hmong held their ground.

Just as Granier had explained in the drawings, the commander retreated until his men had passed the end of the Pathet Lao's flanking line of attack. He ordered his men to climb uphill and form a new line intersecting with the Pathet Lao's flank. It worked like a charm. They opened fire immediately, killing five enemy soldiers and crushing the Pathet Lao's flank.

Hearing the new firefight behind him, Granier ordered his men to leapfrog backward until they reached the commander's half of the company. Granier's half took up offensive positions as the commander continued his flanking attack. The Hmong company now formed one long offensive line. The Pathet Lao and the North Vietnamese were forced to form a long line facing the Hmong company. The fighting continued for another fifteen minutes until Granier told the commander to order his men into a fighting retreat. The Hmong began to withdraw, keeping up a steady barrage to pin the enemy line. Within ten minutes, Granier and the Hmong disappeared into the jungle. The enemy chased after them with little success. The Hmong were experts at hiding in the jungle. They took their time and waited until the enemy had passed their position before taking off in another direction. They were safe for the moment.

A TIME OF CHANGE

Central Highlands, South Vietnam

It was late afternoon, and the sky grew dark. Rain was on its way once again. Le Duan and Suong rode their bicycles along a country road. Le Duan could have requested a car to take them to their destination - Dak Long Commune in Kon Tum Province. While it would have taken less time and effort, he knew the exercise would do him good. Like most field commanders, Duan spent most of his time traveling or sitting on his ass writing reports. The politburo never hesitated to request more reports from the field. It didn't matter that the task chewed up time that could have been spent better training troops or planning raids.

Pedaling through the countryside was a nice change of scenery from his dreary office that constantly leaked during the monsoon season and became sweltering hot during the hot season. The fresh air perked up his mind and brightened his outlook. Without knowing it, the thoughts and doubts that plagued him were placed on pause. He would deal with them later. For now, he would enjoy his escape from the drudgery of command.

The pair was traveling to meet with the former chief of the province, Y'Thong Mlo, a Montagnard tribal leader. Y'Thong had been replaced by Colonel Do Xuan Han, a retired military commander that was not afraid to use force to keep the local civilians in line when required. Han was a Northerner that had migrated to the South during Operation Passage to Freedom. Having converted to Catholicism six years ago, Diem immediately trusted Han and dismissed Y'Thong. The people of Kon Tum Province did not share Diem's enthusiasm for Colonel Han. He was an outsider and worshipped a foreign god. Resistance to his orders was already growing, and several of his militia had been ambushed and beaten.

Le Duan was told that Y'Thong, who still held tremendous respect among his fellow tribesmen, felt he had been mistreated and was angry with the government. Duan hoped to sway him and his followers to join the revolution. If successful, this one man could be responsible for doubling or even tripling the Viet Minh forces in the province.

The rain began as a few heavy drops. Suong was wearing the same dark pajamas she always wore. Le

Duan, following her, could see the drops pelt her back and darken the fabric. They kept pedaling. They were close to the village where Y'Thong was living and hoped to reach it before nightfall. But nature had other plans.

Before long, the drops turned into a downpour. Le Duan could see that Suong's clothes were soaked and clinging to her slender figure. The dirt road was turning to mud, and the tires of their bicycles sank, making it harder to pedal and steer. Le Duan could see that they weren't going to reach the village before sunset. He looked for any structure where they might take shelter. There was none. Suong stopped and turned back, "This is stupid. We must stop."

"I agree," said Le Duan stopping his bike.

They dismounted and guided their bicycles off the road and into the surrounding forest. The canopy of leaves and branches lessened the deluge but not by much. Both Le Duan and Suong were soaked. They were in the hills, and unlike the flatlands, the temperature dropped when it rained. Le Duan shivered. "You should get out of those wet clothes," said Suong.

"Why? Everything is soaked. I have nothing dry to change into," said Duan.

"You'll catch a fever. I'll see if I can find some dry wood, and I'll build a fire."

"It'll be wasted effort. Even if you get it started, it will just smoke."

"It'll be better than nothing. Besides, smoke keeps the bugs away."

"…and hurts my eyes and lungs."

Suong ignored him and searched for dry wood.

The fire was still smoldering in the early morning light. It had rained most of the night and only stopped a few hours before dawn. Le Duan's eyes flittered open. He was warm. Suong was curled up next to him, and his left arm was wrapped around her. He wasn't sure if she sought him for warmth in the night or he her. What he was sure of was that his hand was over her right breast. Her back was facing him. He couldn't see her face or eyes. He hoped she was still asleep. He could hear and feel her breathing. He wasn't sure what to do. He began to slowly remove his hand, and she stopped breathing. She was awake. She whipped around, pushed him, and scrambled to her feet. He, too, climbed to his feet and said, "I'm sorry. I don't know what happened."

She slugged him in the face, and he fell back down. The woman knew how to throw a punch. His nose was bleeding. "Why the hell did you do that?" he said.

"I am your bodyguard, not a cheap prostitute," she snarled.

"I never thought you were a prostitute."

"What did you think?"

"Nothing. I thought nothing. I woke up, and my hand was on your breast. I didn't mean anything by it. It just happened."

"Things like that don't just happen."

"Well, in this case, they did," he said, climbing back to his feet. "Believe me. I'm not interested in you like that."

"Why not?"

"What do you mean, why not? You're my bodyguard. I am your commander."

"You're not my commander. Ho is my commander. I am just doing this because he asked me."

"Whatever. I don't fraternize with my comrades in arms."

"Is there a rule against it?"

"Yes. It's called decency."

"I don't think that was decent."

"As I said, I didn't mean it. It just happened."

"You wouldn't have put your hand on my breast unless you wanted to."

"I suppose on some level… yes. I am a man, and I have urges like all men. But I was asleep and not in control of my thoughts."

"…or your hands."

"… or my hands. Yes. I am sorry."

"Why? Didn't you like how it felt?"

"What?"

"My breast… you didn't like how it felt?"

"No. It felt fine."

"Fine?"

"Yes. Fine. What do you want me to say?"

"That you liked it."

"Yes. Well, I suppose…"

"Don't suppose. You either liked it, or you didn't."

She stepped closer, grabbed his hand, and put it on her breast. "Do you like it?"

He thought for a moment; then, all his inhibitions fell away. He pulled her close and kissed her deeply. He did not remove his hand from her breast, and she didn't push him away. They fell to the forest floor and made love.

Afterward, they lay in the same position as they started, but both were naked. His arm was around her as before, his hand on her breast. "What will you tell your wife?" said Suong.

"Why must I tell her anything?" he said.

"You would lie?"

"No. Not to her. Never."

"Well then?"

"I suppose I will tell her the truth. She will understand as always."

"And what is the truth?"

"That we were lonely, and we fell in love."

"That's what this was? You were lonely?"

"Weren't you?"

"I don't know. I think… yes. I was lonely. But it was more than that to me."

"What was it?"

"It was satisfying. I haven't been with a man in many years."

"Why not?"

"Too involved in the revolution, I guess."

"I understand that. So, why me?"

"You are the revolution."

"Me? No. Ho is the revolution."

"He was. Now, it's you."

Duan shook his head in disbelief. "You're making fun of me."

"No. I mean it. Ho was the only man I ever met that was willing to give everything up to free us from the French. He did that. Now his time has passed.

You are like him. You would give everything to see the revolution continue and reunite the country."

"Great sacrifice is required if we are going to be free."

"I know. That is why I admire you."

"You admire me?"

"Yes," she said, turning back to him and kissing him passionately. "With all my heart."

1959 – Saigon, South Vietnam

With the additional flow of weapons and supplies from the North, the Viet Minh in the South increased their raids against the Diem government and the South Vietnamese Army. Over 150 government officials and army officers were assassinated each month. Diem and his family finally took notice. They could not deny the increase in violence. The Viet Minh were making headway. Diem had to do something, or he would lose the people's support, and even worse… America's.

Diem's solution was Law 10/59. The government decree created mobile military tribunals that resulted in hundreds of men and women being executed by portable guillotines, a leftover from the French, in villages around the country. The idea was to intimidate anyone considering joining the Viet Minh and crush the rebellion before it gained steam. Like many of Diem's heavy-handed methods, it had the opposite effect he intended.

It was the younger Vietnamese that refused to be cowed. They stood defiant as they watched their parents and village elders beheaded. Resolved to stop the madness, they joined the Viet Minh in droves, and with the new arms provided by the North, the revolution grew swiftly. It was a vicious circle - the more repression, the more rebellion.

Phnom Penh, Cambodia

With the Ho Chi Minh Trail expansion, Cambodia was thrust into the middle of the growing war between North and South Vietnam. Having abdicated his king's crown to his father in 1955, Prince Norodom Sihanouk became Prime Minister and Cambodia's de facto leader. It was not an easy job. To prevent his country from being drawn further into the war, Sihanouk walked a four-way political tightrope between Saigon, Hanoi, Beijing, and Washington D.C.

Over the years, Sihanouk had become partial to the socialist cause. He felt that communism offered a way out of the crippling poverty that gripped his country. Pressure from China and North Vietnam undoubtedly influenced his ruling philosophy, but he proved unwilling to become their puppet. He had a mind and will of his own, and he wanted what was best for his people. More than anything, he wanted to save his nation from the ravages of war. While walking the line of diplomacy seemed like the path to save his nation, in fact, he pissed off his neighbors.

Nobody was angrier than Diem. He saw the arms flowing through Cambodia and into his country that threatened his rule. The Viet Minh were growing at an alarming rate. On a hot afternoon, Diem sat with Lansdale on his palace's patio, sipping hot tea. "Would you like some ice for your tea, Colonel?" said Diem.

"Yes, please. How can you drink that in this heat?" said Lansdale.

"It is you that is foolish. Hot makes the body cool, not ice."

"Surely you didn't invite me here to discuss the temperature of my tea."

"No. Of course not. We are both too busy for such niceties. How goes your training of our intelligence group?"

"Very well. But you understand that it is an ongoing process?"

"Yes, yes. I have no complaints. The men are yours to do what you will. There is another covert matter that I would like to discuss."

"Of course. What do you have in mind?"

"Cambodia is becoming more and more of a problem."

"I agree. You have increased patrols at the border?"

"Yes, but they don't seem to have the desired effect. The arms and supplies continue to flow to the Viet Minh. I feel like we are powerless."

"You are far from powerless, Mr. President."

"Perhaps. But Cambodia is still a problem that must be dealt with sooner rather than later. I was hoping for some assistance from the United States."

"What did you have in mind?"

"It seems to me that the problem is with the head of Kouprey."

"Kouprey?"

"A grey ox that lives in the wild. The symbol of Cambodia."

"You are talking about King Suramarit?"

"No. Suramarit is a figurehead, king in name only. I am talking about his son, Prince Sihanouk, the Prime Minister. He holds the real power in Phnom Penh."

"And what do you wish us to do?"

"Assassinate him."

"You want us to assassinate the Prime Minister of Cambodia?"

"Yes, please. With Sihanouk gone, I believe the flow of weapons into my country would be greatly curtailed."

"Mr. President, America does not assassinate heads of state."

"Really? Never?"

"No. Never. It's not something we do."

"If America is serious about stopping communism, perhaps it is time you started?"

"We cannot be involved in an assassination of Prince Sihanouk… at least not directly."

"Not directly?"

"You know that I am always available to advise you, Mr. President."

"You think we should do it?"

"I didn't say that. However, if you were to attempt such a feat, I would hope you plan it meticulously. Failure could be a disaster and expand the war."

"I see. Perhaps we should ask my brother Nhu and his wife to join our discussion?"

"While Madam Nhu's creativity is always an asset in the planning stages of a mission, she is not well known for her discretion."

"Yes. She is a passionate woman. I will invite my brother Nhu alone."

"As you wish, Mr. President."

During the meeting that followed, Nhu was given the responsibility of planning and executing the mission. Lansdale agreed to review Nhu's plan and make suggestions. Diem reserved the right to give the mission the final green light.

It was a relatively simple plan – a parcel bomb. Nhu had his agents purchase two handcrafted lacquered boxes from Hong Kong as presents for the Cambodian Prince Norodom Vakrivan, the chief of protocol, and his brother and Prime Minister, Prince Sihanouk. The parcels were to be addressed as if originating from an American engineer in Hong Kong that had previously worked for the Cambodian government and was known by both princes. The engineer knew nothing of the plan or the parcels. The box in the parcel to be sent to Prince Vakrivan was empty, while the box sent to Prince Sihanouk would contain a bomb made from British explosives. It was designed to explode upon opening the box. It was assumed that as chief of protocol, Vakrivan would open his parcel first and find the beautiful box. Seeing the box, Sihanouk would let his guard down and quickly open his parcel. There was only one small problem with the plan – jealousy.

When the two parcels were delivered to the royal palace, Vakrivan noticed that his brother's parcel was heavier. Upon recognizing the engineer's return address, he immediately opened his present and found the lacquered box just as Nhu had planned. When he opened the box and found it empty, he was slightly disappointed. After all, who sends an empty box? Imagining another gift inside the heavier parcel, Vakrivan opened his brother's parcel. When he opened his brother's lacquered box, the explosion ripped off both his arms and set his clothes on fire. In the next room, the king and queen were visiting friends and barely escaped serious injury. Mortally wounded, Vakrivan stumbled through the door and collapsed on the floor to the sound of his mother's screams. He was dead.

Prince Sihanouk accused Nhu of sending the bomb, but secretly he knew the American CIA was behind it. Relations between Cambodia and America went from bad to worse. It wasn't long before Prince Sihanouk agreed to allow North Vietnamese soldiers to set up staging camps on the Cambodian border with South Vietnam.

Diem put no blame on his brother for the botched mission and instead suggested it was Lansdale's poor suggestions that caused the assassination attempt to fail. Madam Nhu implied that if she had been allowed to help plan the mission, the assassination would have been successful, and a coup would have overthrown Cambodia's government.

A WALL OF GREEN

Mekong Delta, South Vietnam

The heavy fog that hung over the delta was being pushed away by a gentle morning breeze. The bang grass's long reeds tapped against each other with the sound of a THACK like crickets. The grass was taller than most men and made for an effective hiding place. *It won't be long until the fog is gone*, thought ARVN First Lieutenant Phi Hung Ngọc, a company commander from the 23rd Division. *Better. Viet Minh like the fog.*

Nourished by the Mekong River's waters, the ground was moist year-round, causing the boots of his men to sink into the black mud. It was slow going. Phi's company was performing a sweep of the area, searching for the Viet Minh, hoping they wouldn't find them. Everyone knew this was rebel territory and very dangerous, but the commanders in Saigon had insisted. They wanted to end the uprising before it gained more steam in the South's rich rice-growing delta. Too late. The movement was growing fast, with more rebels joining daily.

Phi crouched down in the long grass next to his radioman and gave a sitrep to his commander,

Captain Mạch Thuan Anh. All was clear. Having fought the Japanese and the French, Phi was older and more experienced than Mach. Phi had been part of the Viet Minh force that had overrun Dien Bien Phu. When the war ended, Phi's commanders tried to get him to enlist in the People's Republic Army, but Phi refused. He was proud of the French defeat and hoped they would soon leave Vietnam for good. With the communists firmly in control of the North, Phi saw how the cadre treated anyone who disagreed with them. He didn't like it. Freedom of speech was not something the communists embraced. In the North, one had to watch his tongue or risk having it cut out.

He had done the only sensible thing and headed South along with a million refugees. He had been in the military most of his adult life and had no other skills. In the South, everyone was hunting for work. When he was offered a lieutenant's commission in the South Vietnamese Army, he took it. It was a demotion from his former rank of major, but he was grateful to still be an officer. He knew that his superiors would scrutinize him until he could prove his loyalty. The South Vietnamese Army was very different from the Viet Minh. Bribes, not merit, were the way to get ahead in the ARVN. He was not from a wealthy family and kept his expectations low. He could live with the fact that he would probably never receive another promotion. But what really bothered him was officers like Mach. The young captain was from a good family, a wealthy family. He had risen in rank quickly since he had been accepted into the military. His family paid for his promotions and used their influence to build his reputation as an officer loyal to Diem's government. For Mach, the sky was the limit, no matter his competence or experience.

Despite the unfairness of it all, Phi wanted to help Mach be a better commander. The lives of his men depended on it. Mach had never been in a battle. He was untested. But Mach was not interested in listening to Phi's advice. He saw Phi as a loser that could do nothing to help his career and, therefore, valueless. Earlier that morning, when Phi suggested they wait until the fog burned off before beginning their sweep, Mach had accused Phi of being lazy and a coward. Phi shut his mouth and followed his commander's orders, however dangerous they might have been. He knew better than to make waves with someone like Mach.

Mach was not only in command of the mission; he was in charge of the second company currently finishing a sweep of another sector. The idea was that if one of the companies became engaged by the enemy, the other company could be used as a flanking force. Mach ordered Phi to move to an adjacent sector and begin the next sweep. Phi checked in with each of his platoon commanders as he issued new orders.

Ten minutes later, Phi's company moved to the new sector. Phi didn't like it. It was a marsh of bang grass along the edge of a mangrove forest. Bad ground. He thought about radioing Mach, but he knew what he would say. He wasn't in the mood to be ridiculed twice in one day. The company was using an M formation with two platoons forward and three back as a reserve. Mach had ordered him to use a W formation with three forward and two back so he could cover more ground faster, but Phi didn't like the idea of the bulk of his men being engaged right out of the gate. They would not be able to maneuver if the lead platoons were pinned down. An M formation was safer, and he could always claim that he was following Mach's orders by using an upside-down W. Mach's company was finishing its last sector and was out of position. With no flanking element immediately available, Phi was cautious.

He wondered if Mach had arranged for any air support in the event they came under attack. He doubted Mach would have been that diligent. The ARVN had never encountered an enemy unit larger than a platoon south of the border. With 350 men in the battalion, the ARVN would vastly outnumber any Viet Minh unit they might engage. Phi wondered if Mach had been correct and he was overly protective of his men. Seeing his men deployed and advancing across the swamp, Phi took a deep breath and relaxed.

With the company making good progress, a 3rd platoon scout was moving through heavy grass and heard a sloshing sound a few yards ahead. His first thought was a critter of some sort. Maybe a cat-sized rat or a Binturong. There were plenty that lived by the river. Both were tasty when barbecued. His second thought was a python or crocodile. They, too, lived by the river. He fixed his bayonet on the end of his rifle's barrel without unloading the round in the weapon's chamber. A bad practice, but he wasn't taking any chances. He used the bayonet to part the bang grass and look ahead. A giant catfish wiggled out of the reeds and between his legs. He was startled and fell back on his ass. The catfish swam off. He cursed the fish and retrieved his weapon covered in mud. It would take him an hour to clean his rifle properly once they made camp. As he rose, a woman's face appeared between the grass along with a bamboo pole, its end sliced at an angle, forming a point. The spear plunged forward into his stomach just below the sternum. He swung his rifle around toward the woman and pulled the trigger. Nothing happened. The gun was jammed with mud. *Damn fish*, he thought as he fell back into the shallow water and died. The woman moved forward, kicking the soldier to ensure he was lifeless. She removed his ammunition belt and picked up his muddy rifle. She would clean it up before giving it to her commander. It was a prize. She had little hope of being awarded the weapon. She, like the other women, made their weapons from tree branches and bamboo poles. The Viet Minh made no excuses. They fought with whatever they were given or could make on their own. Rifles were only given to those that were proficient at shooting. She was not. But she knew how to use a spear and a bow for hunting deer and rats in the mangroves... and for killing government soldiers like the one she left in the tall grass.

None of the soldiers in Phi's company heard the death of their scout. They continued their sweep through the long grass and mud, keeping one eye on the mangrove trees on their flank. The thick canopy of leaves made the forest dark as night. The enemy could have been easily hiding in the shadows of the trees, and nobody would have known.

But the Viet Minh weren't under the trees. They were waiting in ambush in the grass. They numbered over one hundred from the Viet Minh 2nd Liberation Battalion. The Viet Minh commander knew that they were outnumbered and outgunned. Their only advantages were surprise and close combat. The Viet Minh wanted to kill the government troops. Some wanted revenge for the savage way their friends and family had been treated. Others wanted their country united. And some believed deeply in the communist propaganda and wanted Ho Chi Minh to lead the people out of poverty. Whatever the reason, they waited in the long grass, still and silent. Some had rifles; most had spears and bows with arrows. In the long grass, spears and bows were almost as good as rifles. The enemy would be close when they attacked. The rebels had studied the government troop's movements and had formed a half-circle directly in their path. They would attack from three sides at once.

Phi's company did not realize they had walked into a trap. The opening volley was arrows and spears, followed by gunshots. In the first minute of the battle, three of Phi's men were killed and four seriously wounded. The ARVN troops returned fire with their rifles, shooting blindly into the long grass. Arrows and spears continued to fly, striking men in the torso, arms, and legs. More men went down wounded and dying. Just as the ARVN platoon commanders formed defensive lines, the Viet Minh facing them melted away and struck from a different angle. Some of the government troops broke and ran wildly through the grass, trying to get away. Most ran directly into the rebels and were killed or captured.

Phi could not see where the enemy was positioned. There was only a wall of green grass surrounding him and his men. Visibility was only a few feet to any side. The Viet Minh seemed to be coming from everywhere. These insurgents were not like the rebel bands he had previously fought. They were far more organized and more numerous. He felt control slipping away as his men fought for their lives in the long grass. He radioed Mach for reinforcements. But Mach and his company were out of position. It would take precious minutes before they could arrive and join the battle. It was time Phi and his men did not have. The enemy had the government troops by the belt. Phi could not order any artillery support for fear of hitting his own men. He needed to separate his men from the rebels if they were going to survive. He ordered his 2nd Platoon to fall back into the mangrove forest so they could give covering fire to the rest of the company as they withdrew.

The 2nd Platoon broke off and moved through the grass toward the tree line. The Viet Minh were waiting. Muzzle bursts flashed from the shadows as the hidden rebels opened fire. The men of the 2nd Platoon returned fire. They could not see the adversary in the shadows, but they could see the flashes that gave away the enemy positions. The 2nd Platoon poured on their fire and drove the enemy back. After a few minutes, the gun flashes from the shadows lessened, then disappeared entirely. 2nd Platoon pushed forward and entered the forest. They took up defensive positions behind the tree trunks and massive roots stretching across the ground. The platoon commander radioed Phi.

Phi ordered the other platoons to withdraw to the forest. 2nd Platoon focused their fire on any of the enemy that broke through the grass in pursuit of the ARVN troops. There weren't many. They knew the grass protected them and chose to stay hidden. Many of the ARVN troops abandoned their weapons to lighten their loads as they fled into the forest.

As the last of Phi's company made it to the forest, Mach and his company arrived and opened fire on the enemy's flank. It was impossible to see the enemy through the grass, but any movement of the top of the long reeds brought a fusillade of ARVN gunfire. With Phi's company now separated from the enemy, Mach called in artillery from a heavy mortar squad stationed in the rear of his company. Bursts of flames and muddy water flew into the air as the mortar shells exploded in the long grass in front of Phi's and Mach's positions.

The Viet Minh commander recognized the danger his soldiers were now facing. With the second ARVN company coming online, the rebels were outnumbered and fighting their enemy on two fronts. He ordered his rebels to withdraw deeper into the plain of reeds. Viet Minh gunfire dissipated and finally disappeared entirely as the rebels retreated. The battle was over.

Phi wondered why Mach and his company did not pursue the Viet Minh. It might have been out of compassion for Phi's men who the rebels had mauled. They were no longer an effective fighting unit and needed to be protected. Many of his men were wounded, and there were dead still on the battlefield. But Phi concluded it was cowardice. Mach didn't have the stomach for fighting, especially against an invisible enemy.

The first major battle between the Viet Minh and the ARVN was lopsided against the government forces. Mach's battalion suffered twelve killed, fourteen seriously wounded, and nine missing or captured. The ARVN also lost a large number of weapons. Viet Minh losses were unknown but presumed to be light.

Saigon, South Vietnam

When word reached the presidential palace of the defeat, Diem was stunned and dismayed. He had always assumed his soldiers were superior to the rebels, especially when armed with superior American weapons. The disastrous battle was evidence of the hard reality – his government troops broke when faced with an organized and determined foe.

Madame Nhu blamed the American advisors that were supposed to be training their men. "The Americans are fighting the wars of the past. They do not understand how to fight against the rebel's guerrilla tactics," said Madame Nhu. "We should use our shoe to send them back to America."

"We cannot do that. We need their weapons and money," said Brother Nhu. "We should be thankful that the enemy has shown us the weakness of our military. It is not the troops' fault as much as their commanders. We should purge all of those that are incompetent and disloyal. I shall make a list."

"Yes, a list of those responsible. And I want the battalion and company commanders punished. We must use them as an example. I will not tolerate cowardice," said Diem.

It never occurred to Diem that the men of the 23rd Division lost because they had no reason to fight. Many of the soldiers didn't believe that Diem cared about them or their families. After Diem's heavy-handed security measures, many soldiers were left wondering who the real enemy was. Diem could have seen the rise in desertions among his troops had their commanders not feared to report the numbers accurately. It was not uncommon for the same commanders to line their pockets with the missing soldiers' pay.

Diem also failed to recognize the communist build-up. His nation was being secretly flooded with communist insurgents from the North. In 1959, 4,500 military officers, non-commissioned officers, and communist cadres crossed the border and entered South Vietnam. Their mission was to bring about open rebellion against the Diem government. They would train and lead tens of thousands of Viet Minh in running battles with ARVN troops through the Southern countryside.

South of Saigon, mass anti-government demonstrations with thousands of protesters gathering in local villages, the people listened to speeches and slogans of the Viet Minh recruiters. Under threat of death, local government officials and their sympathizers were forced to flee. Those that did not were beheaded by the Viet Minh to intimidate any that were tempted to side with the government. The Viet Minh made it clear that they would control any village outside of Hue and Saigon. The villagers felt two nooses around their necks, with the government troops pulling on one side and the Viet Minh pulling on the other.

THE RELENTLESS HUNT

Saigon, South Vietnam

After the ARVN battalion's poor performance in the Mekong Delta, Army commanders were reluctant to engage with the Viet Minh. It was true that great honor would be gained by the next commander that defeated the rebels in a large battle. He could single-handedly restore Diem's reputation as the commander and chief of South Vietnam's military. No doubt the successful commander would be given a hefty promotion and metals to pin on his chest. But like Diem, the generals in Saigon had lost confidence in their troops. Each commander's army could not be defeated if the soldiers stayed in their barracks. The actual losses incurred during the Viet Minh ambush were far less consequential than the damage to the army's reputation.

In the meantime, minor skirmishes between the ARVN patrols and the Viet Minh continued throughout the south. Each time the Viet Minh attacked, they collected more weapons and ammunition that could be used on the next ambush. Knowing that the Americans would give them replacements, the ARVN troops showed no compunction about throwing aside their weapons and ammunition belts to lighten their load as they ran away from a battle.

Not all ARVN troops broke. It was mostly veterans that held their ground and fought the Viet Minh. But as their comrades retreated, they soon found themselves alone battling an aggressive enemy that now outnumbered them. Even the bravest of men would struggle to find a reason to sacrifice his life for a government that he didn't believe in. In the end, most of the Southern soldiers bolted.

Ambassador Elbridge Durbrow called his secretary into his office within the American embassy and dictated a letter to President Eisenhower. He had watched as Diem, and his family created policies and declared laws that made things go from bad to worse. Whatever public support he had achieved after the final departure of the French was now almost gone. Areas of the country were in open revolt, and the Viet Minh were growing in numbers and power. It was far from an ideal situation. Durbrow suggested it was time to remove America's support of the Diem regime.

Durbrow knew that the chances of Eisenhower removing his support for Diem were negligible. Eisenhower had publicly praised Diem during his tour of the United States. In his last year of holding the office of president, Eisenhower was focused on his legacy. He had led a distinguished career in the military and politics. He did not want to be remembered as the guy that threw South Vietnam under the bus. That was better handled by the next president. The man who made it a habit of taking responsibility was now passing the buck to America's next leader. Still, Durbrow felt it was his duty to at least try and change Eisenhower's mind. It didn't work.

Eisenhower wrote back that he wanted Durbrow to meet with Diem and convince him of the need to change course. Durbrow could threaten to remove American support but was not authorized to actually take action. Without a realistic alternative to Diem, it was to be an empty threat, and Durbrow knew that Diem would recognize it as such. But as a loyal follower of Eisenhower, Durbrow phoned the presidential palace and asked to meet with Diem at his earliest convenience. He also requested that their conversation be private, meaning without Diem's family. Durbrow knew that part of his request would not sit well with Diem, who preferred to have his brother Nhu present during all conversations with the Americans. He wished Diem would not inform Nhu or Madame Nhu of the meeting, but he held little hope that the two would not find out anyway and show up unannounced. Durbrow was not afraid of Nhu or Madame Nhu, but he didn't want to anger them unnecessarily. They had the ear of Diem and, more importantly, his trust.

The next day, Durbrow arrived at the Presidential Palace and was escorted to Diem's office by none other than Brother Nhu and his wife. The message was clear; Diem would relay all information garnered from the meeting to his brother and sister-in-law whether the American Ambassador liked it or not. Durbrow supposed that it didn't matter. They would find out sooner or later anyway through their spies. Besides, he was on a mission from the President of the United States and, as such, would not be bullied by the two underlings even if they were Diem relatives.

Nothing was said, but feelings were clear. Durbrow sat. Diem entered and formally greeted the Ambassador. Brother Nhu and Madame Nhu begrudgingly left. After a small bit of diplomatic chit-chat, Diem got to the point. "You bring a message from President Eisenhower?" said Diem.

"I do. My president is concerned by the deteriorating situation in the South, especially the anti-government protests," said Durbrow.

"Peasant troublemakers. Nothing to worry about," said Diem.

"Those troublemakers are joining the Viet Minh."

"Some, perhaps. We are countering the communist cadres with our own propaganda. Colonel Lansdale assures me it will work given enough time."

"Time is not on your side. Our intelligence estimates tell us that the Viet Minh almost outnumber your military forces."

"The Viet Minh do not have the weapons to arm such a force. They are fighting with spears and arrows."

"I agree. But every time they ambush a patrol or supply convoy, their arsenal grows in size. The Chinese and Russians have also stepped up their arms shipments."

"Your advisors assured me that the Royal Lao forces would cut off the North Vietnamese supply line into the South."

"Yes. And with the help of Hmong tribesman, they have made some progress. The flow of arms has slowed."

"But not stopped?"

"Not as of yet. It is reasonable to expect some arms and supplies will always get through. It's a long border between your countries."

"Perhaps it is time that we take matters into our own hands. We could send in our troops."

"That is not advisable. President Eisenhower does not want to see an expansion of the current hostilities. South Vietnamese troops in Laos could trigger a reaction from China. It's better to exercise patience and let our Green Beret advisors in Laos do their job. They will slow arms and supplies to a manageable trickle."

"You have told me what President Eisenhower does not want. Perhaps you should tell me what he does want?"

"President Eisenhower would like you to curb your counterinsurgency policies. You are jailing thousands of South Vietnamese for even the slightest offense without trials. You've locked up anyone that criticizes your regime, and you have muzzled free speech and the press. It's infuriating the populace and fueling the Viet Minh's recruiting efforts. You should include the opposition leaders in your government rather than locking them up."

"One minute, you Americans are telling me to take a firm stand against communism, and the next, you say I am being too tough. Which is it?"

"We admit it is a difficult balancing act."

"It's not difficult. It's impossible. The Vietnamese people respect power. This waffling back and forth only confuses them and creates instability – the very thing we are trying to avoid."

"Mr. President, you must understand, America cannot be seen supporting a heavy-handed dictator."

"I was elected by my people. I am not a dictator."

"My choice of words was unfortunate. But the sentiment is not. If you abuse your power, America cannot continue to supply South Vietnam with military and financial aid."

"I am tired of your threats, Mr. Ambassador. If President Eisenhower wishes to sever our agreement, then he is free to do so. But understand this, my army is the only thing standing in the way of the communists. If you abandon your ideals, they will not only overrun South Vietnam but the rest of Southeast Asia as well. Then where will America be?"

"On the side of freedom and liberty, Mr. President. On the side of the right."

"Abstract concepts do little good in the fight against the communists. I deal in reality, Mr. Ambassador."

"One last issue before I go. The corruption and political favoritism propagated by your family has become an albatross around your neck. Their schemes have diminished your ability to lead your people. As the head of your security force, your Brother Nhu is the most hated man in all of Saigon. And your sister-in-law continues to pour kerosene on a fire that is quickly growing out of control. President Eisenhower suggests it is time for them to leave the country before they bring it down around your feet."

"I wonder how President Eisenhower would feel if I suggested the same treatment of his own family?"

"His family stays out of the limelight and does not undermine our country with loud rhetoric and bad advice."

"Perhaps he would do well to listen to them more and lecture his allies less."

Durbrow knew that Diem had dug in his feet and would be unmoved at this point. It was time to leave before something was said that could not be undone. "Mr. President, thank you for your time. I will relay your words to President Eisenhower," said Durbrow rising to leave.

"Verbatim, if you would be so kind, Mr. Ambassador," said Diem refusing to shake Durbrow's outreached hand.

"Of course, Mr. President," said Durbrow dropping his hand to his side and leaving.

Diem knew that he had pushed Durbrow in the heat of the moment. A diplomatic mistake to say what one really feels. He hoped Durbrow was smart enough to understand that his words were spoken in anger and that he would measure the message he delivered to Eisenhower. South Vietnam could not hope to survive without America's help. He knew Eisenhower, a military man, would understand that simple fact.

Central Highlands, South Vietnam

It had only been a few weeks since Le Duan and Suong had returned to the South when the politburo once again ordered him back to the North for some urgent business. "This is exhausting," said Duan. "How am I supposed to get anything done if I spend all my time traveling back and forth."

"And it's risky," said Suong. "Every time we cross the border, there is a chance that we will be discovered. You won't be much use to anyone in a South Vietnamese prison."

"I can't go back to prison. I'm not a young man anymore. My body will not stand the abuse."

Duan considered for a long moment and said, resigned, "It's time I picked my replacement in the Southern Office."

"That won't be an easy task," said Suong.

"No. But necessary. One more decision on the pile of things that must be done. I need to send a message to the politburo that I will be delayed for four days."

"I'll see that it is done," said Suong.

Saigon, South Vietnam

Conein had used every resource at his disposal to search for Le Duan. He made sure to keep the pressure upon the South Vietnamese intelligence groups throughout the country. He finally found what he was looking for in an action report from a military base near the border in the hills. A woman had been detained when a routine patrol found the conical hat she had been wearing had two bamboo layers. Like many of the soldiers, the soldier who discovered the layers worked on a farm before joining South Vietnam's army. Having worn a conical hat most of his life, he knew the weight by simply holding it. Something was off with the hat. Although it looked like a peasant's hat with plenty of patches and well-worn bamboo strips, it was too heavy. He examined it further and discovered the two layers. Sandwiched between the layers were coded messages on slips of paper.

When the woman realized that her cover had been blown, she ran for it, was shot in the shoulder, and captured. The soldier who discovered the messages had been given an extra ration of rice and fish sauce for an entire week.

The local military intelligence officer could not translate the messages, so he forwarded them to the 5th Bureau for analysis. While Conein was interested in the encrypted letters' contents, he was more interested in the woman now being held at the military base detention center. He decided to have her brought to Saigon, where he could interrogate her personally and find out if she had a connection to Le Duan. He called Lansdale and requested a plane and a flight crew be assigned to his team. "Why?" said Lansdale.

"You said whatever I need," said Conein.

"Yes. But a plane and crew on standby is a big ask."

"I wouldn't ask if I didn't need it."

"Yes, but you didn't say why you needed it."

"It's a big country. I need to track down leads before they get cold."

"Alright. I'll see to it."

Coyle and his crew were loading a C-47 with supplies for the troops in Laos when orders came, temporarily assigning him and his crew to Conein's team. Coyle didn't dislike Conein anymore than any other CIA officer but wasn't happy about the assignment. The idea of being at Conein's beck and call was unsettling. Conein was a well-known wildcard and considered undependable by many officers. "Alright. Change of plans. Unload the supplies. We have a new mission," said Coyle.

"What's that, Boss?" said one of the crew.

"Sit around and wait for King Conein's orders. We're on standby."

Filthy from a mission in the Central Highland jungles, Granier and his team disembarked an aircraft and made a beeline for the food carts just outside the airbase's main gate.

It was surprising how many different dishes a single vendor could make with just a wok, burner, and a can of propane. The ingredients were purchased fresh every morning from the market and cooked to order. Most of the soldiers stationed at the airfield preferred the food carts over the restaurants that lined the street's opposite side. Fewer cockroaches and spiders falling from the rafters ended up in the food.

Overwhelmed by the aroma, the team split up in search of their favorites. Granier headed over to his chosen banh xeo vendor. After three days of rations, he craved the crispy rice crepes filled with shrimp, mint, basil, crunchy bean sprouts, and a tangy red sauce. He was surprised to see Coyle standing beside the cart waiting for his order. The vendor poured the rice batter into the hot oil inside the wok. It popped and sizzled. Bahn xeo didn't take long to cook. That was one of the great things about it besides the taste. It was a hungry man's go-to food. "You're a fan of bahn xeo too?" said Granier walking up behind Coyle.

Coyle turned around, "Oh, hey. I'm a fan of what?"

"Bahn xeo. That's what she's cooking for you."

"So, that's what it's called. I thought they were Vietnamese tacos."

"Good a name as any."

"You've been in the bush again."

"Yeah. Three days. How could you tell?"

"Your odor is a bit rank. Do you mind standing downwind?"

"Yeah, sure. Wouldn't wanna spoil your appetite."

"I appreciate it."

As he moved downwind, Granier caught the vendor's attention, pointed to the shrimp, and held up five fingers. The woman went to work preparing his order. "Can I buy ya a beer?" said Coyle.

"What for?" said Granier.

"You saved our asses in Laos. It's the least I can do."

"It was my job. But I'll take the beer… if it makes you feel better."

"It would."

Coyle ordered two beers. "You done for the day?" said Granier knowing that Coyle never drank before flying.

"Yeah. I just got back from the border. Your buddy Conein's doing. An entire Dakota and aircrew for one prisoner. What a waste of fuel."

"He ain't my buddy… Conein."

"I was kidding. What is it with you two? You're like siblings."

"He's an asshole."

"I'm pretty sure the feeling is mutual."

"Man's got a couple of screws loose."

"Don't we all?"

"Not like him. He's truly fucked up in the noggin."

"I just thought he enjoyed his work a little too much. I can't imagine what he's gonna do to the woman."

"Woman?"

"The prisoner. She's a real beauty from the hill tribes. I hate to think what she's gonna look like once Conein has his way with her. A real waste."

"Why is she so important?"

"I don't know. I heard one of her guards say something about the Viet Minh leader."

"Le Duan?"

"Yeah. She's connected to him somehow."

Alarm bells clanged in Granier's mind. *Suong?* he thought. "Do you know where they took her?" he said.

"They didn't mention it. 5th Bureau detention center, I imagine," said Coyle.

Granier pulled a wad of bills from his pocket and handed them to the food vendor. "I gotta go," he said, moving off without taking his order.

"Hey, what about your tacos?" said Coyle.

"You eat 'em."

Granier stood outside the 5th detention center and watched. He wasn't sure what he was looking for, but he wanted desperately to get inside and find Suong if she was there. It didn't matter that they were now on opposite sides of the growing conflict. He still cared for her and wanted to protect her, especially from a man like Conein.

Even if he was able to get inside, he didn't know where to start looking. It was a large facility with dozens of cells and interrogation rooms. He surmised that Suong would be a priority and was most likely in an interrogation room. That helped, but not much since he had no idea of the exact layout of the structure. This wasn't the type of place people could walk in and look around, even the Americans.

There was one guard at the main gate and two more guards at the building's only entrance. He imagined there were a lot more inside. He looked around the perimeter to find another way inside. There was nothing. Not even a back gate. The fence was capped with rings of barbed wire. He considered cutting through the fence, but that would require him to wait until after dark. Suong didn't have that kind of time. He needed to reach her soon rather than later if he was going to save her. Whatever he was going to do, he had to do it now. He decided on the direct approach but wasn't sure if it would work or even what he would do. He would have to wing it all the way. He hated winging it.

Granier walked up to the main gate. He flashed his credentials at the gate and was waved on in by the guard. He knew the two guards at the entrance would not be so easy. As he approached, he again flashed his credentials and said, "Commander Granier here to see Commander Conein."

"Is Commander Conein expecting you?" asked one of the guards.

"No. But I carry orders from Colonel Lansdale. It's imperative that I talk with Commander Conein immediately."

The two guards exchanged glances. Lansdale was well known at the 5th Bureau. "Commander Conein is occupied with an interrogation," said the guard.

"I don't give a shit if he's having tea with the Queen of England. I need to speak with him. Get him… now!" said Granier in his most threatening tone.

"Of course, Commander Granier," said the guard and opened the entrance door. "You can wait inside while we send someone to find Commander Conein."

Granier pushed past the two guards and entered the building. *So far, so good*, he thought. There was a guard post just inside the doorway. Granier waited next to a guard while a second guard was sent to find Conein. The guard, standing at parade rest, said nothing. Granier spent the time figuring out what to say once Conein arrived. Whatever it was… he didn't expect it to be a pleasant conversation. After a few moments, he heard footsteps approaching from a hallway. Conein appeared. He was pissed and said, "What in the hell are you doing here, Granier?"

"Lansdale sent me to find you."

"What the hell for?"

"To deliver a message."

"And?"

Granier had not come up with anything to say. So, he did the only thing he could think of… "He knows, and he's furious," said Granier.

"Knows what?"

"The money."

"What money?"

"The money you stole."

"What the hell are you talking about? I didn't steal any money."

"Tell it to Lansdale. He's the one that is pissed off."

"This is ridiculous. I haven't done anything. It's got to be some kind of misunderstanding. Wait a minute… is this about the slush fund? He knows about it. Hell, it was his idea. Yeah, it's been growing pretty fast, but it's all meant for operations. He couldn't be mad about that. Could he?"

"How the hell am I supposed to know? I'm just the messenger."

"Right. I probably should have kept him better apprised on the balance."

"Whatever. He wants you front and center ASAP."

"I can't just up and leave right now."

"Why not?"

"I got some unfinished business I need to attend to. I'll head over there as soon as I'm done."

"Okay. It's your funeral."

"He was really angry with me?"

"He was angry like I've never seen him before."

"Maybe I should give him a call on the phone."

"I wouldn't, but hey… that's me."

"Yeah. Some things are better explained in person. I'd better head over to headquarters now before he gets more of his panties in a bunch."

"Good thinking."

"Are you coming?"

"Hell no. A man doesn't walk into a tornado unless he has to. I've got a few errands to run."

"Alright," said Conein turning back down the hallway.

"Where are you headed?"

"I've got to tell the sergeant heading up the interrogation that I've got to go."

"You go. I'll tell him. What's his name?"

"Thanks. It's Sergeant Tuan. Tell him I'll be back as soon as I get things with Lansdale straightened out," said Conein turning around and heading out the entrance.

Granier figured Lansdale's headquarters was located ten minutes away by car. It would only take a few minutes for Conein to find out he had been played and that Lansdale wasn't angry. Another ten minutes back to the detention center. He figured he had about twenty-two minutes to find Suong and get her out of the building. It wasn't much time. He walked down the hallway where Conein had appeared. He didn't know where Suong was being interrogated, but he knew he would figure it out. Interrogations were rarely quick matters.

When he turned a corner, he saw a guard standing outside a door and figured that must be it. He approached the guard and said, "Open the door."

Not knowing Granier, the guard hesitated. "I ain't got all day," said Granier steely-eyed.

Not wanting to mess with the American, the guard opened the door. Inside, the room Sergeant Tuan stood in front of a half-naked woman slumped over in a chair. She was bound with wire. Her tangled hair hung down over her face. Her shoulders and breasts had several burn marks from a cigar. She wasn't moving. "Commander Granier, how can I help you?" said Tuan smoking a half-finished cigar.

"Commander Conein sent me to fetch you. He's going to headquarters to report to Lansdale, and he wants you to go with him."

"To report to Colonel Lansdale?"

"Yes. He said it was important. Something about the progress of the interrogation."

"Progress? It's over. She's dead."

Granier's heart sank. He tried to mask his emotions and said, "Dead?"

"Yeah. She died a few minutes ago. Shock, I imagine. It doesn't matter. We got what we needed."

"And what was that?"

"I am not at liberty to say. You'll have to ask Commander Conein."

Granier snapped. He picked up Tuan and lifted him against the wall using his forearm over the man's throat to pin him in place. "Or you could just answer my fucking question," said Granier with a snarl.

"Le Duan is heading North again. He's using a velocipede to travel by rail."

"And you killed for that?"

"She was a spy."

"We're all spies."

"She was the enemy."

Granier heard the room door being unlocked. He released Tuan. Tuan slid to the floor, coughing and gasping for breath. The door swung open, and Conein entered holding a pistol and said, "I changed my mind and used the phone. You're a fucking liar. Lansdale knew nothing about any missing money. What are you up to, Granier?"

"Why'd you kill her?"

"Who gives a fuck? She was Viet Minh."

"I give a fuck, you sadistic bastard."

"Always thought you were a traitor at heart. But I never understood why."

"She was a human being."

"Save your holier-than-thou attitude. We're at war. People die."

"Nobody deserves to be tortured."

"Now that's where you're wrong, Granier. A patriot does what's necessary to protect his country."

"It ain't our country, Conein. It's theirs."

"You are so full of sanctimonious shit, Granier. Did you know the Viet Minh slaughtered the villagers you convinced to join the fortified hamlet program?"

"What are you talking about?"

"Your human beings are cold-blooded killers. They're just as dedicated to their cause as we are to ours… maybe more so. We either kill them, or they are going to kill us. It's that simple."

"Nothing is simple. Not in this country."

"No. Because people like you cross the line."

"You talk about crossing the line. You're the king of crossing the line."

"I do what needs to be done, and I don't get emotional about it. It's not personal."

Granier took a long moment to consider what Conein was saying. As much as Granier was appalled by what Conein had done, on some level, he agreed with him. They were CIA officers. Their personal concerns were not supposed to be part of the equation once they had been given their orders. An officer in the field could not see the whole picture or even how the pieces fit together. He had to trust his superiors' decisions. That was the deal. Commitment. Fidelity. Even when the missions he was asked to carry out seemed immoral and dishonorable, it was his job to obey and trust the system he was a part of. Granier longed for the clarity of being a simple soldier that he once processed.

Conein walked over to the dead woman and pulled her hair, so her head tilted back. Her hair fell away from her tortured face. It wasn't Suong. "Did you know the bitch?" said Conein.

Granier hid his relief and said, "No. I've never seen her before."

"So, why all the drama?"

"Guess I just wanted to piss you off."

"Well, you succeeded," said Conein raising his pistol to point it at Granier's face."

"Go ahead. If you think you can get away with it."

"Oh, I can get away with it. These men work for me."

"Yeah, but you don't know who I told I was coming here."

Conein thought for a moment, calculating, then said, "Get the fuck out of here, Granier. And don't come back."

"Sure, Conein. Sure."

Granier pushed past him and left the room.

Granier walked back to the barracks at Lansdale's headquarters in downtown Saigon. He wasn't sure what to do. Conein was determined to hunt down Le Duan, which meant Suong as Le Duan's bodyguard, would be in danger. But Conein was right – they were the enemy. As the Viet Minh leader, Le Duan was the one person whose death could change the coming war's outcome. Perhaps even prevent it. There was a big part of him that wanted to resign and go someplace else. Anywhere else. But that was a coward's path, and Granier was no coward. He was in the middle of a fight between good and evil, and even if he couldn't determine which side the players were on, he had to push on. He had to fight through the fog.

When he fell in love with Suong, he didn't imagine he would arrive at this predicament. Granier's desire to protect Suong and his loyalty to America were at a crossroads. It seemed insane that his feeling for this woman would put his patriotism into question. It seemed even more insane that he still had feelings for her after all this time and everything that had happened. After all, she did try to assassinate him. He told himself Ho Chi Minh must have ordered his death. Suong had such respect for Uncle Ho; how could she possibly refuse? What bothered Granier more than anything was that she had chosen her side, and it felt like he still hadn't. He had been straddling the fence, hoping the dilemma would go away. It hadn't. If anything, it was now worse than ever. Vietnam was on the verge of war, and he was protecting the enemy. There was no other way to see it. Conein was right; he was a traitor.

Conein went to Lansdale's office for two purposes. First, was to once again complain about Granier, which fell on deaf ears. Second, to make a request... "I need a dedicated train assigned to my team," said Conein.

"What?" said Lansdale, floored by the request.

"I know it's a big ask, but if you want Le Duan dead, that's what it is going to take."

"A train. What are you going to do... run him over with it?"

"He's heading north by rail on a velocipede. We'll pick up a train on the border and head South. When we meet… the game will be over, and you will have Le Duan's head."

"You know I don't really want Le Duan's head?"

"Yes. You have made that clear. I was speaking figuratively."

"The U.S. Army does not control the trains in South Vietnam."

"I understand that, but I am also sure that you can convince Diem of our need to borrow a train."

"I'm not sure I can convince Diem to do anything nowadays. Although, if I explained why we need it, I'm pretty sure he would oblige me."

"Then you'll get it for us?"

"Are you sure this is going to work?"

"Absolutely."

"Then I'll get you a train."

Outside the office, Granier casually listened to the conversation through the open door. He didn't know precisely what Conein was going to do, but he had a good idea. Over the years, he had observed Conein's tactics and felt he could predict his moves. The one thing Granier was sure of was that Conein would plan out every detail of the mission. Planning was the key to Conein's success.

Dong Hoi, South Vietnam

With his sniper rifle wrapped in a blanket and slung across his chest, Granier stood on the roof of a train car. He had convinced himself that he would attempt to protect Suong one last time. After that, she was on her own. He wasn't sure what he would do. The situation was fluid.

He had hitched a ride with Coyle, claiming he needed to cross the border for a last-minute mission. Climbing aboard Coyle's C-119 boxcar, Granier found the cargo hold filled with barrels of lazy dog bomb darts – two-inch brass projectiles with fins. Coyle's plane was to be used as a spotting plane and a makeshift bomber.

When the plane landed in Hue and taxied next to the C-47 carrying Conein and his team, Granier jumped out and covertly followed Conein to the train yard in Dong Hoi. Conein's team set up in three railcars next to each other. When the train pulled out of the yard, Granier stowed away and climbed onto the roof. He could see one of Conein's scouts, sitting forward on the boxcar in front of him, searching the track ahead with binoculars. Granier, too carried a pair of binoculars in his pack along with extra ammunition. However, the scout was facing forward and did not notice Granier behind him. Granier didn't want to take any unnecessary risks. He climbed back down the ladder and rode the train on the back of the last car. Staying hidden as much as possible, he would pop up periodically to check the track ahead for signs of Suong and Le Duan.

In the sky above, Coyle and his crew flew the C-119 along the railroad tracks ahead of the train, looking for signs of Suong and Le Duan.

Suong and Le Duan rode the velocipede in silence, stealing glances of one another whenever the other wasn't looking. It was Duan's turn cranking the vehicle's drive. He sat on one side with his feet on the pedals and his hands on the handlebar crank. The velocipede required both the arms and legs to drive the steel wheels with a push and pull action. The velocipede was designed for one person, but Le Duan had redesigned the railcar to fit two plus a limited amount of space for supplies. Suong sat on the wooden crossbar that extended to the smaller steel wheel on the opposite side of the tracks. With minimal room for sitting, traveling on the velocipede was far from comfortable, but it was better than riding bicycles on South Vietnam's rain-rutted roads. At least the tracks were smooth, and potholes were non-existent. Riding on the crossbar was a welcome break from pedaling and cranking. The wind created by the velocipede's motion cooled the body down and dried out wet clothes and supplies from unexpected downpours.

The surrounding land was flat and covered with bright green fields, mostly rice paddies with an occasional vegetable field around the edges. Most of the water from the previous rain had been absorbed into the mud exposing the young plants. They would need more rain soon, or they would shrivel up under the sun and die. Rice and rain existed hand-in-hand, both essential to life in Southeast Asia. The sun was welcome but not too much. The heat could be stifling during the hot season. But during the monsoons, the sun dried out the farmer's wet clothes and prevented them from getting a chill. "I wish it would rain again," said Suong breaking the silence.

"I think we should get married," said Duan.

"What?!"

"I think we should get married."

"Why?"

"It's not honest sneaking around. If we are to be together, we should marry."

"How do you think your wife will feel?"

"She will understand as she always does. She is dedicated to the revolution and knows sacrifices must be made."

"That's what I am... a sacrifice?"

"No. Don't play games. You know I didn't mean it that way."

"Of course not. How did you mean it?"

"I meant to say... I love you."

"And I love you too, but that's no reason to get married. We are doing fine without it."

"Suong, if I am to be a leader in the politburo, I must be respected and beyond corruption. A secret that can be exposed can be used to blackmail."

"You're making this sound better and better."

"It's the truth. The members of the politburo frown on concubines. They want everything out in the open whenever possible."

"Where would we live?"

"In my house. Where else?"

"With your wife and children?"

"You can bring your children too if you wish."

"My children are grown. They don't need looking after. As a second wife, I could see being asked to watch over your wife's children."

"You mean my children. Possibly yes. In a family, each person must carry their load."

"And what of my career as a soldier?"

"You wouldn't need that anymore. I would support you."

"I don't do it for the money. I do it for the revolution which last time I looked was not yet over."

"Now you are being difficult."

"Then let me make it simple… no. I will not marry you."

"You don't think I would make a good husband?"

"I already know you would make a terrible husband. You are gone for months or even years at a time. When you are home, you are thinking about work. The only time you pay any attention to your wife is when you want to eat or have sex. That kind of life does not interest me."

"Then why did you start with me in the first place?"

"I never said you were not a good man. You are a great leader that loves his country. I admire you. It's just that you are constantly distracted."

"I have a country to free."

"Yes. And your commitment to your country will always outweigh your commitment to your wife and family."

"So, that's it? You are just going to leave me when we get to Hanoi?"

"Is that what you want… me to leave?"

"No. Of course not."

"Good. Because that's not what I want either. I like sharing your bed even if it's often made of twigs."

It was Suong that first heard the plane overhead. It wasn't a rare occurrence to see planes flying around South Vietnam. And Suong didn't make much of it, except that the plane's flight path seemed to parallel the train tracks. Still, nothing to get too excited about.

In the C-119, the co-pilot spotted the velocipede below and pointed it out to Coyle. Coyle radioed the information to Conein, riding in a railcar with several of his team members. Coyle turned from his search route and began a wide U-turn so as not to alarm the prey below.

Duan looked far down the tracks and spotted a cloud of grey smoke rising from the forest up ahead. "There's a train coming," he said.

Suong studied the map and said, "There's not a sidetrack in this area."

"Damn," said Duan using the hand brake to slow the velocipede to stop.

They climbed off the vehicle and unloaded it. There wasn't much time. Duan leaned the contraption to one side, lifting the small wheel on the opposite side off the rail. Suong pulled the locking pin and swung the extension arm over next to the two larger wheels making it more compact. Together, they lifted the heavy machine off the rail and carried it to the side of the tracks so the train could pass unimpeded.

From the roof of the train, Granier watched through his binoculars. Even at a distance on a moving train, he could clearly see that it was Suong and Le Duan removing the velocipede from the track. The train he was riding was approaching the edge of the forest and would soon be fully exposed. If he was to remain undiscovered, he needed to disembark immediately.

He climbed down the ladder and stopped on the last rung. He leaned over to the side and looked down the side of the railcars. He spotted a large leaf plant approaching as the train continued down the track. He tossed his blanket-wrapped rifle into the plant, hoping it would cushion the impact. Next, he unslung his pack and tossed it to the side of the track. Finally, he jumped from the train just as it left the forest's shadows and entered the sunlight of the open space.

Unhurt by the fall, Granier gathered his pack and rifle. He cut loose the twine holding the blanket around the rifle and did a quick check for damage. It looked good to go. He pulled the telescopic sight from the center of his backpack and removed the towel he had wrapped it in for protection. The sight, too, looked undamaged. He assembled the sight to the rifle. He moved through the forest to the edge of the tree line, so he had a better angle on the train. He lay down in a prone position with his rifle's barrel resting on his pack. He pulled his eyeglasses from a side pocket on his pack, opened the protective case, and slipped them on.

Peering through the scope, he checked on Suong and Le Duan. They were standing by the side of the tracks waiting for the train to pass. Unaware of the approaching danger, they were like sitting ducks. He swung the scope toward the train cars holding Conein's team. The doors were still closed. He had no idea what was inside but suspected they were armed to the teeth. He still wasn't sure what he could do to prevent the coming ambush, but he had to try.

Suong and Le Duan watched the approaching train. They heard the shriek of the brakes being applied to the steel wheels. The train slowed. "That's strange. Why is it slowing down?' said Duan.

Always on guard, Suong considered the potential dangers. She looked around at the surrounding countryside, and it occurred to her that with the exception of the velocipede, there was no cover for hundreds of meters in all directions. She looked back at the approaching train and noticed that it was short with only a few boxcars. Trains in Vietnam were usually loaded down to capacity to prevent wasting fuel. This one wasn't. As the locomotive passed, she looked through the window in the door into the engineer's compartment and saw the engineer crouched down, away from the windows. She looked back at the three boxcars and their sliding cargo doors. They were unlocked on the outside. That was very unusual. If they were empty, the doors would be left open to air out the boxcars, which were prone to mildew from the constant moisture in the air. If the boxcars were loaded with cargo, the doors would be locked from the outside to prevent pilfering. Something was amiss. The train was creeping to a stop. She could calculate that the boxcars would be lined up next to the velocipede when the train finally came to a halt next to them. There wasn't much time. And then it hit her… "It's an ambush," she said.

"What? I don't see——" said Duan.

"The train. We've got to find cover. Now."
"Where?"
The train screeched to a final stop.

Granier figured he was slightly over three hundred yards from Suong and Le Duan's position. There was a gentle breeze. He adjusted for that. He peered through his scope as the boxcar doors slid open, revealing the barrels of three .50cal machine guns, one in each of three boxcars. Even though he had moved off in the forest, he still had a bad angle. He couldn't see the gunners. There was nothing he could do to stop them. He knew that Suong would protect Le Duan with her life. Granier considered killing Le Duan. It would be a relatively easy shot at this distance with little risk of injury to Suong. The problem was that he wasn't sure how Suong would respond. She wasn't the type to just run off on her own. It wasn't that her survival instinct was low. It was that her sense of loyalty to those she fought beside was high. She could try to pull Le Duan out of harm's way. Or seeing the man she had been assigned to protect killed, she could stand her ground and fight for revenge. Either way would end her life for sure. Granier nixed the idea and focused on Conein's team. He was too late. The machine guns opened fire. Fearful of seeing Suong ripped to shreds by the giant bullets, Granier took a deep breath before swinging his scope over to the velocipede. To his surprise, Suong and Le Duan were nowhere in sight.

Conein, frustrated as hell, could see that his machine gunners were shooting into thin air and wasting ammunition. He cursed and yelled, "Ceasefire."

The machine guns went silent. He jumped down from the middle boxcar. He chambered a round in his Thompson machine gun. He walked carefully around the velocipede riddled with bullet dings. Having been fired at close range, the high-velocity bullets had torn through the steel wheels along with the rest of the contraption. He looked over at the side of the train and saw nothing of interest. "Goddammit," he said, looking at the surrounding area.

Granier was looking across the fields next to the train in search of Suong and Le Duan. With little cover beyond the young plants, he could see clearly. They weren't anywhere in sight. He swung his scope back to the train and watched as Conein's team climbed out of the boxcars, formed a long line, and moved across the fields. They, too, had not spotted Suong and Le Duan. Granier methodically searched the train examining the roof and undercarriage of each car, starting with the locomotive. He spotted Suong and Le Duan midway down the boxcars. Each was curled up in a ball behind the boxcars' large steel wheels. They were like scared rabbits. Frozen. Unable to move without being discovered. Granier knew that Suong was no coward, but she also wasn't stupid. The train was the only cover available in the immediate area. Granier considered the situation and settled on a tactic. He would create a diversion hoping that Suong and Le Duan would use the distraction to make their escape. He wished there was some way to communicate with her, but that wasn't an option.

Granier's biggest problem was that he couldn't kill any of Conein's team, although he briefly considered shooting Conein in the ass. He ruled it out. Too much risk of hitting an artery by mistake. He settled on a tree stump that had been pulled out of a field and left on the top of a dike wall. He waited until one of the soldiers got close to the stump and fired. The bullet blew a chunk out of the wood.

"Sniper," yelled Conein. "Hit the dirt."

The entire team dropped into the fields. Most of the soldiers were in rice paddies filled with foul-smelling mud or with a few inches of water filled with human and animal waste for fertilizer. The machine gunners in the boxcars opened fire, shooting randomly across the open fields. They had no target but put down suppressing fire in hopes of protecting the soldiers in the fields.

Although bullets were flying in every direction, Granier was in no real danger. Still, he kept low and out of sight, only popping up to fire. Granier took another shot, landing a bullet in front of Conein, splashing muddy water into his face.

Seeing the water's path hitting him in the face, Conein determined the direction of the sniper. He motioned the direction toward his men, then ordered them to use the dikes as cover. Once in place, they opened fire on the line of trees at the edge of the forest.

The fire on Granier's position increased dramatically, and he kept low. He knew he couldn't stay in his current position. Conein was smart enough to flank him. Granier looked for a way out.

Conein heard the C-119 approaching. He radioed Coyle and ordered him to lay down a blanket of darts on the sniper's position on the edge of the forest.

In the back of the C-119, the cargo boss and his assistant waited for the green light. Each had a bucket filled with lazy dog bomb darts. The rear doors on the cargo hold had been removed. When the light changed, they threw the darts out the back of the cargo hold.

Conein and his team continued to lay down fire on the sniper's position pinning Granier down. Conein watched as the brass projectile fell from the back of the C-119. The darts tumbled for a moment then straightened themselves out in a downward trajectory as the fins caught the air.

Granier heard the plane's engines and a whistling sound. He knew instinctively he was about to get bombarded by something. He remembered the darts from the cargo hold. He rolled under a nearby tree trunk and watched the forest canopy quiver as the projectiles pierced the leaves and branches. Like a cloudburst from hell, they hit the forest floor at

500mph, penetrating anything they hit. Thick branches were torn from trees. Tree roots shattered. Rocks split into pieces. The wave of falling brass marched toward him. There was nowhere to run or hide. He heard the heavy thumbs of the darts hitting the trunk under which he sought shelter. The trunk blew apart with wood shards flying in all directions. A dart penetrated the trunk just a few inches from his head and stuck in the ground as a reminder of how close it had come to ending his life.

As the blanket of brass passed, Granier rolled out from under what was left of the tree trunk. There wasn't much. He felt pain in his side and looked down to see his shirt torn. He pulled the hole in the cloth wider and saw a wooden shard sticking out the side of his waist. He removed the shard, and blood flowed. It wasn't enough to affect his performance, so he left tending to it for later. He picked up his sniper rifle and found a dart had hit the back of the stock chipping off a chunk of wood. It looked ugly, but the rifle was still functional. He turned back to the task at hand and peered through the scope.

Conein and his team had taken the opportunity to advance closer to his position. Granier fired off a couple of rounds just to let them know he was still alive and keep their attention.

Suong didn't know who was firing at the soldiers, but she didn't care. It was an opportunity, and she wasn't going to waste it. She turned to Duan and motioned to the opposite side of the train. He nodded that he understood. They crawled out from underneath the train and ran along the train back toward the forest.

Granier caught sight of them heading in his direction when he poked his head up for a brief moment. He had a decision to make. He could run in the opposite direction in hopes of leading Conein and his team away from Suong and Le Duan, or he could head in the same direction so he could protect them. He considered for a moment and chose to continue with his diversion. Suong was a warrior, and she could defend herself, especially in the forest. He jumped up and ran in the opposite direction so he was sure that Conein and his team would spot him. They did.

As they left the protection of the train shielding their movements, Suong and Duan could see a long stretch of open ground in front of them. There would be no cover until they reached the forest. They ran toward the trees until they heard the engines of the approaching plane. They looked up to see the C-119 flying over the treetops heading straight toward them. Suong was unsure what to do. A big part of her wanted to run back to the safety of the train, but her mind told her that was a dead-end that would result in their capture or death. The trees were their only hope. They continued running as the C-119 bore down on them. As it came closer, she looked up and saw a cloud of dark objects tumble out the back of the plane. Moments later, the projectiles straightened out and resembled distant golden sleet falling through a beam of sunlight. They were beautiful until they started hitting the ground, and she could see their true purpose. She grabbed Duan's arm and stopped him. There was no time to run another way. Only time to watch death on the march.

The brass darts pelted the railway in front of them, moving closer. The darts splintered the wooden railroad ties, sending wooden shards into the air. The rocks in the underbed broke into pieces. The darts broke into pieces and sent sparks into the air when they hit the steel rails. Like a wave, the bombardment moved forward. Suong and Duan couldn't take their eyes away. It wouldn't have mattered. The outcome was certain. Having pulverized the ground in front of them, the last of the darts landed just a few feet in front of them, sticking upright in a wooden tie defiantly. The fins on the projectile stood defiantly like a peacock's tail. Suong and Duan were frozen with fear that there was more coming. But there wasn't. Suong took a moment to reclaim her senses and reached for Duan's hand. They were alive… for the moment.

Hiding behind a thick tree, Granier stopped for a moment to look back toward the train and saw Suong and Duan holding hands. He wasn't sure what infuriated him more, the two holding hands or that they weren't moving. He swung his rifle around, took aim, and fired.

Granier's shot ricocheted off the rail just behind Suong and Duan. Hearing the danger, Suong snapped out of her malaise. They resumed their dash toward the woods.

Satisfied that they were now moving, Granier resumed his decoy journey running through the edge of the tree line in the opposite direction.

Conein was still too far away to see that the sniper was Granier, but there was something in the way the sniper was moving that seemed familiar. He saw the sniper fire a round back toward the train. He turned to see Le Duan and the woman bodyguard running toward the forest. He wanted the sniper, but Le Duan was the mission. He ordered his men to go after Le Duan. They ran through the fields to intersect the fleeing enemy. Conein motioned for the machine gunners to keep firing at the sniper in the tree line.

Bullets ripped through the trees, barely missing Granier as he ran. He stopped for a moment, using a large tree as cover. Bullets chipped away the bark and dug deeply into the wood on the front of the tree. It was a thick tree, and Granier was sure that even the .50-cal bullets would take time to break through the tree's trunk. He turned back toward the train and saw Suong and Le Duan as they entered the tree line next to the tracks. He turned his scope back to where he thought Conein and his men would be in the field and saw that they were no longer there. He scanned the horizon between the fields and the forest. He found the soldiers two hundred yards off heading toward Suong and Le Duan's position. His diversion had failed, and now Suong was in real danger of being hunted down by Conein. He knew Conein would shoot and ask questions later. Resembling a frontiersman, Granier carried his rifle in one hand

and sprinted back through the trees toward where he thought Suong might be heading. It was a big forest, and finding them would be difficult, but it was his only hope of protecting her.

Conein and his men entered the tree line. "Spread out and form a line," he said.

The sixteen soldiers formed a line and moved quickly through the trees hunting their prey. Conein was in the middle behind his best tracker. He knew not to rush the man who studied every detail on the forest floor looking for signs.

Like a deer leaping through the woods, Granier ran flat out. It took all his focus to dodge the exposed roots and rocks scattered across the forest floor. He knew Conein was out there somewhere, and if he ran into him, he would be outgunned and outnumbered. Even with his fighting skills, it wouldn't be much of a brawl. Granier would be a deadman for sure. The key was to find Suong and Le Duan and lead them out of harm's way or find Conein and his men first without being detected. Both were tall orders for a man running wildly to catch up. His peripheral vision caught movement on his right. He slowed and moved more cautiously, searching through the trees and undergrowth. He spotted two soldiers from the far left of Conein's line. He heard a single gunshot deep in the woods. The two soldiers moved off toward the direction of the gunshot. Granier didn't. He knew that soldiers would often shoot at anything that moved in the forest, especially when they were searching for an enemy. He had only heard one gunshot, and there were two targets – Suong and Duan. He figured the missing gunshot meant that the soldier had not found them. He proceeded to move along the line he thought Suong and Duan were heading. Again, he picked up speed.

He heard the sound of a stream and water splashing from footfalls. He knew that Suong would never allow herself to make such a racket, but Le Duan was a different story. He was a fighter but not an experienced woodsman like Suong. Granier approached with caution.

Suong rose from behind a fallen tree laying on the stream's embankment. Le Duan was beside her. Her gun was drawn. Granier's eyes met hers. She looked confused, like she didn't know if Granier was hunting her or saving her. Granier raised his fingers to his lips, signaling for them to keep silent. He looked down at her pistol and shook his head as if saying no. She didn't move. He knew she didn't trust him, and if he was totally honest… he didn't trust her either. It had been too long, and too much had happened. They were enemies. It saddened him. He wanted to hold her one last time, but he knew that was impossible. He would keep the promise he made to himself and help her escape. He again briefly considered killing Le Duan but realized it would give away Suong's position to Conein. He would let Le Duan live. All three heard the snap of a branch nearby. Conein and his men were approaching. Granier motioned for Suong and Le Duan to head west and that he would continue north to lead them away. Suong nodded that she understood. He watched for a moment as they disappeared into the trees and wondered if that would be the last time he saw her. He heard another footfall of a soldier behind him. He sprinted into the trees to the North.

The soldier spotted him and fired off two rounds. Both shots missed, and Granier disappeared into the woods. He continued north, allowing himself to be seen every few minutes so that the soldiers would continue to follow.

It didn't take long for Conein to figure out that they were chasing the sniper and not Le Duan. He considered doubling back but knew that the odds were thin that they would find Le Duan at this point. He had slipped away once again. Conein had failed. Killing the sniper would be little consolation, but at least it was something. They continued the chase for the rest of the day.

When night fell, Conein called off the search. The sniper was dangerous, even more so at night. It wasn't worth losing any of his men to soothe his ego. He had an inkling that the sniper might have been Granier, but there was no evidence. Just a hunch, and Lansdale didn't appreciate hunches. Conein would seek revenge another time. The fight between them wasn't over. It was about to enter a new phase.

That night, Suong and Le Duan made a fireless camp in the woods. They kept their conversations to a minimum and lowered their voices. "Why was the American following us?" said Duan.

"He was trying to protect me," said Suong.

"You knew him then?"

"Yes. A long time ago."

"Was he the sniper that tried to kill me at the warehouse?"

"I don't know. Maybe."

"You lied to me."

"I didn't lie. I just… never mind. Punish me if you must."

"Do you trust him?"

"He won't betray us to the others if that is what you are asking."

"How do you now?"

"I know him. He is honorable."

"And he loves you?"

"Once… yes. But that time is gone between us."

"And yet he still protects you?"

"Yes. It's foolish. I know."

"He saved our lives."

"Yes. He does that."

They fell silent and eventually slept curled up next to each other under the canopy of trees and a blanket of stars.

September 10, 1960 – Hanoi, North Vietnam

When Le Duan and Suong finally made it back to Hanoi, the politburo members were relieved to see them. They had heard the news of the ambush. With no word from the two travelers, some thought them dead or captured. Ho was particularly worried. Le Duan's near capture made many politburo members sympathetic to his arguments about supporting the war in the South.

Ho acknowledged that Duan's arguments had merit even if they weren't completely realistic under the current circumstances in the North. Ho knew when the political winds were changing. A master at politics, he could feel them blowing against him. On some level, he was relieved. After decades of fighting for his people, he had grown tired. He was sixty-nine years old, and his life had been far from easy. Much of the time, he had lived in the jungles and mountains with the Viet Minh. His body was frail, and he felt the aches and pains of age. He didn't want to give up. There was still much to do to ensure the success of his legacy – the revolution. His spirit was strong, but his body was betraying him.

Ho disagreed with Le Duan on many things. While the Americans helped Diem's government with military and financial aid, they were still taking a hands-off posture as far as the international community was concerned. Ho did not want to anger the U.S. diplomats and advisors in Saigon to the point that they would commit American troops to Vietnam. He believed the North could lose everything that it had fought so hard for against the French and Japanese if the Americans fully supported Diem in a civil war over control of Vietnam. Ho had lived in America. He feared America.

But Ho also knew that Duan was the future. He was the only leader capable of uniting the North and South. He was respected by his fellow politburo members and the people, especially in the South, where most of the fighting was taking place and where the war must be won. Duan was the clear choice to replace Ho and Ho knew it.

Duan was rash and impatient. He wanted war now, not ten years from now when the army was well-trained and fully armed. Duan saw the revolution in the South slipping away. Everything he had worked towards was disappearing before his eyes as more and more of his rebels were arrested by the secret service units Brother Nhu controlled. If discovered, being a Viet Minh was a death sentence, usually after torture. Many of Duan's followers had already sacrificed their lives for the cause.

On September 10, 1960, Ho nominated Le Duan as First Secretary of the Communist Party of Vietnam. As first secretary, Duan would become the de facto leader of North Vietnam. If Duan was elected, Ho promised to stay on as chairman and guide the new leader as he took over the massive responsibility of running a country and fighting a war at the same time. The politburo members were relieved that there would not be a fight for power as Ho stepped aside from his day-to-day responsibilities and became the figurehead that everyone loved and respected. Le Duan assured the members that Ho's counsel would always be welcome.

The vote was unanimous, except for General Giap, who continued to fight for what he believed was right. General Giap knew only too well how difficult it was to fight against a western power. Giap was willing to fight both South Vietnamese forces and the American forces but only if both the USSR and China gave their full support to the war effort. But neither of the communist leaders had the stomach for another full-on war. The Chinese and Russian advisors made it clear, if North Vietnam and the Viet Minh went to war against the Americans and South Vietnamese, they would be doing it alone.

Duan's election to party secretary was evidence that Giap was slowly losing his power and influence in the politburo. Under Duan's leadership, Giap would remain as commander of South Vietnam's military forces, but even his command was slowly slipping away. Before long, Giap would be asked to step down to make way for a younger, more aggressive commander.

With Le Duan in charge, everyone knew that the war in the South would proceed at a much faster clip. Already one-third of South Vietnam's population was living under open or secret communist control. Duan was ready to finish the job he had started. The Americans be damned.

November 8, 1960 – Washington D.C., USA

"American frontiers are on the Rhine and the Mekong and the Tigris and the Euphrates and the Amazon. There is no place in the world that is not of concern to all of us. We are responsible for the maintenance of freedom all around the world. The enemy is the communist system itself - implacable, unceasing in its drive for world domination," said John F. Kennedy on the campaign trail.

In a closely contested election, Senator Kennedy beat Vice President Richard M. Nixon for the presidency of the United States of America. Kennedy's Roman Catholic supporters had neutralized Nixon's Protestant supporters. The fact that seventeen million more Democrats registered to vote helped put Kennedy over the finish line with 303 electoral votes to Nixon's 219. With less than a point seventeen percent margin of victory, Kennedy's win was far from a mandate.

What few people knew was that Kennedy was lucky to still be alive. He was tormented by Addison's Disease, a rare disorder of the adrenal glands. His doctor thought it unlikely that Kennedy would live to complete a second term. The doctor was right but for the wrong reason.

JFK, as many called him, came across as open, confident, and self-deprecating. People who met him were often in awe of his smile and tan. He seemed to personally connect with anyone he met, even if it was just for a moment. He was a man that people remembered long after he left their presence. Although not shy, he preferred to engage with small groups of people he respected and trusted. He did not have deep relationships with anyone outside his family. Only his brother Bobby really understood him and shared his confidence. Born to a life of privilege, Kennedy was well-educated and articulate. He had a willingness to listen to others and valued political courage without respect for party affiliation. He learned from experience, and when proven wrong, he accepted counsel from those wiser, always giving credit where due. His absolute self-confidence caused him to stand out among the political giants of his time. Far from being a saint, Kennedy was a man to be reckoned with, an enigma, and a myth.

Kennedy's running mate and vice-president-elect was Lyndon B. Johnson. Unlike Kennedy, who lay down throughout the day to relieve the constant pain in his back, Johnson was tireless. He often worked eighteen to twenty hours a day to get legislation passed. He was wildly ambitious and imposing at six-foot three and a half-inches tall second only to Lincoln in presidential stature. He was a cowboy-boot-wearing chameleon that changed personality according to the situation. In one moment, he was a big-daddy Texan the son of a tenant farmer, and the next, he was the crusader for social justice, the great compromiser, the hard-headed pragmatist, or the preserver of tradition. He bent like a willow or stood firm like an oak; it just depended on the audience. As one of history's most effective majority leaders in the Senate, he had prepared dossiers on all the senators. He knew their ambitions, hopes, and tastes as well as their pet legislation projects. He would apply the "Johnson Treatment" of cajoling, badgering, promising, and reminding of past favors to get his way.

Johnson respected Kennedy as a politician, having run and lost to him in the primary. But Johnson saw Kennedy as something of a lightweight as far as accomplishments during his time in the Senate. Johnson was miserable as vice-president, feeling that his hands were tied until Kennedy gave his blessing on anything that needed to get done. He also felt awkward and gangly around Kennedy's Ivy League advisors and cabinet members.

Saigon, South Vietnam

On hearing the news of Kennedy's victory, Diem was elated. Surely, if any American could understand Diem and what he was attempting to accomplish, it was Kennedy. The two had met during the Indochina War, when as a young congressman, Kennedy and his brother Bobby had toured Saigon on a fact-finding mission. When Diem had become prime minister, Senator Kennedy had been one of his strongest American supporters. The two had met and talked again when Diem toured the United States at President Eisenhower's invitation. Because of his previous visit, Kennedy was considered an expert on Vietnam to whom the other senators and even the president listened. Like many politicians at the time, Kennedy was an anti-communist and supported American efforts against Chinese expansion into Southeast Asia.

But more important than anything, Kennedy was a Roman Catholic like Diem. Diem was sure that their common faith would be an unbreakable bond between the two leaders. Diem was a defender of the faith and went out of his way to protect Catholic refugees from the North. He often placed Catholic leaders in charge of important programs because he believed them to be loyal. Diem was excited and looked forward to a renewed partnership with America. His mood would change drastically three days later.

THE GATHERING STORM

November 11, 1960 – Saigon, South Vietnam

Twenty-eight-year-old Lieutenant Colonel Vuong Van Dong rode in a jeep at the head of a military column snaking its way through Saigon's streets in the early morning light. He was quiet and thoughtful. His mind elsewhere, going over the plans he and his commander, Colonel Nguyen Chanh Thi, had developed over the last year. Theory was about to become reality.

A Northerner, Dong had fought for the French against the Viet Minh in the Indochina War. Later, he had been chosen to train at Fort Leavenworth in the United States. His American instructors and advisors regarded Dong as a brilliant tactician with strong military prospects as he served in the Airborne Division. But Dong, along with other young officers, had become disenchanted with Diem's government. Diem and his family were constantly interfering with the internal affairs of the military. Dong had watched as officers far less skilled and experienced than he had been promoted because of their loyalty to the family. Diem played senior officers against one another to prevent them from challenging his rule and weakening their leadership. Dong's discontent was also shared by his brother-in-law, Lieutenant Colonel Nguyen Trieu Hong, the training director at the Joint General Staff School in Saigon.

In the preceding months, the American embassy's intelligence officers had noticed the increase in reports about political disillusionment in the ARVN officer corps. It wasn't difficult to see how the South Vietnamese government's promotions of incompetent officers through political favoritism was having a disastrous effect on military morale. Internal security and unit readiness were becoming alarmingly lax. Ambassador Durbrow's warning had fallen on deaf ears as Diem refused to acknowledge the problems in his military and shunned American interference in his government's affairs.

The MAAG inside the embassy stood in stark contrast to the intelligence reports and Durbrow's warnings. The American military advisors believed that Diem was correct to use strong-arm tactics to control his military and thereby the Viet Minh. South Vietnam needed an authoritarian leader if it was going to win the war against the communists.

There was nothing unusual about military vehicles traveling through the city. It was the size of the column that was surprising – several hundred trucks, armored cars, and even tanks. Inside the trucks were three battalions of paratroopers and a battalion of marines. The tanks and armored cars were from an armored regiment just outside of Saigon.

The soldiers in the convoy knew nothing about their commanders' plans. When their journey began in the middle of the night, they were told they were traveling to the countryside to fight the Viet Minh. It was still dark when the convoy was ordered to a halt. A radio message had been received that ordered them back to Saigon to rescue President Diem and his family from a coup thrown by the mutinous Presidential Guards. Many of the ARVN soldiers were unexpectedly relieved to be fighting their own men rather than the Viet Minh. Recent conflicts with the rebels had not gone well for the ARVN, and few were thrilled to once again risk their lives against the communists that seemed to be growing stronger by the day.

Dong had arranged for the radio message to be sent. He played along and acted shocked by the news of the mutiny. The convoy was rerouted to Independence Palace.

To the soldiers guarding the palace gates and exterior walls, it was the end of another night of monotonous patrolling of the presidential compound, snapping a firm salute to passing officers and wondering how long until breakfast. The two soldiers standing at the palace's front entrance, which was elevated by a flight of stairs, were the first to spot the convoy's distant headlights as it rounded the corner onto the main boulevard leading to the palace. It was almost a mile away, and the sun had not broken the horizon making it difficult to see. Their vantage point was unique. In the early morning light, they could see one vehicle after another turning the corner and joining the long line heading straight for them. It was the first appearance of a tank that focused their attention. Tanks on Saigon's streets were frowned upon except during emergencies and parades because the treads dug up the asphalt. They reported their sighting to their commander, who at first thought his men were exaggerating. Once he reached the top of the stairs, it only took a moment before realizing the potential danger. He immediately sounded the alarm for all soldiers in the barracks to report to their stations. He barked out orders to close the palace gates and for his men to take up defensive positions. It was not a drill. It was a coup.

Inside the palace, Diem was still asleep. Nobody had yet thought to wake him. They were too busy preparing for the coming assault. It was the tremors from the approaching tanks that woke him. The room's drapes were closed, leaving only a sliver of light. He opened his eyes to see the chandelier in front of his bed swaying slightly. It was a strange sight, and he didn't know what to make of it. He could hear the faint rumbling in the distance. That too was confusing for his clouded mind, not totally awake. It was all too much before his morning tea. He closed his eyes and went back to sleep, confident his staff would deal with whatever problems arose.

Outside, as the convoy arrived, the tanks kept their distance and took up positions in an outer ring facing away from the palace. They would fend off any potential attack from Diem loyalist troops that might make it to the palace. The troop trucks formed an inner siege ring surrounding the palace. Thousands of soldiers jumped out of the back of the trucks.

Hoping to avoid unnecessary bloodshed on both sides, Dong ordered his men to hold their fire until he personally gave the order to engage. Heavy mortar teams set up their ordnance and stacked their shells. Machine gun teams set up their weapons to cover every entrance to the palace compound from multiple angles. Airborne and marine platoons took up firing positions behind whatever cover they could find. The inner siege ring was beyond crowded. Not even a rat could sneak out of the palace.

The palace guards also held their fire. Even with the latest American weapons, they were vastly outnumbered and outgunned. In all, there were less than one hundred soldiers guarding the palace. The only advantage they had was that they were Vietnamese, and none of the commanders on either side wanted to shed their countrymen's blood.

A rebel paratrooper lieutenant took it upon himself to order his men to assault the front gate. They advanced with purpose, firing at the guards, driving them behind cover. One overanxious paratrooper raked the front of the palace with machine-gun fire breaking windows and piercing the walls.

With the broken glass of his bedroom windows crashing to the floor, Diem woke. He watched as bullets stitched their way down his walls. He dove to the floor beside his bed on the opposite side of the windows. Feathers flew as the thick mattress protected him. He crawled into the bathroom and slammed the door shut.

The palace was not the only building being overrun. Over 5,000 soldiers took part in the coup operations throughout Saigon. Platoons took over the radio stations, post office, and police headquarters, then set up roadblocks around the city. It only took over an hour for all of Dong's forces to report that they were in position and ready to engage.

A battalion of paratroopers overwhelmed the perimeter guards and crashed through the gates around Tan Son Nhut Air Base. They surrounded the barracks of the Air Force personnel and grounded all military flights. The base armory was locked down and heavily guarded.

Near the airbase, the paratroopers captured the Joint General Staff's headquarters and placed all officers under house arrest, confiscating radios and ripping out telephones.

A platoon of marines crashed through the front doors of Saigon's central telephone exchange. With their guns leveled, the soldiers ordered the operators to pull the cables out of the switchboards cutting off all phone service in and out of Saigon. The lieutenant in charge knew little about the technology. It never occurred to him that there might be a backup system. There was.

When everything seemed well in hand, Dong radioed the lieutenant at the phone exchange and ordered him to put a call through to Ambassador Durbrow at the American embassy.

Just minutes before the phone call from Dong, Durbrow had been informed by Lansdale, who was at his downtown residence near the palace, that heavily armed soldiers and tanks had surrounded the palace. Durbrow immediately sent a cable to Washington reporting the coup attempt and asking for instructions. He hadn't heard back when Dong's call was relayed through the embassy switchboard.

Dong's call was polite but firm. He informed Durbrow that no harm would come to any Americans in South Vietnam as long as they stayed out of the internal conflict. He also told the Ambassador that the coup leaders were determined to take the palace by force if necessary. He asked Durbrow to intervene and convince Diem to surrender without bloodshed. While Durbrow had been a persistent critic of Diem, he also understood his duty as the Ambassador was to convey his government's position to support Diem and avoid harm to America's standing in the international community. Like a true diplomat, Durbrow responded, "We support this government until it falls."

Dong understood the cryptic message from Durbrow to mean that America would support whatever government was firmly in charge in South Vietnam. The coup leaders had been correct in concluding that the Americans would stay out of it, offering no help to either side until the battle was over and a victor declared. Dong thanked the Ambassador for his time and hung up. It was good news for Dong and his co-conspirators, who feared America more than Diem and his army.

After the initial shock of being assaulted by mutinous government troops, the director of operations at the phone exchange, a Diem loyalist, asked the paratrooper corporal in charge of the detail guarding him and his people to allow those in need to use the toilet. The corporal agreed to groups of twelve led by two paratroopers.

After the first group returned, the director joined the second group. As they waited to enter the toilet, the director slipped through a doorway and climbed down a flight of stairs to the basement. Flipping on the light, he sat down at the backup switchboard in front of several banks of equipment. He rerouted a phone line and called the palace to inform Diem's staff that several phone lines would remain open for the president's use.

When Lansdale phoned the Ambassador to get an update, he was told by Durbrow to stand down along with all the Americans in South Vietnam until the coup was successful or failed. But Lansdale did not report to Durbrow. He reported directly to Allan Dulles, the CIA director in Washington D.C. Lansdale had invested a great deal of effort in bolstering Diem and his regime. He believed that Diem was South Vietnam's best hope of defeating the communist expansion. He found it more than difficult to standby while Diem was under attack. He ordered the men under his command to stay in the house he was assigned as a headquarters for his covert teams. He grabbed his car keys and headed out the door.

As Lansdale approached Independence Palace, he saw a roadblock manned by paratroopers with an armored car. The armored vehicle was French – a Panard 178 leftover from the Indochina War. It had a 25mm cannon mounted on a turret and a 7.5mm machine gun as a secondary weapon. One-shot from the cannon would blow his car to bits and him along with it. He decided not to risk running the blockade and turned down a side street.

He traveled to the next corner and found another roadblock obstructing his way. The rebel paratroopers were well organized. The fact that their leaders had thought through their plan did not bode well for Diem's chances. He drove across the four-way street to the next block and parked his car in front of an upscale apartment building. He took out his street map and gave it a quick review. He figured he was five blocks from the palace. He tucked the map in the pocket of his trousers and exited the car. He looked both ways to ensure that nobody was watching before heading inside the apartment building.

A Vietnamese doorman met him. "Can I help you?" said the doorman in French.

"Do you have a back entrance?" said Lansdale in English.

The doorman looked confused, like he didn't understand what Lansdale was saying. "Never mind. I'll find out for myself," said Lansdale pushing past the man.

The doorman objected with a string of French as he followed Lansdale through the lobby toward the back of the building. Lansdale didn't respond as he disappeared through the backdoor into an alley.

Crossing the alley, Lansdale checked several backdoors. They were all locked. He spotted an open window, stacked a couple of crates, and climbed through the window.

He found himself in a bathroom stall, standing on a toilet. He climbed down and exited the stall to find a foreign woman using the mirror to apply a new coat of lipstick. Her eyes went wide, seeing the handsome American in uniform emerge from the stall and walk out the door without saying a word.

Lansdale weaved his way through several more buildings until he reached the last building on the street bordering the palace. He entered through the backdoor and made his way toward the front. When he walked into the lobby, he found a platoon of paratroopers in firing positions facing the twelve-foot palace wall across the street. He ducked into a doorway to avoid being seen. He was lucky; the paratroopers were focused on the palace, not the hallway behind them. He quickly realized that even if he could make it past the rebel paratroopers and over the wall, he would most likely be shot by the Presidential Guard. They were crack troops, the best of the best. He doubted they would hesitate to shoot long enough to recognize him as an advisor to

President Diem. He wasn't a coward but didn't see the value of sacrificing his life on a fool's errand. He turned back and abandoned his quest to enter the palace. At least he was able to access the situation somewhat. There was little doubt that Diem and his family were surrounded by a superior force. They wouldn't last long if the Coup leaders decided to press their position.

When Lansdale arrived back at his house/office, he found Conein and Granier waiting when he walked through the front door. "Diem has been calling," said Granier.

"What?! How? The paratroopers overran the telephone exchange. They shut down all the phone lines," said Lansdale.

"Someone in the exchange rerouted the palace's call through a backup switchboard. Diem's called three times. He really wants to speak with you," said Conein.

"I would imagine. So, what do I do? Use the same number to call him?"

"Yeah. That's what he said."

Lansdale picked up the phone in the living room and dialed the number for the palace. After a few moments, someone on the other end picked up. It was Madame Nhu. "This is Colonel Lansdale for President Diem," said Lansdale.

"Where have you been, Colonel?" said Madam Nhu. "The president is in grave danger while you sit on your veranda having lunch."

"I assure you, Madame Nhu, I have been trying to reach the palace. It's surrounded."

"You state the obvious, Colonel. We do not care what you saw. We want to know what you and the Americans plan to do about it?"

"May I speak with the President, Madame?"

A few moments later, Diem was on the phone, "Colonel, it is good to hear from you."

"Thank you, Mr. President. It is good to hear from you too. Are you and your family all right?"

"Yes. Yes. A bit shaken by the events of the day, but we are unhurt."

"Good. I pray it stays that way."

"Thank you, Colonel. Have you talked with President Eisenhower?"

"No, sir. But I have talked with Ambassador Durbrow."

"A useless effort, I am sure."

"Not at all, Mr. President. He has pledged America's support for you and your regime."

"Words mean nothing when guns are pointed at you, Colonel."

"I understand your concern, Mr. President. I will do everything I can to assure your safety. Have you made contact with the coup leaders?"

"Yes. Lieutenant Colonel Dong seems to be in charge. He has demanded my immediate surrender."

"As I would suspect. I hope you understand that surrender at this point would be a mistake. Once you are in their custody, you lose all power of negotiations."

"I have no intention of surrendering to a bunch of thugs, Colonel."

"Good. Any word from your commanders outside of Saigon?"

"Not yet, but we are attempting to communicate with them."

"It is essential that they send a relief force. Our intelligence estimates the rebel force to be a regiment. Any force confronting them would need to be a much larger size."

"Yes. Yes. We have already considered that."

"What about your Air Force?"

"The rebels have overrun the airbase. All flights are grounded."

"I see. I might be able to do something about that."

"Yes?"

"Maybe. I will get back to you as soon as I know."

"Very well, Colonel. A word of support directly from President Eisenhower would greatly strengthen our position."

"I understand, Mr. President. I will see what I can do."

"Thank you, Colonel. I look forward to seeing you again when this is all over."

"And I you, Mr. President. Please stay safe and keep me informed of any developments. I will do the same on my end."

"Very well, Colonel. Thank you for your support."

"Of course, Mr. President."

Lansdale hung up. His mind raced. "Times like these require bold action," said Lansdale to his two team commanders. "Officers Conein and Granier, I want you and your team to round up as many loyal Vietnamese as you can find."

"For what purpose, Colonel?" said Granier.

"We are going to rescue President Diem and his family."

Granier and Conein exchanged a doubtful look. "You understand that the rebels have tanks and thousands of men surrounding the palace?" said Conein.

"Of course, I do. That's why we're going to retake the airfield and perform a low-level parachute drop into the palace compound."

"And the ambassador approves of your plan?" said Conein.

"I don't need the Ambassador's approval. I report to CIA Director Allen Dulles."

"And he approves of it?" said Granier.

"He will. What is it with you two? You know Diem is the only leader currently available that is capable of defeating the communists."

"Kinda hard to defeat anybody if you don't have an army," said Conein.

"I assure you; this is just a small band of troublemakers."

"A small band? You said it yourself; there's an entire regiment surrounding the palace."

"And President Diem has substantial, loyal forces outside of Saigon. It's just a matter of time before they arrive."

"If that's true, why are we getting involved?" said Granier.

"I hate to agree, but Granier's right. We should just stand down and let the Vietnamese settle this one," said Conein.

"When the dust settles, and Diem has regained control, I want to make sure he recognizes that his ally did not stand idly by in his moment of need. You have been given your orders. Now carry them out."

"Yes, sir," said both team leaders and left.

Outside the house, Conein and Granier moved to their vehicles. They knew they were being tossed into the soup together. While they hated each other, they also had a sort of mutual respect. "I don't like this," said Conein.

"Neither do I. It feels rushed," said Granier.

"It was his job to detect the rebellion. He missed the signs. That's not like him."

"Yeah. It sounds like he's determined to do something to save face."

"You know retaking that airfield is not going to be a walk in the park."

"Yeah. It'll be difficult but not impossible. There will be far fewer rebels guarding the airfield than surrounding the palace. A parachute drop is not out of the question either."

"Gonna be a tight drop zone and under heavy fire to boot."

"Hero shit, that's for sure. We should get Coyle to pilot the plane."

"Yeah. Coyle's good. A night drop would be safer."

"Yeah. A night drop sounds good. I'm still not clear why we're getting involved in a civil war."

"I find it best not to question the brass. They have their reasons. Truce until this is over?"

"Yeah. But when it's done, I'm still going to kill you."

"I suspect you'll try," said Conein offering his hand.

Granier looked down at Conein's outstretched hand like it was a bad piece of meat and said, "Yeah, that ain't gonna happen."

Granier hopped in his jeep and drove away without shaking hands. Conein chuckled and said to himself, "At least he's consistent."

Saigon, South Vietnam

A platoon of crack, heavily armed ARVN troops surrounded Brigadier General Nguyen Khanh as they made their way through Saigon's streets toward the palace. Appointed by Diem as the ARVN's Chief of Staff, Khanh was loyal to the president and his family. He carried a portable radio tuned to the frequency that he and the Presidential Guard commander had agreed to use in time of emergency.

The coup plotters had sent a squad to place Khanh under house arrest before the first shots were fired, but unknown to the plotters, Khanh had recently moved to a different house in downtown Saigon. When the rebel troops had arrived, they found a frightened older couple in their nightclothes, but no Khanh. It was a significant oversight considering Khanh's importance to the chain of command.

Just as Lansdale had done, Khanh and his escorts used the buildings to travel unseen past the ring of roadblocks and armored vehicles. When they reached the last building across the street from the palace, they encountered a squad with their weapons pointed toward the palace wall. Khanh calculated correctly that the rebel commanders had placed the bulk of their forces at the palace's entrances. He avoided those positions and instead decided to climb the twelve-foot wall surrounding the presidential compound's perimeter. It was risky. But Khanh was used to putting his life on the line for his country.

His men quietly took up firing positions behind the rebel squad. Khanh silently pressed the radio's transmit button three times, waited for a beat, then twice again. It was a code to signal to the compound commander that he was coming in and not to shoot. One of the rebel paratroopers rose on his way to relieve himself. His eyes went wide when he turned to see the ARVN troops behind him. He raised his weapon but was shredded by loyalist gunfire before he could get a shot off. The rest of the battle lasted only a few seconds as the ARVN troops surprised the rebel paratroopers with a barrage of bullets, killing or severely wounding all of them. The brief skirmish was so lopsided that no loyalist troops were even injured. Khanh knew that luck wouldn't last.

The ARVN troops moved forward and through the building's front door and broken windows with purpose. They formed a defensive corridor crossing the street with two lines facing opposite directions. It didn't take long before they were under heavy fire from the rebel paratroopers on both sides. An ARVN sapper ran to the wall and threw a grappling hook over the top of the wall. He pulled the rope until the tri-pronged hook caught on something. He pulled hard to make sure it was secure then signaled Khanh that it was ready. Several of the general's escorts had been severely wounded and killed. Khanh would make sure their sacrifice would not go unrewarded. Khanh sprinted across the street, keeping his head low. Enemy bullets ricocheted off the pavement and whizzed past him as he ran. He grabbed the rope and started his climb up the wall. It felt like an eternity as more enemy fire chipped away at the wall around him. One bullet nicked the rope and he wondered if it would break, sending back it to the pavement. It didn't. He grabbed the top of the wall and pulled himself over.

Inside the compound, Khanh dropped to the grass. Several guardsmen ran to his side and escorted him inside the palace. Enemy mortar shells rained down, exploding, kicking up dirt and grass as they ran. They climbed the stairs and entered the palace through the front doors.

Khanh was led down to the basement, where Diem and his family were sheltered. "I'm pleased to see you, General," said Diem shaking his hand.

"No more than I you, Mr. President," said Khanh. "Are you and your family well?"

"All things considered… yes. We are unharmed. Please, update me on your progress."

"I have contacted Ky Quang Liem, your deputy director of the Civil Guard. He remains loyal and is standing by to assist you when ordered."

"So, order him to attack the rebels immediately," said Madame Nhu interrupting.

"That may not be prudent. Even with his tanks, I doubt Liem has the forces required to capture the rebels," said Khanh.

"Then what good are he and his men if they will not fight for their president?" said Madame Nhu.

"He could do a great deal of good if he is joined with other forces in a coordinated attack. We should not waste his men because of impatience."

"Impatience? We are surrounded by enemy soldiers wanting to decapitate our regime," said Brother Nhu. "I hardly think this is time for patience."

"I understand your anxiety. But we should not attack until we are sure we can win. We do not have reserves if we lose."

"How long before you can get enough additional forces into the city?" said Diem.

"Thirty-six to forty-eight hours if they do not meet with heavy resistance."

"And what are the odds of that?"

"Surprisingly good. My intelligence reports that while the rebel forces have set up roadblocks near the palace, they have not cut off the major roads leading into the city."

"That's unusual," said Diem.

"Why would they make such an amateurish mistake?" said Nhu. "Everything else seems to have been planned very well."

"War is a strange thing. People make mistakes."

"It could be a trap," said Madame Nhu. "A ploy to lead your forces into an early demise."

"I have considered that. But I think a more likely explanation is that the rebel leaders thought it would be over by now. That you would have surrendered before any loyalist forces could be mustered and therefore the main roads did not need roadblocks."

"Stupidity," said Madame Nhu. "We are obviously dealing with rebel idiots."

"Possibly. But I don't think we should underestimate them at this point. We need to be cautious. I have two divisions on their way to the capital - the Fifth Division of Colonel Thieu and the Seventh Division of Colonel Khiem. We need to buy time for their arrival."

"And when they arrive?" said Diem.

"Our forces will be far superior to the rebel forces surrounding the palace. They will have no choice but to surrender."

"We will hang them all," said Madame Nhu. "The Americans included. The coup plotters would not have been so bold if they did not have approval from the Americans."

"I'm not sure that's true," said Khanh. "The Americans have issued a message of support for you and your regime."

"The Americans often say one thing and do another," said Madame Nhu.

"I agree with my wife. I'm not so sure that it wasn't the Americans that planned the entire operation," said Nhu.

"Conjecture is of little use at this point," said Khanh. "An investigation when this is over will certainly undercover the truth."

Diem listened to the arguments without comment, weighing the merits of each side in his mind.

"How can we buy time?" said Nhu.

"That I don't know," said Khanh.

"I do," said Diem.

As the sun rose and the temperature climbed, Radio Saigon, under the rebels' control, announced that a military coup had been successfully achieved. A revolutionary council was now in control of the government. Hundreds of banner-waving civilians approached the siege ring, verbally encouraging the rebel troops and their leaders to take the palace by force. The mob wanted Diem placed under arrest and his brother and sister-in-law executed.

Over a thousand Saigon-based ARVN troops made their way to the palace and joined the insurgents. They had enough of Diem and his family's interference in military affairs. Rebel support was growing, just as its leaders had predicted. The coup was less than a day old, and it already looked like they had won.

Diem's private secretary Vo Van Hai volunteered to negotiate on the president's behalf. He appeared at the front gate and was escorted to a nearby building where Dong and Thi were waiting. "What is it that you hope to accomplish?" said Hai starting the negotiations.

"We want Diem and his family to surrender to the revolutionary council," said Dong.

Hai pulled out a pen and paper. He wrote down the response and said, "What guarantees would the president have that he and his family would be unharmed and treated fairly?"

"None," said Thi. "The palace is surrounded, and we are prepared to take it by force if necessary. Diem must surrender at once to prevent bloodshed."

"President Diem will not leave the palace until the details of his surrender have been presented and accepted."

"That is fine with us. You may stay here if you wish. We will attack immediately."

"Mr. Hai, if I may have a minute with my associate," said Dong.

"Of course," said Hai taking more notes.

Dong and Thi moved off to another room while Hai stayed seated under guard.

"What is your plan once they surrender?" said Dong.

"To kill them as we discussed," said Thi.

"You would make Diem a martyr?"

"We cannot allow Diem or his family to live. The risk is too great."

"I disagree. Diem still has value if we hobble him and leave him in power."

"Hobble him? You can't be serious."

"How dangerous is Diem without his brother and sister-in-law?"

"…as president? Plenty. He controls the military."

"And if we take that away… his control of the military?"

"Stop playing games. What are you purposing?"

"We require that he replaces his prime minister with a general, and command of the military lies with him."

"Which general?"

"Brigadier General Kim."

"The head of the Vietnamese National Military Academy?"

"He is well respected."

"Yes. He's a good man. Do you think he would accept?"

"I know he would. I have already approached him."

"Why wasn't I consulted?"

"I wanted to make sure it was a real possibility before I asked you."

"And are you… asking me?"

"Of course. We are in this thing together."

Thi thought for a long moment before responding, "All right. I agree. As long as Nhu and his wife are executed before Diem returns to power."

"Colonel, we need to be reasonable. We cannot expect Diem not to retaliate if we murder his brother and sister-in-law. For our own safety, we should send them into permanent exile."

"No. That is non-negotiable. The people will demand their deaths."

"The people will accept whatever we agree to in order to keep the peace."

"Even overseas, they can still cause trouble."

"Yes. But not nearly as much as they do now. They will have no power and cannot bully their enemies."

"I don't like it."

"Neither do I, but the alternative is to spend the rest of our lives looking over our shoulders."

"I'm not afraid of Diem or Nhu. It's that damned woman that scares me."

"I agree. She's so little."

"So is a cobra."

"Then we are agreed?"

"All right. We'll do it your way. I was never any good with politics."

Dong and Thi walked back in and presented their proposal. Hai took meticulous notes. "It's an interesting proposal. I shall be happy to present it to the president once we have worked out the other details," said Hai.

"What other details?" said Thi, suspicious.

"Well, for starters, you cannot expect President Diem and his family to accept your demands without knowing how they will be treated."

"Of course not. What does the president wish to know?" said Dong.

"I have a list," said Hai pulling out and unfolding several pieces of paper.

Negotiations continued for another three hours as Hai took notes over everything said and even asked that some things be repeated. Thi lost his patience several times and left the room to cool off while Dong continued to move things forward with Hai.

Satisfied that he had everything well documented, Hai was sent back to the palace with the rebel's terms and the responses to the president's questions. "That man tries my patience," said Thi relieved it was over.

"Yes. He's an interesting choice as a negotiator," said Dong.

Tan Son Nhut Air Base, South Vietnam

It was night when Granier, Conein, and their two CIA teams approached the forest's edge surrounding the airbase. Accompanying them, Coyle and his aircrew had agreed to join the mission. Behind the Americans were fifty Vietnamese soldiers loyal to Diem, most coming from the 5th Bureau. Even with the addition of the South Vietnamese troops, they were vastly outnumbered by the paratroopers now in control of the base. Stealth was their only hope.

Conein, Granier, and Coyle all pulled out their binoculars and surveyed the area. There was a strip of cleared ground between the tree line and the perimeter fence—two hundred yards with nothing to hide behind. A team of four paratroopers patrolled the perimeter fence. "As far as I can tell, the patrol schedule is random and unpredictable," said Conein in a whisper. "We are gonna have to take them out if we are going to have any hope of making through the perimeter fence."

"I agree," said Granier removing his sniper rifle from his shoulder. "I can do it from here."

"All four at the same time?" said Conein. "That'd be some magic trick."

"It ain't magic. I can do it."

"It's over four hundred yards from here, ya know?"

"I said I can do it."

"All right. I'll lead the insertion team."

"You should probably let the Vietnamese go first. In case something goes wrong. It's better that no Americans are involved."

"Kind of a chicken-shit attitude. Besides, nothing is going to go wrong while I'm in charge."

"I forget… you think you're God."

"No. Just effective."

"Whatever. Let's get this show on the road. We need to execute the drop at the palace before sunrise."

"Coyle, where are we headed once we get through the fence?" said Conein.

"Third hangar to the left. There's a C-119 parked in front of it. The parachutes should be inside the hangar. We're gonna need to remove the back doors on the plane before we take off."

"That's gonna take some time," said Granier.

"You guys wanna all jump at the same time, right?"

"Yeah."

"Then we need to remove the doors."

"All right. We'll remove the doors while you prep the plane."

"Works for me. Do you have a plan for what we're gonna do if they try and block the runway with vehicles?"

"We thought we'd wing it," said Conein.

"Wing it?"

"What can I tell you? I think good under stress."

"Great. This is shaping up to be a real adventure," said Coyle with a weak smile.

Ten minutes later, a South Vietnamese sapper had belly-crawled to the fence and cut the wire with his cutters. He was almost finished when he heard the approaching paratrooper team. He bowed his head and froze. He hoped they wouldn't notice the long hole in the fence wire. It was a foolish wish.

Back at the tree line, Granier slipped on his glasses and aimed. "I hope you are as good as you like to think you are," whispered Conein.

"You do your part. I'll do mine," said Granier adjusting his sight for distance.

Granier aimed and followed the rebel paratroopers as they approached. "Get ready," he said to Conein and the rest of the unit. "This is gonna be fast."

As the paratroopers saw the opening in the fence and moved forward to investigate, Granier took final aim on the team leader. He took in a half-breath and slowly squeezed the trigger. He already knew where his next target was positioned. He wouldn't hesitate or second guess his first shot. He would move to the second target before the bullet hit the first target. It was his discipline to kill.

Inside the perimeter fence, the team leader heard the rifle's crack a moment after the bullet struck him in the side of the head. He crumbled to the ground, dead.

The next three bullets left Granier's barrel in less than three seconds. All three hit their intended targets before they comprehended what was happening. They, too, were trained killers, but they had never encountered someone like Granier. What he did was beyond skill. It was art. All three hit the ground dead.

Seeing the four paratroopers drop dead, the sapper finished cutting the wire to open the fence. He dove through the opening, unslung his rifle, and took up a firing position to cover his comrades as they too dove through the opening. Each took a firing position to fend off the assault they knew was coming. The Americans followed. Granier was the last man through the fence. Still, no assault.

They headed across the runway toward the hangar in the distance. Shots rang out. The paratroopers had located them. The teams kept running. A few returned fire at the muzzle flashes of the paratroopers in the distance. It was hard to see. The runway lights had all been extinguished.

They reached the hangar and the C-119. The Americans went to work removing the cargo doors off the back of the plane, revealing the empty hull. Coyle and the flight crew went to work, prepping the aircraft for takeoff. Coyle sat down in the pilot's chair and immediately checked the fuel levels. The tanks were half full. That was enough. The South Vietnamese soldiers took up firing positions using whatever they could as cover. They returned fire on the advancing paratroopers.

The paratroopers were elite troops, brave beyond reason, and well trained to fight as a unit. They leapfrogged forward toward the intruders, one team firing, while another team advanced. Ten yards at a time, closing the distance between themselves and the enemy. They were flawless in their execution.

As the doors were finally removed, Conein led the two teams to gather the parachutes in the hangar. They formed a line handing them forward and tossing them into the back of the aircraft.

Granier slipped his glasses back on, unslung his weapon, and opened fire. Even in the darkness, he dropped a paratrooper with every other shot and moved onto the next without thinking or remorse. He was a machine.

Seeing a number of their comrades fall to the tarmac, the paratroopers recoiled and took up defensive positions, seeking whatever cover they could find.

Coyle cranked the C-119's twin engines to life. They sputtered, caught, and roared. "Let's go!" he shouted out the side window.

The last of the parachutes were loaded in the back, and the Americans climbed in. On Conein's signal, the Vietnamese fell back and climbed onboard. Granier held his ground and continued to fire at the paratroopers, keeping them pinned down. Coyle's crew chief removed the wheel blocks and climbed in through the side door. The plane began to roll. "Move your ass, Granier," shouted Conein. "Train's leaving the station."

Granier finished his clip, and the rifle's bolt locked back. He sprinted for the back of the plane as it picked up speed, taxing across the tarmac toward the runway. Shots from the paratroopers zinged past his head as he ran. When he caught up, he handed his rifle to Conein and climbed on board with two of his team members' help. He was out of breath and exhausted.

Conein looked out the side window and saw what he feared. A jeep and two troop trucks were speeding toward the runway attempting to cut off the plane. He ran through the cockpit doorway and said, "You see 'em?"

"Yeah, I see 'em. What's your plan, smart-ass?" said Coyle as he steered the plane onto the runway and stopped.

"Why are you stopping?"

"Cuz you ain't got a plan, do ya?"

"I'm working on it, but it doesn't involve stopping."

Coyle locked the brakes and increased power to the engines. The engines thundered as the aircraft's frame groaned under the strain. Coyle released the brakes, and the plane rolled down the runway, picking up speed quickly.

The jeep and the trucks turned onto the concrete runway and headed toward the approaching plane. The machine gun mounted on the jeep opened fire at the cockpit.

Coyle and his crew ducked as several bullets smashed through the windshield and hit the radio. Sparks flew. "This ain't gonna work," said Coyle throttling down, steering the aircraft off the runway and crossing the grass back onto the ramp paralleling the runway. He gunned the engines once again and sped down the ramp. His wingtips were just a couple of feet from hitting the rudders of several planes parked on the ramp. The aircraft's wheel was dangerously close to the edge of the ramp. A miscalculation could send the aircraft into a horizontal spin if the landing gear dug into the grass. "This is crazy," said Concin wide-eyed.

"Kinda. I'm open for better ideas," said Coyle continuing. There were none.

Paratroopers running along the tarmac fired at the back of the plane, the cargo hold open. The aircraft picked up speed. Bullets from the jeep's machine gun stitched across the aircraft's fuselage, punching holes through the metal skin.

Inside, bullets were flying from every direction. A Vietnamese soldier was hit in the shoulder. Another hit in the thigh. Both fell to the deck, moaning in pain. Everyone in the cargo area followed suit and hit the deck, making themselves smaller targets.

An armored car sped across the ramp and stopped blocking the aircraft's path. It swung its turret around and aimed at the nose of the cockpit with its 25mm cannon.

Coyle gunned the throttle squeezing out every last bit of power. Still, he waited, allowing the aircraft to pick up speed. It was a deadly game of chicken with the armored car preparing to fire at any moment. There would be no surviving the explosion from the shell if it pierced the cockpit. After another two seconds, Coyle lifted the aircraft off the ground and roared over the armored car as it fired its cannon, just missing the plane's tail. They were airborne. They were safe. He banked the plane toward the palace. Now came the hard part.

"You know, if there really is a battalion or more outside the palace, you and your guys are going to be jumping into thousands of guns all pointed at you?" said Coyle.

"We are well aware," said Conein.

"You'll be lucky if half your team isn't wiped out before it ever makes it to the ground."

"We are aware of that too."

"So, I gotta ask… Why?"

"Duty."

"Duty to who? Diem's people hate him, and his army has him surrounded."

Considering for a moment, Conein said, "We have our orders."

"You're a civilian, Lou. It's not like Lansdale can court-martial you."

"Granier's jumping. I'm jumping with him. I ain't no coward."

"Stupidest reason I've ever heard of jumping out of a plane."

"Just do your job and get us over the damned palace," said Conein leaving the cockpit, slamming the door shut.

Conein moved back into the cargo hold. Granier caught his eyes and could see his frustration. They looked long and hard at each other. Neither wanted to admit it openly, but each knew that they and their men stood a much better chance at surviving if they worked together. Between them, they had decades of fighting experience and knew how to get out of tight situations. The only real question was if they could trust each other after everything that had happened between them. Conein broke the stare down and sat down deep in thought. He was pretty sure he was about to die.

When Lansdale received the radio signal that the first part of the mission had been successful, he knew it was only a matter of minutes before his men would be over the presidential palace. He picked up the phone and called the number Diem had given him. Two minutes later, Diem was on the phone. "Mr.

President, I hope all is well, and you are safe?" said Lansdale.

"Yes, Colonel. By God's grace, we are still safe," said Diem.

"Good. I am calling to inform you that we have mounted a rescue operation."

"Rescue operation?"

"Yes, sir. A team of Americans and members of the 5th Bureau are on their way to you now. They will be parachuting into the palace compound in the next few minutes. Please make your guard aware of their intent."

"And what is their intent, Colonel?"

Lansdale was surprised by the phrasing of Diem's question and said, "To retrieve you and your family from the palace. Once our team is in place, we have arranged for a diversion that will allow you to escape."

"I believe there has been a misunderstanding, Colonel. I, nor my family have any intention of leaving the palace."

"I don't understand. You're surrounded by hostile forces meant to do you harm."

"Yes, but while I am in the palace, I am still in control of my country. My family and I will not run like cowards. We have made our own arrangements to end the coup."

"And what are those arrangements, Mr. President?"

"I would rather not say, Colonel. There are some in my government that believe the coup leaders would not have acted without permission from the American government."

"You can't be serious, Mr. President. The American government had nothing to do with this coup."

"And how do you know that, Colonel? You are not privy to all conversations between Washington and its embassies."

"No. I am not. But it would be a public relations disaster if America ever betrayed an ally in such a matter."

"I agree with you, Colonel. And yet, here we are."

"Mr. President, I believe you are being given bad counsel. America is your loyal ally. We have a great deal at stake in your continued success."

"Nevertheless, I am sure you see my conundrum. Who can I trust when the wolves are at my gates?"

"You can trust me, Mr. President."

"Can I, Colonel?"

"Yes. Absolutely."

"Just the same, until I have determined who is behind these traitors, I have ordered my guards to fire upon anyone who enters my compound, and that includes from the sky."

"Mr. President, those are my men."

"Yes, Colonel. Please recall them. I would not wish any of them to die through a misinterpretation of events."

"Of course, Mr. President. But you are making a big mistake. America is on your side."

"So, you say, Colonel. So, you say."

Diem hung up. Lansdale was dumbfounded. He considered what Diem had told him and wondered if some of it might be true. *Could Durbrow and the MAAG advisors have covertly encouraged and even helped the coup leaders in their plans to overthrow Diem? Could they have purposely left him out of the loop, fearful of his close relationship with Diem? And if so, would the rescue mission in progress be perceived as an act of treason against America?* Lansdale knew that the conspiracy theories of America's betrayal were coming from Madame Nhu. She had shown her distrust of the Americans in the past. He also knew that her weasel of a husband was probably supporting her theories. Tearing down the trust between Diem and the Americans gave the Nhu's more power, and power was something they valued.

Above the palace, the C-119 approached. Inside the aircraft, the men wearing their parachutes rose, moved toward the center of the plane, and hooked their parachute release lines to the overhead wire that ran the length of the cargo area. Granier and Conein looked out through the doorless opening. Below, the lights of the buildings near the palace zoomed past. "You know, if you're having second thoughts…" said Conein.

"What in the hell are you talking about?" said Granier.

"I'm just saying… Coyle brought up some good points. Diem is not our responsibility. We don't owe him loyalty."

"I ain't doin' this for Diem. I signed up for this shit. It's my job."

"Right. You're right. It's the job."

"So, are you coming?"

"Hell yes, I'm coming."

"Maybe you should step to the end of the line and make sure everyone makes it out okay."

"Fuck you, Granier."

"That's what I thought. Let's get on with it."

They both turned to watch the jump light, currently red. "Standby," said the crew chief to the soldiers, some praying, some trying not to piss themselves.

The faint sound of gunshots popped from below. Dull thuds revealed bullets were piercing the aircraft's outer skin, entering and exiting the cargo hull, missing the men like a magician's sword trick. A bullet nicked the rim of Santana's helmet; only his chin strap kept it from falling off. A Vietnamese soldier grunted and fell to the deck when a bullet punctured his crotch and traveled vertically inside his body cavity, shredding his organs. The men standing beside him knelt to help. It was useless. He would die of internal bleeding in thirty seconds. There was nothing anyone could do but wait for the damned jump light.

The plane suddenly banked hard to one side, knocking some of the men off their feet. Granier unhooked his release line, pushed his way past the soldiers, and entered the cockpit. "What the hell are you doing?" said Granier.

"We're getting the hell out of here. I just got word from Lansdale. Mission has been called off," said Coyle.

"Why?"

"How the hell should I know? He's your boss, not mine."

A .50 Cal bullet punched through the cockpit deck and tore off the front half of the navigator's foot. He screamed more from the shock of seeing the bloody stump that was once his foot than from the pain which hadn't really hit him yet. The radioman knelt and applied pressure to the wound to keep the navigator from bleeding out. "Your dressing," said the radioman turning to Granier.

Granier pulled the emergency dressing from the band on his helmet, ripped open the paper cover, and handed the dressing to the radioman. The gauze turned completely red the moment it made contact with what was left of the navigator's foot.

Granier left the cockpit to tell the others. He knew they'd be relieved, especially Conein. Granier knew that Conein wasn't a coward. But something or someone had unnerved him this time. He just wasn't sure what or who it was.

In the early hours of the morning, Hai returned from the palace with Diem's response. He again was escorted inside, where Dong and Thi were waiting. "Well?" said Thi, growing impatient.

"You will be happy to know that President Diem has graciously accepted your proposal of General Kim as prime minister," said Hai. "He has asked that we flesh out the new prime minister's responsibilities and guidelines in hopes of avoiding confusion when he takes office."

"What are you talking about? Kim's responsibilities will be the same as any prime minister. He will run the country and the military in Diem's name," said Thi.

"President Diem has also asked that I convey his objection to exiling his brother and sister-in-law from the palace."

"Not just the palace, the country."

"Yes, I understand. However, the president questions the need for them to leave with the new prime minister in control of the military. His brother Nhu will be powerless and therefore harmless, except for the president's personal security and intelligence, of course."

"Nhu is not going to be in charge of anything, especially security and intelligence," said Dong.

"Ah, I see. There has been a misunderstanding. Perhaps it was the manner in which I conveyed your request to the president."

"These are not requests. They are demands. If he refuses, we will take the palace by force and depose the president."

Hai wrote several notes on a piece of paper. "What the hell are you writing?" said Thi.

"I want to make sure I correctly convey your message to the president. These notes will help me remember. You are welcome to read them once I am done to ensure their accuracy."

"I don't want to read your damned notes. You're obviously stalling for time."

"I assure you my only desire is to record an accurate account of the matters we discuss so I may convey them correctly to President Diem and his family."

"Family? Diem's family has nothing to do with these discussions."

"So, you are saying that you do not want President Diem's family to read my notes?"

"No. No note reading, especially by the Nhu's."

"I see. Let me make a note of that," said Hai, again taking up his pen and paper.

Thi was furious. He grabbed the paper and ripped it to pieces. "Get out before I have you hanged," said Thi.

Hai genuinely looked shocked. Dong jumped in, trying to calm things down, "Mr. Hai, while we respect your desire for accuracy, our time is limited. Please inform President Diem that he has one hour to surrender, or we will take the palace by force."

"And what of his questions?" said Hai.

"No more questions. Diem and his family will surrender unconditionally within the hour, or we will blow them into oblivion."

"That is unfortunate. I will convey your message."

"See that you do," said Thi.

Hai collected his papers, including the torn pieces, and left. Once the secretary left, Thi turned to Dong and said, "He's obviously stalling."

"Of course, he is. But why?" said Dong, his mind whirling. "We have scouts watching all the main roads in the South?"

"Yes. Marine recon units. Nothing will get into Saigon without us knowing first," said Thi.

Countryside Saigon, South Vietnam

With their jeep parked under a tree and camouflaged with a net, a rebel Marine reconnaissance team watched the highway below. There was a line of car and truck headlights driving on the road. Just normal traffic. "I think I got something," said a private peering through his binoculars.

The team commander, a sergeant, crawled over and looked through his own binoculars at the highway below and said, "Where?"

"Look at that knoll to the Northwest. A scout is surveying the valley. You can see the reflection of headlights on his binoculars."

"I see 'em. A single soldier is hardly something to get excited about."

"Yeah, but if you were going to move a column, you'd send out scouts, right?"

"So?"

"So, I'm just saying… it could be something."

"Fine. Keep your eye on him. Tell me if you see anything else."

"Will do."

A radio crackled. The sergeant crawled back toward the jeep, slipped under the camouflage net, and rose once he was sure he wouldn't be seen. The radio operator at headquarters was checking in. The sergeant pulled a slip of paper from his shirt pocket. He ran his finger down a list of code words next to the time of day. He found the corresponding code and responded to the command center's request for an update that included the code word. He decided not to mention the private's observation until he had something more concrete to report. Finished, he hung up the radio's handset. He grabbed his canteen from the jeep and took a long pull of water. He heard a thud as something hit the ground next to him. Unconcerned, he looked over. It was a satchel charge with the fuse burning. "Down," he shouted to his men.

It didn't matter. The explosion from the charge meant to breach thick walls, steel-reinforced doors, and bridge support beams killed his entire team and flipped the jeep off the side of the hill crushing the radio.

A few moments later, the scout that the marine private had been watching reported the success of the ambush to his commander, who in turn reported to Colonel Thieu, the Commander of the 5th Division and a Diem loyalist. With the eyes of coup leaders now blinded, the ARVN column of armored vehicles and trucks began its final leg toward the outskirts of Saigon.

Saigon, South Vietnam

Thi and Dong watched as five rebel tanks were repositioned in front of the palace gates to show that they meant business as the final hour ticked down. They were ready to shell Diem into submission. "We should have done this at the start," said Thi.

"Excellent afterthought," said Dong.

"Don't be a smart-ass. Diem was never going to give up."

"Then he will die."

"...and his family."

"Agreed."

Both colonels turned when they heard multiple explosions to the Northeast. "What in the hell is that?" said Thi.

An out-of-breath soldier ran up to Thi and said, "Commander, we have just received word. A large loyalist force has entered Saigon."

"How large and what is their current position?" said Thi.

"Our scouts are unsure as to the size, but they believe it is the 5th Division."

"Colonel Thieu's division," said Dong.

"Loyalist tanks have taken up positions along the Saigon River around the Cau Binh Loi rail bridge."

"How did they get so close without us knowing?"

"It doesn't matter. They're here, and if they take that bridge, we are done for. We must immediately reposition our forces to repel them."

"Not all our forces. We must take the palace. With Diem as a hostage, they would not dare to attack us."

Dong thought for a moment, then nodded in agreement.

With explosions continuing their march toward the rebel forces, a presidential guard stepped out of the palace's front door holding a white flag. General Khanh followed him. They approached the front gate. "What the hell does he want?" said Dong.

"To gloat, I would imagine," said Thi as he signaled his men to let the general pass.

Khanh passed through the gate and was escorted to Thi and Dong, who both saluted out of respect. "How may we help you, General?" said Dong.

"Surrendering would be a good start," said Khanh.

"I believe your eyesight is fading with age, sir," said Thi. "You are still surrounded by a superior force."

"Not for long. Those explosions are from our tanks. They will be here in short order. President Diem has graciously offered to spare your lives if you surrender now."

"Please thank President Diem and inform him that he can go to Hell," said Dong.

"I concur," said Thi.

"Gentlemen, you should consider your position. You are facing two divisions and their armor."

"Two divisions?" said Thi.

"Ah. You thought it one?"

"It doesn't matter. This will all be over before they arrive."

"That is your decision?"

The colonels nodded. "Very well then. I shall convey your response to President Diem," said Khanh.

"No. You will stay here as our prisoner," said Thi. "Your flag bearer can tell Diem our response."

"I am under a flag of truce," said Khanh. "Or have you lost your respect for the rules of war?"

"He's right. We have to let him go," said Dong.

"I am not giving Diem a general to lead his defense. Besides, we may need him as a hostage."

"No. He came here with honor. He shall leave with honor," said Dong, firmly.

After a moment of frustration with his co-conspirator, Thi reluctantly nodded, and Khanh was escorted back through the palace gates.

His head poking out of the armored car's open hatchway, Colonel Khiem rode at the front of the column. His 7th Division had come up from the Mekong Delta south of Saigon. They had been traveling at top speed through the night, and he knew his men, especially the drivers of the armored vehicles and troop trucks, would be almost exhausted. He was cautious as he entered Saigon, wondering where the rebel forces would choose to attack his men. His recon platoons scouted the streets ahead. He knew time was of the essence if he were to participate in the battle that would save the president and his family, but he did not want to risk an ambush by the well-trained and well-armed rebel paratroopers.

Outside the palace, Thi and Dong heard radio reports of Colonel Khiem's 7th Division entering Saigon from the South. But that news concerned them far less than Colonel Thieu's 5th Division, which was a far more immediate threat. Thi ordered half of his available forces and all but five of his tanks to defend the Cau Binh Loi rail bridge. The bridge was just six kilometers from the palace. If the bridge were to fall, the loyalist forces could arrive in less than an hour. Thi and Dong needed as much time as possible to breach the palace walls.

The rebel forces began their attack with the tanks blowing open the front gates. The civilians crowded around the palace grounds cheered encouragement to a company of rebel troops as they rushed through the breached gate. As the soldiers entered the compound, they were met with a hail of gunfire from the presidential guards' machine guns positions at the top of the front steps. Taking heavy losses, the rebel troops were forced to leave their wounded and dead on the palace lawn as they were driven back outside the compound. The presidential guards cheered.

Khanh, commanding the guards, knew it was a well-fought but short-lived victory. He knew Thi to be overly aggressive in his first moves during battle, a fault he had mentioned to the colonel on more than one occasion. Thi was probing the palace defenses. His next assault would be executed far better and from multiple points. Even with half his forces leaving to protect the bridge, the rebel paratroopers still vastly outnumber the loyalist guards—time is not on Diem's side.

American Embassy, Saigon, South Vietnam

After the aborted rescue mission, Lansdale headed for the embassy. Entering the front gate, he demanded to see Ambassador Durbrow immediately. He was escorted inside and brought to the ambassador's office.

Durbrow was more than a little displeased, "I heard about your little air rescue stunt at the palace. You disobeyed a direct order to stand down," said Durbrow.

"And you should be grateful I did. It showed Diem that America was a true friend in his time of great need. Now, the tables have turned. Two loyalist divisions have now entered the city and are on their way to the palace," said Lansdale. "We should immediately declare our full support for President Diem before it is too late."

"I stand by my earlier statement," said Durbrow.

"That is a mistake. Diem will see it for what it truly is… hedging our bets."

"Regardless. President Eisenhower has made it clear; he wishes us to stay out of this fiasco until one side, or the other, has complete control of the government."

"If we wait for that, then we will lose whatever influence we still have with Diem."

"You mean you will lose whatever influence you have with Diem."

"You are going to blow up America's best chance at stopping the communist expansion into Southeast Asia."

"We will wait for clarity. A lot can still happen."

"You mean the rebels can still kill Diem and his family?"

"You must admit, it is a possibility. Maybe even a probability."

"Of course, it is. That is why we must act. If America throws its weight behind Diem, it will give the rebels pause. Those few minutes could save Diem's life and our best hope."

"You are assuming Diem is our best hope. I am not convinced."

"And what if you are wrong, Ambassador?"

"Then I will have done my duty as President Eisenhower has dictated. I suggest you do the same. Get onboard the ship, Colonel, or you will be left on the pier."

Lansdale walked out of the embassy compound and climbed into his car. He pulled the handset of the portable AN/PRC-10 on the floor of the passenger seat and turned the radio on. "Bulldog One, Bulldog One, this is Bulldog Six, over," said Lansdale.

On a building rooftop near the palace, his sniper rifle slung across his back and the radio over his shoulder, Granier emerged from a doorway and answered, "Bulldog Six, this is Bulldog One, copy."

"What is your sitrep?"

"In position."

"Do you have eyes on the target?"

"Not yet."

"Keep me advised."

"Affirmative. Out."

Lansdale had ordered Granier to assassinate the two colonels leading the coup. He hoped that by decapitating the leadership, the coup forces would be disheartened and crumble, or at least hesitate long enough for the loyalist forces to arrive and save Diem.

Granier wasn't sure how he felt about the order since both officers were South Vietnamese and supposedly American allies. It was true; they were also traitors to the current government. But it was also true that they could quickly become the current government if they were successful in overthrowing Diem and his family. It was these types of dilemmas that Granier often faced since joining the CIA. Since he did not have enough information to solve the puzzle, he decided to obey Lansdale's order and let his commander deal with the ethics.

He moved to the edge of the rooftop, set down the radio, and removed his sniper rifle. He peered through the scope and surveyed the area. He could clearly see the palace and the rebel forces surrounding it. He knew it was a long shot at spotting the coup leaders among the hundreds of soldiers. That type of thing usually required hours or even days of surveillance to locate their position. He didn't have that kind of time. The coup would probably be over in the next hour or two. If he were going to affect the outcome, he would need to execute the officers within the next few minutes. He surmised that he stood the best chance of locating the two officers behind the firing positions near the front of the palace gate, which was now blown off its hinges. He had photos of the two officers that he could check once he found the suspects. He continued his search through the rebel ranks.

At the Cau Binh Loi rail bridge, Thieu watched the opposite side of the Saigon River with his binoculars. He was suspicious when his recon teams had crossed the river upstream in small boats and reported no rebel units around the bridge. It had all been too easy. Stupidly easy. *Why had the rebel commanders not placed roadblocks on the main roads leading into Saigon? And why no rebel units at one of the few bridges that could support the weight of armored vehicles? They could easily have created a bottleneck and stopped his advance.* Thieu was convinced it was a trap. *Maybe the rebels were hiding and waiting until his first units crossed the river before springing their ambush.*

Even with time running short for the president and his family, Thieu decided on the side of caution. He ordered his artillery to set up. If it were a trap, he would blow the rebels to kingdom come when they finally came out of hiding. From their position along the river and with a maximum firing range of seven miles, the American-made M101 howitzers could cover the Division's move to the palace. Once in position, the 105mm howitzers could be set up in just a few minutes. They were reliable and accurate if operated properly. While not ideal, the howitzers could destroy or disable the enemy's tanks and armored cars if their shells made a direct hit or landed close enough to send hot shrapnel through the vehicle's armor or into its tires or treads.

In the meantime, the commander gave his men some much-needed rest before they entered what he was sure would be a fierce battle around the palace. Thieu's 5th Division was mainly made up of soldiers from the Nung – a Central Tai ethnic group living in the Northeast of South Vietnam. They were brave, experienced fighters, fiercely loyal to one another. He had trained them well, and they were devoted to their commander. He didn't want to risk losing any of them unnecessarily.

The rebel paratroopers were a worthy enemy. Their skills and experience as an elite fighting unit were perfectly matched for a mission such as the one they were executing. They were trained to take ground and hold it until the battle was won, or they were relieved by a stronger infantry force. Like a dog with a bone, the paratroopers had a mean bite, and underestimating their determination was often a deadly mistake.

As the last loyalist howitzer was set up, a rebel tank across the river appeared on the boulevard leading to the bridge and opened fire. Its cannon belched flame, sending a shell across the water. It was a hurried shot, more like suppressing fire to keep the loyalist units from crossing the bridge. The hastily aimed shell crashed into an apartment building and exploded. Bricks and cement rained down on the street below. None of the loyalist troops were hurt, but an entire family living in the building was killed when the shell landed in their kitchen.

Thieu ordered his tanks and artillery to return fire. Shells cascaded down and exploded across the river destroying several storefronts and a restaurant sending burning chairs and tables tumbling into the river. Within ten seconds, the opposite bank's tank was hit and exploded in a ball of flames. Another shell made a direct hit sending what remained of the burning hulk flying up in the air and landing in a heap of torn metal.

More rebel tanks and armored cars peaked out from side streets and opened fire on the loyalists. The loyalist tanks, artillery, and troops returned fire. Unable to do much damage to the rebel tanks, the loyalist heavy machine guns focused on the armored cars. The .50 Cal bullets pierced the thin armor of the vehicles like Swiss cheese killing the crews inside. The loyalist tanks and artillery focused on the rebel tanks. Tanks on both sides were less than three hundred yards from their enemy. It was hard to miss at that range.

Both sides made their mark on the other, but it was the rebels that were outgunned and outmanned by five to one. Tracer rounds soared across the river. The rebel paratroopers were more lightly armed with light machine guns, recoilless rifles, and mortars as their artillery. The rebel armored regiment had set up their battery in the park across from the palace. Howitzer shells poured down on both banks of the river, several hitting the bridge but doing little damage to the heavy steel structure designed to carry cargo-laden trains. Civilians brave enough to risk leaving their buildings, ran for their lives, fleeing the battle. Many were caught in the crossfire between the two combatants. Hit by high caliber ammunition and the jagged fragments from exploding shells, most of the wounds were lethal. As with all urban fighting, it was mayhem and vicious.

With the rebel armored regiment reporting heavy damage, Thi decided to save what he could and ordered his men to perform a fighting retreat to buy as much time as possible.

Half of the paratroopers fell back, taking up new firing positions in the buildings one street back from the river's edge with a concentration of the main boulevard. Two recoilless rifles teams moved halfway down the block of the side streets leading to the main boulevard. They took up new firing positions that would give them a clear shot at the loyalist armor as it passed on the main boulevard. The paratroopers would do whatever they could to slow down the loyalist advance, sacrificing their lives for time if necessary.

Next, the rebel armor began their retreat by re-orienting their guns at the bridge—a last-ditch effort to damage the structure. Twelve high-explosive tank shells exploded on the bridge doing surprisingly little damage to the French-built structure. The tank commanders gave up hope of stopping the loyalist tanks from crossing the river. They pulled their tanks back, retreating up side streets, and taking up new firing positions within the alleys between buildings.

Thieu knew that the rebel armor was not done. Not yet. Their tanks would be waiting for him and his men as they crossed the river. It would be a bloody assault. But it had to be done. There was no other way. He ordered his Division forward, the vanguard taking the lead and crossing the bridge first. They had armored cars that, if immobilized, could be pushed off the bridge by the tanks that would follow.

Several rebel anti-tank units set up their recoilless rifles down the boulevard protected by the surrounding buildings. They had clear shots at the vehicles crossing the bridge. They waited for the right moment before revealing their position, hoping to get off one or two shots before they became a target.

Rebel machine guns raked the loyalist troops escorting the vehicles. The troops took cover behind the vehicles and the bridge's girders as they advanced, firing back and then ducking to cover again. Many were hit by ricochets off the steel structure. When they finally reached the mouth of the bridge on the opposite side, they spread out quickly, taking cover behind whatever they could find. Many of their comrades still lay on the bridge, groaning from wounds or dead. As the newly-formed bridgehead, their job was to provide covering fire to protect the next group of loyalist troops crossing the bridge.

One by one, the remaining rebel firing positions along the riverbank were taken out by the loyalists. Recoilless rifles and machine guns went silent. Resistance faded. Gunfire trickled to almost nothing. The loyalist companies formed up and prepared to advance once again. There would be no rest until they reached the palace and the president and his family were safe.

Thieu ordered his men already across the river to hold their positions. He knew that the rebel forces would be taking up new firing positions to ambush his armor and escorting infantry. He sent scouts forward to spot their firing positions, then ordered his artillery to unleash a rolling bombardment one block ahead of his forces as they advanced. It was tight, and there was a risk of hitting his own men. He figured that it was safer for his men even with the additional risk, especially if his artillery could take out the enemy positions. All his artillery opened fire at the same time.

The shells came crashing down on the side streets perpendicular to the boulevard. They also hit several buildings, causing a torrent of bricks and tiles to fall into the street, crushing rebel soldiers and fleeing civilians. It was merciless. The rebel paratroopers' ambush positions were destroyed. They had little choice but to retreat or die. They pulled back, using the buildings and houses for cover when possible. The paratroopers did not flee. They were not a rabble. They fought their way back, making the loyalists pay for every block.

Outside the palace, Thi and Dong listened to the reports over the radio. Time was short. Thi ordered his men forward through the breached gates once again, and once again, they were driven back by the palace guard. Unknown to Thi and Dong, the loyalist guards were almost out of ammunition and down to their last few grenades. Soon, they would have no choice but to surrender.

Granier watched through his scope on a nearby building rooftop, still searching for the two rebel commanders, still trying to make a difference.

Watching his men retreat from the palace, Thi refused to give up. Without killing Diem and his family, he knew he would be a hunted man forced to live on the run. He surveyed the area, searching for a way. He saw the civilian supporters that had come to cheer on the paratroopers. They were shouting and waving their banners that read – Down with Diem and Death to Madame Nhu. Thi ran toward them.

On the rooftop, Granier spotted Thi as he stopped in front of the crowd. His scope's view was slightly obscured by a tree, the leaves swaying in the breeze. One moment he could see Thi clearly; the next, Thi's face was hidden by the leaves. He waited, hoping to get a clean shot.

Standing in front of the people, Thi shouted, "The time has come to show your love for your country and take the palace. Follow me!"

Thi turned, waved them forward, and ran toward the front gates. Knowing that he might be alone, he dared not turn around.

Granier tracked Thi with his scope as he moved out into the open. He centered his sight on Thi's head and slowly squeezed his trigger.

As he approached the palace walls, Thi wasn't alone. The people ran to catch up with him. Some ran past him wanting to be the first into the palace. The first to lay hands on Madame Nhu and her husband. Thi slowed his advance, letting the mob take the lead.

The people around Thi again obscured Granier's scope. Granier cursed to himself.

The people poured through the front gate and ran toward the palace steps.

Khanh stood defiant. He knew the ammunition wouldn't last, but he was determined to fight until the last cartridge was spent. He ordered his men to open fire on the mob running toward them.

Hearing the guards open fire, Thi slowed to a stop as he entered the gateway, the pillar of one of the gates obscuring him from view, unknowingly saving his life.

Granier cursed again as he saw Thi disappear next to the gate pillar. He surveyed the area just inside palace walls hoping to reacquire his target. Instead, he watched the massacre of unarmed civilians. They dropped by the dozens, mowed down by the murderous rifle fire of the guards.

Safely behind the pillar, Thi watched the carnage he had created as bullets ripped through the mob. Dead and wounded lay on the grass, bleeding. "Keep going!" he shouted.

Khanh watched as his men's rifles emptied. He pulled out his pistol and fired the remaining rounds. It, too, clicked empty.

The mob reached the steps and climbed upward, each person hesitant to continue but feeling the others nearby, giving them courage. The gunfire seemed to be fading. They continued to climb, closing the distance to the front doors. Once inside, there was little the palace guards could do as they hunted Diem and his family down like animals.

Khanh saw a grenade in a dead soldier's hand, the safety ring still attached. He snatched it up, pulled the ring, and hurled it down at the mob. The grenade bounced off several steps and exploded mid-air. Shrapnel flew into the faces of the mob, killing a half dozen, blinding several more. The mob recoiled as screams of pain shrilled through their ears. They had enough, turned, and ran for their lives back through the gate, leaving their wounded and dying comrades on the palace lawn and steps.

Just as the civilians abandoned their assault on the palace, rebel paratroopers and armored vehicles appeared on the main boulevard. They were engaged in a fighting retreat against Colonel Thieu's loyalist division. Outnumbered and outgunned by the loyalist forces, the rebels were losing ground rapidly. The elite soldiers were at the end of their rope, their confidence shattered. It wouldn't be long until the paratroopers' flimsy defensive line broke, and they stampeded in a full rout.

As the paratroopers passed him, Thi knew it was over. There was no taking the palace or killing Diem and his family. The coup was done. Dazed, he moved back, bumped as people and soldiers ran past. Diem and his brother Nhu were sure to want revenge for his betrayal.

Surprised by the needless bloodbath of civilians, Granier once again spotted Thi as he walked away from the palace. Dong appeared too. Dong grabbed Thi and pulled him behind a truck. Granier lost sight of the two. *I guess it doesn't matter much now. It's done,* thought Granier as he collected his rifle and retreated from the rooftop. In a way, he was relieved. The sight of the civilians being massacred made him wonder which side should be the rightful rulers of South Vietnam. *None,* he thought, looking back down at the bodies before leaving.

The artillery from Colonel Khiem's 7th Division unleashed an intense bombardment from the Southwest. His tanks and troops were closing in on the palace from a different direction.

The rebel paratroopers and their armor were now facing an advancing enemy from two directions. It was an impossible situation as either force the rebels were facing was strong enough to wipe them out. It was just a matter of time.

Dong could see that Thi seemed dazed and wasn't thinking straight. "We've got to regroup," said Dong.

"Why?" said Thi. "It's over."

"No. It can't be. We will find another way. We just need time."

A captain ran up to Thi and said, "Commander, your orders?"

Thi didn't respond. The captain looked panicked. Dong could see that Thi was useless; his confidence shattered. The captain turned to Dong as if he were now in charge. Dong said, "Captain, have the men fall back to the park and form a defensive ring. You must protect the artillery."

The captain ran off to carry out Dong's orders. Dong wanted to smack Thi across the face but thought better of it. The paratroopers were already demoralized and didn't need to see their commander discouraged. Dong realized that he needed to take over, but he needed Thi beside him to command authority. He turned to the radioman and said, "Call all the unit commanders and have all our remaining forces regroup at the park."

The radioman nodded and went to work. With everyone occupied in the retreat to the park, Dong pulled Thi over to the truck cab and forced him to sit on the runner. "Colonel, can you hear me?" he said, looking Thi in the eyes.

"Of course, I can hear you," said Thi.

"Good. We need to leave."

"What do you mean leave?"

"Our forces will soon be surrounded by a far superior force. Nhu will demand that we, as the coup leaders, are found and brought to him. If that happens, we are dead."

"I'm not afraid to die."

"I know that, but are you afraid to live?"

"I don't understand."

"This isn't over. Nothing has changed. The people still hate the president and his family. They will follow us again once we have a new army."

"A new army? You want me to abandon my men? Never."

"Think about it. If we leave, we will be saving the lives of our men. They were just following our orders. They thought the presidential guard was behind the coup. They knew nothing. It's the truth, especially if we are not there to deny it. Nhu will focus on finding us, not punishing our men."

"Where will we go?"

"We will find a place to hide with someone we can trust. Trust is everything at this point. But we've got to go now."

Thi thought for a long moment, then nodded slowly. Dong looked around to see who might be watching. It seemed clear. He took off, heading for a side street. Thi followed.

Within an hour, the rebel forces were surrounded by the two loyalist divisions. Loyalist artillery shells exploded around the park, destroying the rebel artillery and armored vehicles. The rebel paratroopers sought cover wherever they could and fought back, keeping the loyalist forces from overrunning their position. When word came that Thi and Dong were nowhere to be found, the remaining rebel commanders surrendered. There was no point in more men dying.

It was as Dong had suspected. The rebel paratroopers claimed Thi and Dong had duped them into believing they were saving Diem and his family from a rebellious palace guard. Colonel Thieu had heard similar rumors in his ranks and believed the paratroopers were telling the truth. Diem wasn't so sure but was focused on finding the coup leaders. Madame Nhu thought it best if all the rebel paratroopers were shot as an example. Diem allowed General Khanh, who had proven his loyalty, to decide the fate of the paratroopers. Brother Nhu suspected that Khanh would be too lenient on his fellow officers and soldiers. Exercising an abundance of caution, the battalion commanders were jailed until a complete investigation could be completed. The rest of the paratroopers were disarmed and escorted back to the barracks. The coup was over. Khanh knew that he would need the elite paratroopers to fight the Viet Minh and had little interest in disheartening them with further punishment.

Diem ordered his brother Nhu to use all his forces to locate the coup leaders. He gave him complete control of any army units if required to hunt down the traitors. Torturing those that might have information was encouraged.

Granier returned to Lansdale's headquarters and reported to his commander. "You've really screwed the pooch, Granier," said Lansdale.

"How's that?" said Granier in no mood for a dressing down by Lansdale.

"Diem and Nhu are obsessed with finding the coup leaders. They are preoccupied with internal struggles when what they need to be concerned about are the Viet Minh. There is little question the Viet Minh leaders will take advantage of the government's distraction."

"I don't see how that is my fault."

"If you had killed the coup leaders, it would have been over once and for all. Now things will drag on."

"I did my best under the circumstances. There was no clear shot… not without hitting civilians."

"Granier, sacrifices must be made in times of war. That includes civilians."

"This is bullshit, sir. If I could have accomplished my mission, I would have."

"But you didn't accomplish your mission. Now, I have to figure out how to clean up the mess you've created. It's not going to be easy," said Lansdale as he considered his options. "On your way out, tell Conein I'd like to see him."

Granier left the office, leaving Lansdale deep in thought, searching for an angle to attack the problem. A few moments later, Conein entered and said, "You wanted to see me?"

"Yes. You were instrumental in the escape of Bay Vien," said Lansdale.

"I made some arrangements."

"Could you do it again?"

"Of course. Who do you have in mind?"

"The coup leaders… if we can find them."

"I don't understand. I thought Diem wanted their heads on a platter."

"He does. But the last thing this country needs is a pair of martyrs. They are a distraction as long as they remain in Vietnam. It would be better for everyone if they were to make it across the border."

"Yeah, but doesn't that leave them to recruit a new army?"

"Once they are out of Vietnam, they will have a difficult time recruiting anyone to join their cause."

"And if you're wrong?"

"Then we eliminate them… discreetly. An accident, perhaps. But not while they are in South Vietnam. I don't want to give rise to any opposition now that Diem has eliminated the threat. He has a war to win. He needs to focus."

"I might have some contacts that could help locate them. But we would need to make assurances that the coup leaders would come to no harm. These aren't the type of people you want to piss off."

"The Corsicans?"

"Yes. If anyone could find them, they could."

"Do it."

"I have your word you won't kill them?"

"You do. I assume the Corsicans will want something in return?"

"They will. Let me take care of that," said Conein as he exited.

Coyle and Conein sat in the officer's club at the airbase. Coyle was always suspicious when someone offered to buy him a drink, especially if that someone was Lucien Conein. He was right to be suspicious. "No way. Not again," said Coyle, hearing Conein's proposal to fly the two coup leaders to Cambodia.

"Lansdale wants it done," said Conein.

"Last time I looked, I don't work for Lansdale."

"I know that. And I am sure Lansdale would take it up with your commander, but the fewer people that know about this, the better."

"I am through being your errand boy, Conein. And I sure as hell ain't no drug runner."

"That was unfortunate."

"So, you're saying no drugs this time?"

Conein shrugs off the question to continue his argument, "Diem and his goons are going to imprison and torture hundreds, maybe thousands of civilians to find Thi and Dong. We'd be preventing that."

"You're not gonna guilt me into this."

"It's not guilt. It's hero stuff."

"You are so full of shit folks can smell you from a mile away."

"It's the truth, Coyle. The world needs guys like you and me. We do the things, however distasteful, that keep the wheels turnings."

"Distasteful? Smuggling drugs is illegal, not to mention immoral."

"You need to focus on the bigger picture, Coyle."

"I am. That's why I ain't doing it. Find yourself another pilot."

"I would if I could, but time is short. The Corsicans have found Thi and Dong. They're ready to go. We need to get them out of the country before Diem finds them. He'll kill 'em for sure, and that's gonna make them martyrs. This whole thing is gonna start again, there'll be another coup, and more innocent people are gonna die. And I know you don't want that."

"I don't. But I don't wanna smuggle drugs either."

"I gotta see that the Corsicans get paid for arranging things."

"How about cash? I'm sure they like cash."

"There is no way Lansdale can get that kind of money approved without a lot of people knowing. Diem might find out about it, and then we're really screwed. 'Sides, the Corsicans don't want money. They want their opium transported out of the country. They've got commitments."

"Where's it going… the opium?"

"I don't know, and I don't care. And you shouldn't either. We get it across the border, and we're done. End of story."

"What about the Cambodians? I hear Cambodian prison is just as bad as Vietnamese prison."

"Worse, I imagine. But that doesn't matter. Prince Sihanouk has agreed to look the other way. He hates Diem and his family, especially after they attempted to assassinate him."

"So, what's he gonna do with Thi and Dong?"

"That falls under the I don't know, and I don't care rule. It ain't our concern."

"Dammit, Conein. This is the last time. I want your word on it."

"You gotta. Cross my heart and hope to die."

"I like the dying part."

"So… you're in?"

Coyle thinks for a long moment, then sighs with a nod. Conein slapped him on the back and said, "I knew I could count on you, Coyle. You're one hell of a patriot."

"Since when is smuggling drugs an act of patriotism?" said Coyle.

"Since they invented the CIA!" said Conein with a big grin.

Phnom Penh, Cambodia

At an airfield just outside Phnom Penh, Coyle set down the C-47 on the compacted dirt runway. It was raining, making the potholes covered by muddy water almost invisible. Coyle did what he could to avoid the puddles hoping those that he couldn't dodge were only a few inches deep. It was a bumpy landing. The plane pulled to a stop near the building that served as a terminal and was immediately surrounded by government troops, all pointing their weapons at the plane. "I thought you said Prince Sihanouk was okay with this," said Coyle to Conein, who just entered the cockpit.

"He is. That don't mean he's not cautious," said Conein.

"And if you're wrong?"

"I'm not wrong. Of course, his people could have been lying."

"And you're just thinking about that possibility now?"

"No. It occurred to me, but if we're obsessed about all the things that could go wrong on a mission, I don't think we'd ever get anything done."

"That's not very reassuring."

"Look, the Cambodians aren't gonna shoot a bunch of Americans and start a war."

"No, but they might toss a bunch of drug smugglers into prison and throw away the keys."

"That's a fair point," said Conein shrugging.

Coyle and Conein climbed back through the doorway into the cargo area. In the center of the hold was a stack of canvas bags containing the opium and lashed to the deck. Wondering what they had gotten themselves into, Thi and Dong stood by the windows and stared out at the Cambodian soldiers. "It's alright, gentlemen. They're here to protect you," said Conein trying to reassure them.

"Then why are their guns pointing at us and not away?" said Dong.

"They just have a strange way of doing things here in Cambodia. I'm sure you will get used to it."

Coyle's cargo boss opened the cargo doors and put the step ladder down. He, too, stared out at the soldiers, still pointing their weapons. "This situation doesn't seem to be improving much," said Coyle taking another look at the portal.

"Gotta have faith, Coyle. Gotta have faith," said Conein.

A four-door 1956 Citroen DS pulled onto the airfield and stopped next to the plane. The driver, a lieutenant with an umbrella, opened the back door as a Cambodian general emerged from the backseat, followed by a Corsican dressed in a white suit and carrying a satchel and his umbrella. The lieutenant held the umbrella over the general, who didn't look too happy to be out in the poor weather.

The Corsican walked over to the open cargo doors on the C47 and pointed to one of the bags of opium. Conein picked it up and set it in front of the businessman. The Corsican pulled out a pocketknife and used it to cut a small hole in the canvas bag's side and retrieve a sample of the black tar inside. He licked the tar and winced. Satisfied, he turned back to the general and nodded.

The general barked out some orders to the officer in charge of the soldiers. In turn, the officer barked out orders to his men. The soldiers slung their rifles and moved to form a line between the C47 and the only other plane, a three-engine French Toucan, parked on the airfield. The Corsican watched as the cargo was transferred from one aircraft to another, counting each bag.

Inside the C47, Conein turned to Thi and Dong and said, "Gentlemen, your carriage awaits."

The two colonels exchanged worried glances before stepping out the aircraft doorway. Four soldiers escorted them to the car. They climbed in the back, followed by the Cambodian general. The Citroen sped off, leaving the airfield. As Coyle and Conein stepped from the C47, Coyle said, "Do you think those two are long for this world?"

"Hard to say. They are guests of Prince Sihanouk, and I hear he can be a bit erratic," said Conein. "Not our concern anyway. The mission was to get them out of South Vietnam alive. We did that. You can pat yourself on the back."

As the last of the opium was unloaded, the Corsican handed Conein the satchel, spoke a few words in French, and shook his hand. The Corsican climbed into the French Toucan, and the plane fired up its engines and took off from the airfield. "What's in that?" said Coyle motioning to the satchel in Conein's hand.

"Coyle, have you ever considered that you ask too many questions?" said Conein climbing back into the aircraft.

Coyle followed, and a few minutes later, the plane took off back to South Vietnam.

December 6, 1960 - Washington D.C., USA

Overcoats were the dress of the day when President Dwight D. Eisenhower and President-Elect John F. Kennedy met at the White House for the first of two meetings before Kennedy took office. Hundreds of reporters and photographers gathered around the steps as Ike emerged from his home for the last eight years and Kennedy's limousine pulled up. Ike greeted Kennedy with an outstretched hand and a big smile. Kennedy took the president's hand and smiled even bigger.

It was a facade for America. Neither man liked the other much. Ike thought Kennedy was too young and inexperienced to be president. He hated how the Kennedy family had used their money and influence to get him elected. Ike was a stickler for fairness, and there was little question that he valued experience. In his mind, Kennedy had neither. Ike also disliked Kennedy's overwhelming confidence. "You can always tell a Harvard man, but you can't tell him much," said Ike on several occasions during the hotly contested election between Kennedy and Nixon.

Kennedy hated how Ike referred to him as "the boy" and "the young whippersnapper." He felt like Ike was portraying himself in the father role. Kennedy already had an overbearing father. He didn't need another one, and it certainly wouldn't have been Ike, even if he was a war hero like himself. Kennedy also felt like Ike's ideas on governing were old-fashioned and inflexible. Kennedy was not afraid to experiment, and that worried Ike. America was too big and too powerful to become Kennedy's childhood chemistry set.

Ike escorted Kenned inside the White House and into the oval office, leaving the press outside to deal with the cold December weather. Their conversion was cordial and light until the doors closed. Then things got uncomfortably quiet as coffee was served, and both men lit their preferred smokes – Ike, his Camel cigarettes, and Kennedy, his Cuban-made H. Upman Vitola cigars. They were sizing each other up as warriors often do before battle.

Ike felt like this might be the last time he was able to influence Kennedy, and there were vitally important things that they needed to discuss. The world was not in good shape, and the tide was turning against America. Ike knew that Kennedy had a somewhat liberal domestic agenda that he disagreed with and had little hope of changing Kennedy's mind. So, he didn't even try. Besides, there were many more pressing issues that needed the incoming president's focus.

Ike started the conversation, and Kennedy listened, occasionally asking intelligent questions. Ike warmed up to Kennedy when he realized how bright he was and that he really cared what Ike had to say. They mostly talked about global politics, including the threats to America and communist expansion. The growing conflict in Vietnam was left until last as Ike felt it was one of the most important topics of discussion. Having toured Vietnam when he was a senator, Kennedy felt like he had a grasp of the current situation but wanted to hear Ike's take on what was happening. "Although the growing unpopularity of President Diem and his family is vitally important and of great concern, they are not what keeps me up at night when it comes to Southeast Asia," said Ike.

"What is?" asked Kennedy.

"Laos."

Kennedy nodded and said, "Yeah, Laos."

Ike was slightly annoyed that Kennedy thought he knew what was going on in Laos when Ike knew he didn't. Ike decided to press on, "The problem is two-fold. First, the Royal Lao government is on shaky ground. The Pathet Lao rebels are growing in number, and the North Vietnamese are supporting them."

"When you say 'supporting' them, you mean weapons and training?"

"Not just that. The North Vietnamese have committed ground troops to fight beside the Pathet Lao and in some cases… in front of them."

"The North Vietnamese lead the attacks?"

"When it is an important installation… yes. The Pathet Lao are strong defenders, but many of the North Vietnamese troops are veterans and far superior when it comes to assaults."

"I didn't know that. It's a troubling development."

"You're telling me. If the civil war in Laos continues as it is, the government could fall at any time, which would be a disaster for America and South Vietnam. The communists would finally have their foothold in Southeast Asia. Which brings me to the second problem… The North Vietnamese have developed an extensive supply network through Laos."

"The Ho Chi Minh Trail."

"That's what we're calling it. What few know is that North Vietnamese are expanding their supply lines all the way into Cambodia. If that happens, the front lines facing the South Vietnamese will have grown from a thirty-mile border to over 2,000 miles, with dozens of mountain passes leading deep into South Vietnam. They will be able to ship as many weapons and supplies as they wish. The Viet Minh are growing in number, and soon they will have the weapons they need to overpower the South Vietnamese Army."

"Jesus."

"We've been stepping up our arms shipments and training, but it's too little."

"So, you think I should step up our efforts?"

"I think you need to be careful. I don't believe we can win a ground war in Vietnam. Jungle fighting is the worst and will take a heavy toll on our troops. My advice is to stay out of it."

"Wait… you think I should throw the towel in before the war even starts?"

"I think you should avoid putting real boots on the ground. It's a losing proposition. That doesn't mean just handing the South over to the communists, but you need to let the South Vietnamese fight for themselves. I would suggest more advisors in Vietnam and more Special Forces in Laos. You need to buy time while trying to keep the pot from boiling over."

"I'm not sure what good that will do in the long run."

"It may do a lot of good. The Soviets and the Chinese don't want a war in Vietnam. But Ho Chi Minh cannot win a war with the South without their help. Keep up the international pressure on the communists to stay out of Vietnam."

"I see."

"I know it's not an ideal situation I'm leaving you, but continued independence in the South is achievable if you handle it right. Buy time and cut off the Ho Chi Minh Trail. That's my advice."

Kennedy always believed that Ike was a man of action. Ike's suggestion to "Buy time" seemed overly soft and surprised Kennedy. The meeting was initially scheduled for twenty minutes, but the two continued to talk for one and a half hours before they finally included their staff and advisors in for additional discussions.

Over the coming years, Kennedy and Ike's relationship would suffer and at times fracture from strong rhetoric. But neither man lost respect for the other. Kennedy called Ike several times during his presidency, usually asking his opinion on military matters, especially during the Bay of Pigs incident and the Cuban Missile Crisis.

December 20, 1960 - Tan Lap, Tay Ninh Province, South Vietnam

Most of the Viet Minh in the North had joined the North Vietnamese regular army when it was formed. The original purpose of the Viet Minh was to gain independence from the French and Japanese. That goal had been accomplished. However, the country was still divided. The time had come for a new army designed to win the coming civil war and reunite the country.

Le Duan had fought most of his life for independence and sacrificed more than most to build up the rebel movement in the South. He was deeply saddened when he was asked not to attend the historic meeting in Tan Lap. Duan was now the head of the communist party in the North, having replaced Ho Chi Minh. His attendance would support the suspicion that it was the politburo in North Vietnam that actually controlled the rebel forces in the South. He understood, but it didn't soften the blow. His baby was about to become an adult, and he wouldn't be there to witness it.

The site of the meeting was symbolic, and security was incredibly tight. Suong had been reassigned temporarily to protect the delegates attending the conference. It was deep in the South, less than a hundred miles from the heart of Saigon and the Presidential Palace. The rebels demonstrated to the world that they could go anywhere and do anything, and there was nothing Diem and his army could do to stop them. While hesitant to support the rebels in an all-out war, the Soviets and the Chinese were impressed by the bold move. That alone was a victory for the rebel leaders.

Discussions between the delegates went on for days, each declaring their support for reunification and with it the overthrow of Diem and his government. Vietnamese politics were in full swing, with many of the delegates vying for the political positions that would surely be available once the new party and army were officially formed. While officially frowned upon, bribes were offered and taken for the best positions.

The name of the new political organization would be "National Liberation Front of Southern Vietnam," while the name of the new rebel military, formally the Viet Minh, would be "Liberation Army of South Vietnam." Both were a mouthful, as was the Vietnamese way.

Lieutenant General Nguyen Huu Xuyen was promoted as the new head of the liberation army and would lead the revolutionary effort in the South. Born in the village of Dinh Bang village in the Ninh province, Xuyen's family were peasant farmers that struggled to survive. In 1937, at the age of 22, he left his village for Saigon, joined the communist party, and fought against the French. Upon receiving his new commission as leader of the Viet Minh, he was renamed Tam Kien Quoc. Within one year after its official recognition, the liberation army's membership would swell to over 300,000. The days of bringing about change through propaganda were over. It was time for war.

"Viet Cong" was the new term the Americans were using to describe the new rebels. It stuck, and now the ARVN used the term which loosely translated meant "Traitor Communist of Vietnam." It just made things easier when talking to the American advisors that had been training them. The Americans saw the Viet Cong as communists, while the ARVN saw them as traitors against the government in the South. Either way, the Viet Cong were the bad guys and needed to be eradicated.

The Viet Cong thought otherwise. Regardless of what anyone thought, a new phase in the conflict between North and South was about to begin...

Dear Reader,

I hope you enjoyed *The Willful Slaughter of Hope*.

Our heroes will be back in <u>*Kennedy's War*</u> - Book 10 of the Airmen Series. Newly elected president John F. Kennedy and the forces under his command are faced with overwhelming challenges as the conflict against the Viet Cong heats up. President Diem and his corrupt family continue to persecute their own people making civil war more likely. Something's got to give…

You can find the entire Airmen Series on <u>Amazon</u> and on <u>Shopify</u>, available in eBook and Paperback.

Reviews on Amazon or Goodreads are always appreciated. Thank you for your consideration, and I hope to hear from you.

In gratitude,

David Lee Corley

Next in the Airmen Series:

Kennedy's War

Author's Biography

Born in 1958, David grew up on a horse ranch in Northern California, breeding and training appaloosas. He has had all his toes broken at least once and survived numerous falls and kicks from ornery colts and fillies. David started writing professionally as a copywriter in his early 20's. At thirty-two, he packed up his family and moved to Malibu, California, to live his dream of writing and directing motion pictures. He has four motion picture screenwriting credits and two directing credits. His movies have been viewed by over fifty million movie-goers worldwide and won a multitude of awards, including the Malibu, Palm Springs, and San Jose Film Festivals. In addition to his twenty-three screenplays, he has written ten novels. He developed his simplistic writing style after re-reading his two favorite books, Ernest Hemingway's *The Old Man and the Sea* and Cormac McCarthy's *No Country For Old Men*. An avid student of world culture, David lived as an ex-pat in both Thailand and Mexico. At fifty-six, he sold all his possessions and became a nomad for four years. He circumnavigated the globe three times and visited fifty-six countries. Known for his detailed descriptions, his stories often include actual experiences and characters from his journeys.

9 781959 534082